# A
# Sword for
# Defense

# A
# Sword for
# Defense

Sherlock Holmes and
His London
Through the Eyes
of Scotland Yard

## by Marcia Wilson

Edited by David Marcum

MX Publishing

ISBN Paperback 978-1-80424-650-4
ISBN AUK ePub 978-1-80424-651-1
ISBN AUK PDF 978-1-80424-652-8

Published by
**MX Publishing**
335 Princess Park Manor, Royal Drive,
London, N11 3GX
www.mxpublishing.co.uk

David Marcum can be reached at:
*thepapersofsherlockholmes@gmail.com*

Cover Design by Awan
Illustration of The Yarders by Marcia Wilson

# Sherlock Holmes and the Scotland Yarders
### by Marcia Wilson

1. *You Buy Bones*
2. *Test of the Professionals: The Adventure of the Flying Blue Pidgeon*
3. *Test of the Professionals: The Peaceful Night Poisonings*
4. *Test of the Professionals: Leap Year*
5. *The MoonCursers*
6. *A Sword for Defense*
7. *The Narrow Path: The First Storm*
8. *The End of All Things*
9. *A Fanged and Bitter Thing*

*Further adventures forthcoming . . . .*

# Author Foreword
## by Marcia Wilson

Looking back, it was a strange time. High school in the late 1980's meant Tolkien, King, Christie, and Poe were always checked out of the school library, but we had multiple copies of Sherlock Holmes on the shelf. If students were going to apply for English-oriented scholarships, by gosh, we were going to read the good stuff, and that meant short stories with murder and mayhem. In emulation of the masters, our choices were usually ACD or . . . Hemingway. It wasn't much of a contest. Hemingway didn't have a demon glowing Death Hound on the moors.

High school segued into college, but we had *Mystery!* re-runs on PBS, even if we had to visit people to watch it, and besides Jeremy Brett, we had Christopher Plummer's compassionate Holmes against Jack the Ripper, a role that shattered the domination of Rathbone and Bruce. Our classmates swore it was necessary for our sincerity as fans of Sir Arthur to see it.

If that sounds like pithy stuff for high schoolers, my generation had a flexible relationship with media – or even power grids. Even if they existed, they weren't exactly as reliable as the sun coming up every morning. The further into the West Virginia panhandle you got, the bigger the library room in the house. Even the poorest of houses, be they on blocks or wheels, had at least one shelf of sanity to rely on when the power was out, or the brownouts made hash of anything but AM radio. When a flood took out the local libraries, it was devastation.

There was media, but there wasn't enough – there's never enough – but as far as the books printed in the wake of Sir Arthur . . . it really was never enough. You were lucky to find something in a thrift store or library sale, and your odds were no worse than combing the bookstores in the mall. Oh, for the days when there was more than one bookstore in a mall. If something was found, readers had to buy it on faith that it wasn't a waste of their time.

Look, our standards weren't low, they were desperate. We made a lot of poor book-buying choices, which were hastily returned to the ecosystem of flea market sales for some other poor shmuck to buy up. One girl, bless her, would donate the books after carefully penciling in every sin the authors made against Canon, history, plot contrivance,

1

and attempts to pair Holmes up with a romantic partner. I like to think she cackled as she returned the much-improved dreck to the public. She always cited her sources . . . .

It shouldn't be a surprise when we wound up obsessing, ever so slightly, with what little we could find that wasn't terrible, and (*Hooray!*) didn't go against The Canon. I wonder if anyone has ever tried to list all the knockoffs and illicit print runs out there. Probably not – I'd like to think nobody could be that crazy.

Fan fiction was the outlet for a crying need that had hit breaking point. Paper fanzines of decent quality were even harder to find than a decent paperback on the shelf – you have never bought a pig in a poke until you've combed through a hand-printed zine catalog, squinted at the type, and decided to spend your allowance on what sounded the most promising – and too bad the cover art was rarely as good on the inside.

Fanzine editors lived in the twilight, trying to put out their passion projects between the obligations of home, family, and keeping a roof over their head, as well as hanging on to entire drawers of receipts to make sure a rival 'ziner didn't get spiteful and report them to the IRS. (That actually happened.) Zines were non-profit only, which is partly why the zines we could afford were always shipped Media Mail on whatever paper was on sale. If you were very lucky, you got your order in three weeks.

Maybe we shouldn't talk about the pastichery in animation . . . .

The Internet found its feet and bloomed with forums and places to hide and talk about the lack of stories, and that led to posting paper zines online, and people began writing fresh stuff, online, and showing it for reading and/or critiquing. Almost overnight there were clubs, groups, and social organizations that could get their fix on the stories between the boom-and-bust world of conventions and newsletters.

There were friendships made that I miss to this very day. The sheer power of a small number of people who were intelligent, thoughtful, and mindful of Canon encouraged so many of us. They helped with research, knew how to spell, and learned different languages in this world. They reviewed books, scrounged supplies, and let us know if someone was copying our plots just a little too much for comfort. Plagiarism and how to address it was a real eye-opener when it came to intellectual property that wasn't yours to begin with, but you could claim the OC's (Original Characters) were yours, and debatably, your unique perspective on the people, places, and things created under the pen of Sir Arthur.

I was a fan of these fans. They were amazing and – honestly – damn good writers. *Damn* good. They were role models. They read the whole Canon, and they kept track of everything, and they led us to places like *fanfiction.net*, where we could post with a minimum of fussing.

I could write about anyone I wanted, but it was partially out of respect for these writers that I began to veer away from making just one more story about Sherlock Holmes and Dr. Watson. I loved the stories, but part of their appeal was their world. And there was a lot to that world that was relevant today. Methods may alter crime, but motives rarely do.

At the time, there was a pretty well-represented group that was pro-Watson, and they wrote some of those "damn good stories" with Watson as the protagonist – or at least, a powerful, equal voice. The Granada series was a huge influence, as well as the Russian series, and throw in some of "the radio show" for good measure.

These fan writers may have loved the tight scripts and drama of the Rathbone and Bruce approach, but as they grew up, they said, collectively, "Man, that was bad for Watson!" There were other words, much less polite. Burke and Hardwicke were a positive force for the shift in the thinking that pointed out Watson was *not* an idiot and we couldn't do a decent job showing how smart Holmes was by surrounding him by idiots. This had already been tried, during Classic Dr Who, and nobody had been left happy about it. Nobody blamed the actors for doing their job too well.

*Fine,* I thought, *there are a lot of really good writers writing for Watson. I can do that.* But I also caught on that if Watson illuminated Holmes by writing of the man from his point-of-view, *maybe I could write about Watson through other people's eyes.* The question was: *Who?*

Enter a re-visit to the Granada Series, and "The Norwood Builder".

I make no secret of the fact that I am heavily synesthetic. Face blindedness comes with its own challenge, and I have to train myself to recognize people. With an irony that approaches opera-grade comedy, I literally could not tell Holmes from Lestrade in Granada's "The Norwood Builder". Also, Lestrade made me angry when I was a hero-worshipping teenager watching the show with other hero-worshipping teenagers. *How dare Lestrade challenge Holmes? Couldn't anyone see Holmes was the smartest man in the room?*

Older adult me revisited that part of my life and went *Oops!* because there were some of those Fanfiction Demigods that rather liked Lestrade and had plenty of backup reasons. I wish I could remember the name of the one who mused, *"Colin Jeavons is the only actor who could be bulldog-like and also ferrety."* I was doing a lot of research at my job, and that included the Victorian era and law enforcement. Somehow it all started clicking together, piece by piece.

A writer whom I regret losing (her entire message board went the way of LiveJournal – only, it vanished for good. Poof. No trace) challenged me on whether or not Lestrade was stupid. He knew more than he let on, she said, and I . . . kind of said, *"Oh? Prove it."*

*Ouch.* She did, lining out events in "The Boscombe Valley Mystery" and "The Second Stain" and a few other bits and pieces, and I ate crow. A lot of it. I was wrong. Still, I could at least write with this new perspective. Bad as it was to be wrong, it would be worse to stay with it.

Add to this a sleep disorder that can politely be called *insomnia*, and a marriage turning into a nightmare of violence, and no health insurance – but writing was the cheapest therapy out there . . . Lestrade slowly woke up and came to life. I'll blame Colin Jeavons for knowing what the writers wanted out of the scripts. It's on him.

*"Trust your characters,"* my old English teacher would say, sternly, so I did. I wrote short stories that could connect with others to make a fuller piece. A necklace is made one bead at a time. I wrote at night. I had to. I needed to stay awake, listening to any sounds that might be my ex-husband's return to stalk us – tampering with my car, crawling under the house, draining the well his own children needed to drink from, and taunts to the police that tried their best, but could only work within the limits of the system. They failed, but it was the system that failed. They cared, and they shared my rage that when the ex was finally brought to justice, it was too late for one of his victims.

There is only so much a policeman can do against so much collective injustice out there. If Sherlock Holmes had existed on that force, they would have begged for his help against my ex-husband. They knew he could go where they couldn't, and they would know when not to ask the awkward questions about how information was collected. They would have sniffed and said, "Well, that's a pity," and shrugged and did things according to the law – *their* law – but not expecting civilians to follow the same oaths they swore.

I empathized with Gregson's ability to buck the rules, and I empathized for Lestrade's inability to do so. The Yarders took on their own lives and, without knowing it, the job had changed. I was now sitting back and watching the stories unfold, writing them as fast as they told them. They had a lot to say. They still do, but the stories are whispering now. We are safer, there is no need to listen for danger. I am learning how to sleep.

More years ago than I'd like to recollect, I received an email so startling I forwarded it to my sister before a family dinner at the pizza parlour. It wasn't a fantastic day. Before long I would be needing their help to flee across the country in the middle of a winter snowstorm. The mood was glum. We were subdued.

My sister looked at me over the table and said with uncharacteristic bluntness, "You impressed that man."

That man was David Marcum.

Marcia Wilson
February 2025

# Scotland Yard's Story
## *Editor Foreword*
## by David Marcum

Back in 2008, it was still a different Sherlockian world from today.

In those days, the quest for more excellent Holmes adventures beyond the pitifully few sixty Canonical adventures was still quite difficult. Each year, only a few slipped through the needle's-eye clutch of the moribund major publisher model. (In fact, if one is still publishing by that route, then this fact remains true.) But there were many Holmes adventures waiting to be revealed, and they just needed an outlet. Is it any wonder that the Internet was that path?

Holmes pastiches have been around since William Gillette's 1899 play, *Sherlock Holmes*, showing that Our Heroes' adventures did *not* have to pass across the first Literary Agent's desk. Some amazing and accurate adventures appeared on the radio in the 1930's, courtesy of visionary Edith Meiser. And the door kept getting wider, with more radio shows, films, and the occasional book giving us more traditional, authentic, and Canonical Holmes.

*But it was not enough.*

In 1998, *fanfiction.net* was created, allowing another outlet for sharing Holmes's adventures, wherein those who had discovered them could get them directly to starving readers immediately, without facing the impossible discouragement of the faceless soul-dead major publishing model. I was fortunate to discover the site a few years after that, and began to visit regularly to read and print and archive stories about the True Holmes. There are thousands of Holmes stories located there, but many are parodies, or anachronistic, or related to modernized and offensive simulacrums, or with incorrect ghost-busting leanings. Others were clearly written by individuals who have no clue about Sherlock Holmes, or have hijacked him for their own agendas. These stories may be ignored, even if they have to be waded through – for buried in the muck of this backyard goose lot, for those who take time to look, are some true and rare jewels.

And in April 2008, the beginning of a couple of stories were posted, "An Ordinary Meeting" on the tenth, and "Truth is the Critic" the next day, both as written by an author going under the curious sobriquet of *aragonite*.

"An Ordinary Meeting" gives details of Lestrade's first consultation with Sherlock Holmes, and "Truth is the Critic" is written from the perspective of the Scotland Yard inspectors as they read *A Study in Scarlet* – and providing their reactions when see how Watson has described them. These were well written and interesting, and this approach really hadn't been attempted before.

(To be accurate, there had been some stories about the Yarders, but they were inconsistent. For instance, M.J. Trow's long Lestrade series veers wildly from legitimate mysteries to unreadable parodies, with particularly bogus attacks on Sherlock Holmes, and Trow inexplicably gives Inspector G. Lestrade the first name of "Sholto".

In "Truth is the Critic", *aragonite* was already painting the Yarders – Inspectors Lestrade, Gregson, Bradstreet, and Hopkins in particular – in well-rounded and respectful ways that hadn't been seen before. They had their own life stories beyond The Canon, and weren't just the inspector *du jour* appearing in this-or-that Canonical tale. Who knew then that this new author, slipping quietly onto the scene, had such an overall vision for these individuals, with fully realized details about their personal lives, their backgrounds and histories . . . and a plan for a massive overarching adventure that would span decades in their lives?

Over the next few months, more stories quickly followed – "A Cookout in Cornwall", "Route to Madness", and "Just Inspector Will Do" (my all-time favorite of these works, relating the events on the Paddington platform when Mary Watson awaits her husband's return from the Continent in mid-May 1891. I re-read it every year on Reichenbach Day.) But on April 17th, 2008, *aragonite* raised the stakes, publishing the first chapter of a novel, *A Sword for Defense*, the first of a massive story arc relating what Watson and Lestrade and the other Yarders faced in the months after Holmes's supposed death at the Reichenbach Falls.

While keeping one story going would overwhelm many authors, *aragonite* – whomever he or she was – had even greater ambitions. New stories and chapters began to be posted at a feverish pace. A week after *Sword* started, another serialized novel began, *You Buy Bones*, telling how Watson, in early 1882 and fresh from his first year living with Holmes in Baker Street, comes across a monstrous crime that directly and personally affects the Scotland Yard inspectors. And a few months after that, *aragonite* started another novel that served as a prequel leading to *Sword* called *The MoonCursers*, telling of Lestrade's own terrifying adventures in late April and early May 1891, occurring at the same time Holmes and Watson were playing cat-and-mouse with Moriarty, on their way to a fateful encounter in Meiringen.

Over the course of that summer, nearly every day brought some new chapter: Sometimes another episode in *A Sword for Defense* or *You Buy Bones* or *The MoonCursers*, and at other times a seemingly stand-alone story that that filled in some crucial and interesting aspect about the Scotland Yarders that only made the overall painting richer and deeper.

Imagine if Charles Dickens were writing and publishing three serialized novels at once, and adding in short stories too. And they were going straight from being written to being posted for public consumption as soon as they were complete. And clearly the overall storyline wasn't being generated along the way – there was a *plan*, for little threads mentioned here and there about Lestrade's boyhood or Bradstreet's family had massive importance much later.

Over many months during this time, *aragonite* was also constructing another massive work, *Test of the Professionals*, which related the events after *You Buy Bones* and served as a set-up for *A Sword for Defense*, telling us much more about Lestrade's past, his unfortunate and dangerous life-long connection with Professor Moriarty's agent, the truly evil Jethro Quimper, and the escalating and terrifying events surrounding his courtship with Clea Cheatham.

In August 2008, with all of this going on, *aragonite* started another brilliant novella, *A Secondary Stain*, the *other* events of "The Second Stain", in which Lestrade was not as clueless as he appears in Watson's manuscript, actually working behind the scenes to assist Holmes's investigation. It was the brilliance of this story that finally prompted me to write a fan letter.

Using the fan fiction website's messenger feature, I emailed an extensive message to *aragonite* in October 2008, and soon received a wonderful and informative reply.

First, I learned that *aragonite* was really Marcia Wilson. In subsequent communications, I learned that *aragonite* – which curiously I'd never looked up before then – is calcium carbonate used by marine organisms to build their shells and skeletons. Since aragonite can be found in cave formations, and since Marcy is a caver – the evidence of which can be found in some of her stories brilliantly dealing with caverns and London's Lost Rivers – I suspect that's why she chose the unusual pen-name.

Over many emails over many years, Marcy has explained to me that she wrote so prolifically in those early years because she had insomnia, and that was a very productive time to write. She also could *see* all of these scenes, and almost couldn't write fast enough to convey them. In her very first reply to me in October 2008, she explained, how she approached telling the Yarders' story, and why she named Inspector G. Lestrade *Geoffrey*:

> *I've never liked the playing down of characters. It's a lazy way to pump up the character in your mind. I have to be very careful not to wander into the Fangirlyverse. Usually I deal with it by giving a character a name I dislike, and for some reason, I dislike Geoffrey so naturally I stuck it on the poor guy.*

She also explained that:

> *I was so bleeding tired of writing against another person's notions on Holmes and Watson that I just went to another character that I rather liked. (When I was younger, I hated Lestrade. He should have been kowtowing to Holmes' genius like all of us!) Later on, I realized that it took a pretty remarkable man to refuse to see Holmes in a reverent light. [The] clues about Lestrade were subtle and interesting. There had to be a reason for someone who was supposed to be such a good cop to stay a police inspector after his initial promotion. I made him a Celtic Breton out of a half-thought. I was seeing Colin Jeavons in my head, and he's so Welsh he's probably half-Neanderthal! Being a Breton or a Channel Islander would have made [Lestrade] an English citizen, but he would not have been accepted as an equal in race or status by many people.*

Our communications continued, as did her writing. By early 2009, *A Sword for Defense* was complete, and the next book in the ongoing saga, *The Narrow Path* had commenced. Those were great days to be a Sherlockian and to be reading *fanfiction.net*, as there were other great authors there as well – *Westron Wynde* and *KCS* among them, all with powerful and correct understandings of the *True Holmes*. These authors were writing for the fans, and also for each other, and I was privileged to be in contact with many of them. In a few years, Marcy and *Westron*

*Wynde* – who turned out to be amazing pasticheur Sarah Bennett, whose works are slowly being made available from Belanger Books – began to take down their online works and publish them in real books. (It was at this time that I let Marcy and Sarah read my first Sherlock Holmes pastiches, written in 2008 and at that point seen by no one but my wife, and with their encouragement I started publicly publishing my stories too.)

Marcy initially published *You Buy Bones*, along with some related short stories, in 2010 (from Lulu Publishing. That version is now out of print.) Next came *Test of the Professionals: Leap Year* (2013, also from Lulu and out of print), also collecting the original online novel and working in some supplementary material.

In 2015, I came up with the idea of *The MX Book of New Sherlock Holmes Stories*, and of course Marcy was in the initial list of invitees. Since then, much of her writing has been turned to contributing stories to these anthologies, having submitted nearly two-dozen. Through these books, she became associated with MX Publishing, who issued a new edition of *You Buy Bones* in 2015, as well as splitting *Test of the Professionals: Leap Year* into three planned smaller volumes. The first two, *The Adventure of the Flying Blue Pidgeon* and *The Peaceful Night Poisonings*, were published by MX in 2016 and 2017, respectively. Unfortunately, due to a combination of events, the third part of *Test* – the much larger piece called *Leap Year* that relates the exciting conclusion to that narrative – was not published.

So for the wider public, those who were never able to read Marcy's massive *ouvré* on *fanfiction.net*, her available works consisted of these three novels, and her well-respected stories in the MX anthologies. (Unfortunately, Marcy, Sarah Bennett, and several others were forced to pull their Sherlockian content from *fanfiction.net* several years ago after some of their works were stolen – copied-and-pasted and then republished under other author names by way of Amazon's self-publishing program.)

In late 2024, I was in the process of working toward assembling and editing the final volumes, Parts 49, 50, 51, and 52 of the MX anthologies, a process which would continue into early 2025. While looking around in my computer files, I found something I'd forgotten: Years earlier, I had saved and formatted the files for five of Marcy's novels – those relating to Watson and Lestrade's adventures during The Great Hiatus. Since the late 1990's, I've printed and archived every traditional Canonical Holmes adventure that I've found online –

thousands of them – and I have over 175 binders of pure Holmes adventures – including all of Marcy's now-withdrawn stories. But luckily I had these novels as Word files. And I had an idea . . . .

I contacted Marcy, who hadn't had time in several years to think about publishing more of her works, and asked if I could shepherd these five novels to publication – *pro-bono*, just because I was passionate about other people reading these incredible stories. Marcy was willing, and so I started editing with great enthusiasm – even as I was supposed to be editing the final MX volumes, stories for which were rolling in every day.

It soon became apparent to me that to publish these five novels without readers knowing the events of the missing *Leap Year* would be a confusing mess. Too much happened in these books that continued from what happened in *Leap Year*. Clearly, that missing volume would need to be edited and published too. And while I was at it, why not re-edit the previously published three books – *You Buy Bones*, *The Adventure of the Flying Blue Pidgeon*, and *The Peaceful Night Poisonings* – into an overall cohesive narrative?

MX Publisher Extraordinaire Steve Emecz, THE Sherlockian publisher and the Sherlockian Gutenberg – the man who made Sherlockian publishing accessible to real people instead of guarding a narrow doorway, or deciding that Sherlockian publishing should only be available for a very narrow cadre of self-described elites – was enthusiastic, and ready to proceed immediately. But I needed to actually finish editing the nine books first. It was a joy, and a labor of love to do so.

I had read all of these books serially as published, hopping from story to story as new chapters appeared, back in 2008-2011. But to read the story now, in one place, in order and available in its entirety, made it even more amazing – and exciting for the thought of new readers able to discover this magnificent world: *Sherlock Holmes's London, as seen through the eyes of the Scotland Yarders.*

Even as I dug deeper into Marcy's Scotland Yard adventures, I was remembering the other stories – the previously mentioned *A Secondary Stain*. Her Yarder's Christmas novels, *Gunnysack Goose for Christmas* and *A Mouth of Ivy*. Short-story collections like *Devilry* and *It's All in a Name*. Other novels and novellas like *The Muse of History*, *Ghosts in the Making*, *Courage Rises*, *The Kings and Queens of London*, and the World War I narrative, *The Days of Our Years*. I had amazing fun editing the first nine books that are being published in

2025, and with any luck, I hope to be able to edit the rest of these, along with a collection of Marcy's MX anthology contributions, over the next year or so, in order to fill in Marcy's *Great Scotland Yard Tapestry*.

There are certain authors who "own" other Canonical characters by taking hold of them and defining them. The late Carole Nelson Douglas was Irene Adler's chronicler. Michael Kurland gives us the best portrait of Professor Moriarty. Will Thomas has absolutely defined Barker, Holmes's hated rival on the Surrey Side. The late Gerard Williams claimed Dr. Mortimer (even if only for two books), and Susan Knight is easily becoming the definitive voice of Mrs. Hudson.

But Marcia Wilson tells the True Story of the Scotland Yarders – and presents an amazing viewpoint of Holmes and Watson along the way.

I've said it many times before, and can't say it any better now:

*Marcia Wilson has found Scotland Yard's Tin Dispatch Box.*

David Marcum
January 2025

# A Sword for Defense

# Chapter I – Unpleasant Business

"You are Inspector Lestrade," said the mourning-black man in the doorframe.

Lestrade was well-used to the cautious contempt his social betters carried for him. Unlike the true gentlemen, this one would have him use the tradesman's entrance rather than sully his honor by permitting him in the front door.

Lestrade knew how to play the game. Although he was still quite exhausted from the Henley Royal Regatta [1] of two days previously, he rose to his feet, his clothes sticking to his body in the wilting heat of July. He *could* have remained seated – a show of his own personal power in his office – but it would have quickly turned into a battle of wills neither man would truly win. Only hardness of feeling would result, and that invariably reaped harsh rewards. Besides, the mourning-black was a dead giveaway that he should be treated cautiously.

Despite the weather – which was enough to paralyze a man – his visitor was clad in the deep black of grief suitable to the cooler months. The graying black hair receding from his dome only increased the ferocity of his leathery face.

"I am indeed Inspector Lestrade, sir." He nodded his head formally. The other was so ramrod-erect he appeared to have no real spine at all. An iron pipe was more suited to that body.

His visitor stepped inside, once, and did not remove his hat. A metal circle rested at his breast right where a posset would normally be placed: Victoria Cross. Military, Lestrade was unsurprised to notice.

"I am here to report a liability of truth, Inspector. You have a reputation for tenacity that even your enemies admit to. This is a matter of tenacity."

Lestrade's sense of unease grew although he hid it well. "And what would that be, sir?"

"My name is Colonel James Moriarty, West Station."

Lestrade hoped his reaction did not show. In truth, he had been wondering when something of this nature would finally happen.

Moriarty he might be, but he bore little kinship to the slump-shouldered nemesis of the late Sherlock Holmes. Where the Professor had been pallid and glittering, a product of mind without little personal movement, this man was bronzed to his cuffs and collar from activity. His health burned the same way his brother's intellect had burned. Coldly and self-driven. Holmes had described the professor as giving the impression of being much larger than he really was merely by his presence. With this brother, there was no impression. He *was* bigger. Bigger in a way that actually discomfited Lestrade.

Lestrade was a small man. He knew it and was unbothered by it. Being described as little was only a fact. There was no point in any other attitude. Yet Moriarty was conjuring feelings he had thought were left behind in his past as the smallest child on the street, the one to be tormented simply because it was natural to destroy the weakest member.

"Colonel Moriarty." Lestrade nodded his head again. "Please, would you care to sit down?"

"I have no interest in lingering with unpleasant business." The Colonel reached inside his black coat and pulled out a large rectangle of pale paper – an envelope, tied with string and sealed with a ring. "It is unpleasant business that brings me here."

"Very well, sir." Lestrade answered him with as much tact as his nature would allow. "I have no desire to delay you or interfere with your valuable time."

A grunt was his reward. "You have worked in the past with Sherlock Holmes and Dr. Watson. Your peers assure me you are immune to prejudice and work evenly with friend and foe. Very well. I am reporting a crime to you that involves a man you may or may not think highly of."

"Go on, sir." Lestrade felt his chest constrict at an old instinct. He knew nothing good was about to happen.

"Dr. Watson in his florid accounts has given the world a description of his wounding in the Second Afghan Campaign. I am here to tell you, as the same Colonel Moriarty who was at the Battle of Maiwand, his account is fictitious. I wish to see his falsehoods addressed."

"Falsehoods," Lestrade repeated numbly, his mind for once not obeying his need for the situation. "Falsehoods in what way?"

"To begin with, he was reprimanded before the battle for failing to perform his duties as a surgeon." The envelope tapped Lestrade's desk with an absurd lightness for the weight it carried. "He was flogged, Inspector. Flogged for willful disobedience on part of his superior officers. The report is inside this folder. And secondly, if he was indeed wounded honorably in battle, in his left shoulder and opposing leg by Jezail bullets, I would much like to know the reasoning behind *this*."

Moriarty had pulled out another rectangle, bound in pasteboard. He held it over Lestrade's desk like a board. Lestrade's hand did not quite shake as he took the object – he would have far rather closed his fingers around a coiled serpent.

A serpent, after all, might have a chance of missing its strike.

Moriarty remained where he was, imperiously waiting. He watched as Lestrade slowly turned the pasteboard over, and opened its folded leaves like a book. His lips tightened in satisfaction as the Inspector turned white.

"Stragglers of the 66th (Berkshires) Coming into Kandahar"
by Harry Payne

## NOTE

1.    Regatta on the Thames, usually first week of July.

# Chapter II – Talents and Character

*"Talents are best nurtured in solitude, but character
is best formed in the stormy billows of the world"*
– Goethe

*Kensington Practice, 1891:*

Mary saw him idling in the new consulting room, gnawing on a problem like a dog with a bone. She smiled slightly to see him that way. Their friends often referred to him as a bulldog when a puzzle presented itself. While she thought he looked nothing like a canine, there was a way his dark brows knit together and his jaw stuck out, as if he expected a battle to gird against. Her father had been of a similar bend, she'd been told, when his sailing presented a particularly difficult tack against the wind. It was something men were prone to.

He was so absorbed in whatever was bothering him, he did not see her pause by the jamb. For a moment she simply watched him. He was pleasant enough to observe, and she could admit that as his wife. The sunlight pulled the gold threads out of his hair and illuminated his skin – skin that would never lose that light brown tang from the harsh foreign suns. What had been burned on him as a boy in Australia had only been topped off by India and the desert. Proof positive, he joked, that a north-countryman could actually be more than pale.

The seven pounds she'd worked so hard to put on him looked as though they would actually stay, but for a year she had despaired. He was fond of his meals more than most, and was always looking forward to the next plate, but he never ate above small portions at any given time. Indeed, he seemed as incapable of pushing himself at the table, and he apologized profusely for it. The one time he had spoken to her of the war had been over the subject of food. He had admitted that knowing there was a meal nearby was almost more important than the eating of it – that followed with another apology, for he did not want to make her understand the desperations of war. But she had. Eating meant security to him in from a time when there were no guarantees on anything.

But what she truly enjoyed was seeing him lean back in a position that was impossible when he was feeling the ache of his wounds. The moments were far too rare. Without the pull of pain he was calmer, his tension thoughtful rather than distracted.

Were John a selfish man, he would have been mourning the loss of his closest friend as deeply as he had when he stepped onto the train platform. She had no doubt the wound was still as deep as it ever was, but it was beginning to close over, bit by bit. His own pain came second after the responsibilities he'd set for himself, and he would not shirk his attentions to his wife and his practice.

His wife, his practice . . . and perhaps . . . Mary allowed herself a private smile for the hope they shared.

John's being at odds was natural. Her husband was an introvert, comfortable with knowing his place in the scheme of things, and if he did not know his place, his demeanor soon took on the aspect of a man who is in the middle of a combat zone – too busy to comment or reflect until long after, and then it would be to shake his head in detached wonder at his own actions. He'd worn that look quite often in the past two weeks from their move to this practice.

She still missed their old place at Paddington. It had been a bit more convenient for their small circle of friends and clients, but not overly successful. Competition was quite fierce around the Station, and they had always known that a move would occur the second John found better. Still, she liked living on the other side of Hyde Park, and the fact they could arrange an occasional jaunt on the Serpentine when the weather was good. But Mary's strong, unvoiced feelings were that John had pushed their change of address with a determination that was outside his usual capacity. He had enacted such a change once before: To uproot himself from his Army life into the strange world of London. Paddington had been more reachable in his memories of the past. Paddington was a link backwards in his old life with Sherlock Holmes, and he must needs take a step away from that old life for his very sanity.

It was impossible not to think of the man who had, however indirectly, brought them together. Mary often wondered if her upbringing had been a bit harsher than was expected of a proper lady, for she had long found herself immune to his reputation as a callous-tongued misanthrope There were enough people in the world who possessed a gift that made them gleam like torches, but those gifts seemed to be priced highly. Mary was no stranger to geniuses, and they were all united in a lack of skills the rest of the world did not.

*Paddington Practice, 1888:*

*"He just thinks so swiftly, you know." Her husband had commented almost idly in her presence as he wrapped the hand of an injured constable at Paddington. A case with*

*Holmes, and the man – no more than a boy – had suffered an agonizing blow from a common but clever thief. Holmes had dropped the poor man off without ceremony and took off with no other word, leaving a patient friend to explain and patch to a bewildered comrade. "Holmes is so far ahead of us mere mortals that he has no real comprehension of how intelligent he really is. He honestly believes we can all see the world the same way he does." John shook his head and smiled at his patient's disbelief. "I've had plenty of time to think about this, Hopkins. The main reason why he has so little patience for us common men is that he has no idea of his real value to the world."*

*And Hopkins was bandaged, given a shot of whisky, and packed back to Scotland Yard with no doubt a new tale to add to the collection growing in what John swore was Holmes's personal file cabinet sitting within an easy lunge of Inspector Gregson's office.*

*"Do they have a file on you?" she murmured with a smile as she stepped inside the warmth of his arm.*

*"Me?" He looked down at her with a surprised laugh. "Why would they have a file on me?"*

*"Oh, nothing, dear." Mary smiled back up at him, thinking that no one could say that Sherlock Holmes the only man who lived ignorant of his own worth.*

*Kensington Practice, 1891:*

"James," She paused in the doorway and he stopped his fugue, startled to be pulled out of his mind and into his own house. "Darling, dinner is almost ready. Would you like a cup of tea first?"

Watson – "James" as his wife privately called him – smiled and put a calling-card in his pocket. "I'd be delighted," he announced in overdone and deliberate formality – a joke that made her giggle like a schoolgirl every time. "I'm afraid you've made me a wretch over tea." He sighed as he pointed to the card still protruding. "It looks like I'll have a late caller, no doubt of a confidential nature, when you and Ivy are snug abed. Tea would be a great help."

"Then we'll be sure it's a proper cup, and I shall leave a tray with you when I take myself upstairs tonight," she scolded fondly, and brought the tray in. Tonight it was a cup of Darjeeling, a ship's voyage away from the first flush of spring. It was a tradition, the doctor and his wife, to sit and enjoy a cup before the last meal of the day. She took such pleasure in the custom he did as well. There were not enough such moments in anyone's life.

# Chapter III – A Rumble of Thunder

*Kensington, London, 1891*

The doctor was already tired when the card came upon its tray by Ivy – *"Poor Ivy"*, as he and his wife said in reference for her earnest yet uninspiring skills as a maid. Were she not earnest and lacking the nurturing instinct, they would have been forced to find some polite excuse for her dismissal. Still, she meant well. It was largely her terror of making a mistake that led to her utter lack of confidence around the house and the practice.

He picked up the card with an absent "Thank you" to the girl, but the feel of the paper surprised him slightly out of his fatigue. It was rich paper, textured with skill and the tint of old ivory – the thought made him pause, as something touched his memory, but it fled as fast as it came.

*J.M., Cl.*
*West Station – Master*

Only one name came to mind. He turned the card over. On the back the message was clear: 9:15 p.m.

"James," She paused in the doorway and he stopped his fugue, startled to be pulled out of his mind and into his own house. "Darling, dinner is almost ready. Would you like a cup of tea first?"

"James" smiled and put the calling-card in his pocket. "I'd be delighted," he said . . . .

*Nine p.m.*

His consulting room clock rang first, soft and slow chimes of heavy brass. The hall-clock Mary was so proud of followed seconds after in a lighter, rainfall patter. It was almost time for his guest.

Watson leaned back in his chair, eyes closed, listening to the church bells pick up and scatter notes across Hyde Park. It was quiet in this affluent street.

Long moments passed, and his eyes opened. He rested his hand on the left-hand drawer by his desk and pulled it open in a sudden impulse. It took no more than a second to pull out his Adams Mark III [1] and tuck it into his pocket.

Instinct.

24

He had learned to listen to his instincts a long time ago. What was it about this small white rectangle that conjured up feelings he hadn't stared at since his Army days?

A flash of memory: A cold moor in a lonely part of the world. A predator that glowed with hate and phosphorous, and a human that was even worse.

The man lifted his hat over his head, and the doctor felt a sword of ice stab him in the heart.

"Colonel." The old days would never leave him.

The ferocious gaze softened slightly, perhaps in surprise, as the other man honored him with a taut military stance and a crisp nod of the head. Did he not think he would give him that respect?

The older man regarded him in silence for a moment. Colonel James Moriarty. Officer of the Second Afghan Campaign.

"Colonel Moriarty." The doctor nodded his head. "Would you like a cup of tea?"

"That would be agreeable." The man settled himself down, back erect against his chair, and watched the doctor pour the cups. It gave both men the period of silence they needed for the moment.

"I'd heard you were master of the West Station." Dr. Watson said quietly.

"Yes. A satisfying position." The Colonel held the cup in his hands, letting the heat sink in. Those hands were exactly as Watson remembered – strong and tough and capable of doing as much work as the hardest infantryman. "I recall you from the campaign." Something glittered deep in those eyes. "You did your share."

Watson took the safest response to such sere praise. He nodded once without taking his eyes off the other.

"Perhaps you have divined the purpose of my visit."

Watson was a moment replying. "It is an unusual time for a visit, but you wanted to make it late enough, I'm sure, to ensure privacy."

Moriarty grunted. "I will not allow the slander of my brother's good name, Major."

Major. No one had called him by his rank in years. It was a clever cut. It reminded them both of his inferior status to the Colonel. It reminded him of what his life's work would have been without the invention of the Jezail bullet.

"Nor would I wish to see anyone slandered, Colonel," Watson answered him quietly.

"I lack my brother's skills in many ways." The deep voice grumbled. "But I was always a man who preferred direct action, rather than those who arrange it in unseemly and indirect methods." The dark gaze raked him up and down. "And it would have been hard indeed not to recall you, even before the incident with the saber. [2] You were a good fighter, Watson. A good soldier. I remember."

"As I recall you." Dr. Watson passed the teacup forward. His face was nothing but the perfect mirror of military respect. "I remember the murmurs of your retirement . . . There were those who felt a loss by your absence."

Another grunt. "You know why I am here, then."

"I would not presume to speak for you, Colonel."

A snort of amusement. "I hear you are writing again."

The doctor merely tilted his head slightly to one side.

"I hope you are not formulating a rebuttal against my beloved brother, Major Watson."

It was the second time his lower rank had been noted, and his life's title ignored.

Watson held the cup close to his face. The steam curled under his chin and he breathed in the scents of a world far removed from the cold eyes facing him. "I am a writer, Colonel." He pointed out the obvious gently, refusing to use any emotions that the old veteran would read as an insult – or worse, a challenge of some sort. "And I was there with Sherlock Holmes almost to the end. I have the facts as were presented to me. If you have other facts, then I welcome your use of them. I can say no more on the subject."

The metallic face did not seem to move, but something fierce jumped on the other side of those burning eyes. "If you seek your own destruction, I have no means by which to save you," he announced. "I confess you have not disappointed my expectations." The Colonel took a sip of his tea, and he must have noted the high quality of Mary's choice, for he took another sip soon after. "A pity that your discretion is not always well directed. I noticed that at your trial."

"My discretion, as you put it." Watson heard the iron leak into his voice, "has never been for sale."

"Everyone is for sale." Moriarty rose with a ponderousness that absurdly reminded Watson of Mycroft Holmes. "You are merely unaware of your personal value." His eyes narrowed as he turned his head, and Watson breathed out in relief of finding himself alone again.

*Private Journal – J.H.W.*

*I must have sat there with my thoughts for a half-hour while the fire died down. The Colonel's absence had left a cold hole in the room.*

*I have no doubt he can make my life unpleasant – and that of Mary's. Our funds are not deep. I do not have many reserves and Mary has only the Agra Pearls, which she would sell if I were to ask her, but things will never come to this. I will see to that.*

*Colonel James Moriarty served as a man of distinction in each and all campaigns abroad. That he took an early semi-retirement as a station-master for West might suggest he was not above the cloud of suspicion his brother endured as a mathematician. This news would hardly surprise anyone who has personally encountered him.*

*No matter how well one can cover their tracks and pretend to live a wholesome life above suspicion, I believe something will always endure, and people will notice. Perhaps such a cloud is over the Colonel. I would have to make discreet inquiries.*

*I do not wish this. I am sick at heart to think that Holmes's actions must be defended from beyond the grave. And were he here, I can well hear his chiding at the stance I take: My responsibilities as a physician, as a husband, as a writer. I can not well afford a stance of solitude and fruitless bravery.*

*But every instinct I possess is telling me I must not show Moriarty weakness.*

*And although writing of his death hurts on every level in my being, I must tell the world the events as I know them to have happened.*

## NOTES

1. Firearms experts generally hold that Watson's "service revolver" was most likely an Adams Mark III .45 service revolver. It was adopted as the official service revolver on January 25, 1878. A tough weapon, it had a rod ejector and a loading gate, weighed close to three pounds, and had a six-inch barrel. It took a cartridge that was acceptable for both the Mark II and Mark III. By the time Watson was being shipped home, the Mark II was being replaced by the Mark I, but the II was still being issued. No matter which model, it is clear no one wanted to be on the wrong side of the bullet.
2. A clue to that little flogging incident referred to in Chapter I.

# Chapter IV – Close as Two Brothers

*"Tell your friend a lie. If he keeps it secret, then tell him the truth."*
– Proverb

*Near Reigate, Surrey:*

"**I**nspector Lestrade, I am pleased to finally meet you." Colonel Hayter proved a diametric opposite of Colonel Moriarty by producing his hand in a quite un-military manner, and Lestrade was shocked out of his defensive reserve long enough to shake it. The grip reminded him of Watson instantly: Quick and firm and of a hand that was very warm with health. "You are not an infrequent name in John's letters to me."

Lestrade caught himself swallowing, caught somewhere between flattery and panic. "He writes to you often, then?" He'd thought he had been a little clever, researching the names of the officers who had attended this military trial in the records. Hayter's name had come up practically next door to London.

Hayter laughed. "I may be a free bachelor, but my days are still lonely enough! John writes me as often as the mood strikes – as do I."

That was encouraging. "Well, I trust that you could deduce from my wire the purpose of my visit," Lestrade cleared his throat.

"Hmmph." Hayter continued to confuse the Inspector by patiently regarding the clouds rolling over their heads. "That I do. Well, shall we go inside, then? Or would you be more comfortable out here? I have noticed many of my more urbane guests are a bit taken aback by all the greenery I cultivate."

"It fair outbids Hyde Park," Lestrade said honestly. He couldn't recall ever seeing so much . . . stuff . . . in a single plot of earth.

"I once referred to my retirement as becoming a full-time gardener," Hayter explained succinctly.

"Ah." Lestrade blinked a bit as a bevy of red squirrels conducted a complicated-looking maneuver in the trees by the small fountain.

"Watch out for those little blighters. As soon as you turn your back, they'll fan your pockets and run off with your watch!" Hayter warned. "I'm afraid my housekeeper has spoiled them dreadfully and they associate all humans with blind benefice. When we fail to show them proper respect, they grow as aggressive as a Hindu asked to attend an ox-roast." Hayter waved his stick in the air as he spoke. "Once in a while I conduct a little target-practice for my cooking pot, but it seems that for every one that makes it into the mulligatawny, three others move in." Hayter paused as a thought struck him. "Do you like squirrel?" he asked hopefully.

"I don't know if I do or not." Lestrade figured that was the best tactic to take – not that anyone really knew what was served up in the sausages off Fleet Street.

"Very healthful. I'll send some home with you." Hayter looked fantastically pleased at the notion of ridding himself of a problem by being a good host, and patted the pistol-shaped gun in his pocket.

"*Ahem*." Lestrade cleared his throat. "You . . . are too kind. But I don't want to take up any of your valuable time, Colonel . . . ."

"You have business to conduct. I understand." Hayter paused at the outdoors chairs set upon the lawn by a rather strange statue of a faun and threw himself down. "Do have a seat. What may I help you with?" The shrewd eyes were knowing. "It involves John, I'm sure, or you wouldn't be here – and you certainly wouldn't look like you were about to hang your best friend."

Lestrade rubbed the back of his neck, telling himself the pollen made him itch. "A complaint was raised to us at the Yard about some details of Dr. Watson's service days," he began hesitantly. "A charge that he was not being truthful about his account of the Battle of Maiwand."

"Balderdash!" Hayter pronounced. "I was there – Watson told the utter truth."

"I'm glad to hear you say so." Lestrade relaxed. "But the man who had charged the complaint has produced a strange bit of evidence that I must confirm or deny."

"You intrigue me, sir. By all means, present your problem and I will do my best to help you."

Lestrade silently handed over the chromolithograph and the report.

The report only made Hayter lift his brows. He snorted once and set it aside – clearly he already knew of the contents. The chromolithograph was another matter. For a moment surprise slashed his face, and then a deep sorrow before the image was put away.

"I can answer many of your questions, I'm sure." Hayter said gravely. "But you must ask them."

"Was Dr. Watson flogged for some sort of failure before the battle?" Lestrade decided to pick the worst question first.

Hayter sighed. "Yes. Flogging was allegedly abolished the year after Watson's trial," he said grimly. "I am afraid the practice still continues."

"Colonel Moriarty intimated there was more to the trial than what was in the report," Lestrade said, carefully using that name for the first time.

"Moriarty." Hayter snorted with enough force to wave his waxed moustaches. "Is *that* his little game?" he retorted. "God spare me from his type. I tell you, it is the men of his stamp that made me regret retiring when I did. I never felt comfortable with leaving the lambs in charge of the hybrid wolves . . . ." Hayter's long fingers rapped a staccato on the arm of his chair. "If you'll forgive the perspective of a man who was at the trial, I would be honored to give you my own account – within reason, of course. There are still some details that I would prefer not to divulge in order to protect the privacy of some innocents."

"Colonel Hayter," Lestrade's voice was grim with emotion, "whatever you see fit to tell me, I assure you, will be far more than what I have now."

Hayter seemed pleased with the answer. "To begin with, are you aware of the laws that bind the Medical Surgeon in the British Army?"

"I know precious little, although I have a reference at Scotland Yard."

"Then you already have more than most." Hayter approved. "I shall start with the subject that began this wretched affair. The officer's saber. It is mandatory for officers to distinguish themselves in their rank – besides the extra gold braid, the different hat and leg-stripe – to carry a saber that befits their rank." Hayter shook his head wryly. "Even the Medical officers are expected to carry a saber. However, there is an interesting little rule in their conduct: *No medical officer is permitted to use his saber, save in self-defense.*"

Lestrade realized he had stopped blinking. Hayter remained silent, patiently waiting for his brain to process. "Sir . . . are you *joking*?"

"It is a joke, but not an amusing one." Hayter said calmly. "I see your imagination is conjuring up the logical conclusions as to that situation."

"The report says that Major Watson was guilty of unbecoming conduct with his dress saber. I thought it meant something like . . . well, forgetting to polish it, or leaving it out in the rain or something like that." Lestrade's face turned red as he realized that sounded completely unlike Watson.

Hayter threw back his head and roared. "For all Watson cared, he could have used it to peel a pomegranate! – Oh, my, that did conjure a vivid mental image, didn't it?" To Lestrade's confusion, Hayter turned as red as the roses crawling up the trellis. "Forgive me, that was quite uncalled for."

"Quite all right," Lestrade wondered what in the world had just happened with Hayter's embarrassment. As far as he knew, pomegranates had precious little to do with impropriety. [1]

"Back to the subject, the report says that Major Watson ran afoul of another officer, who himself was a Major. What the report does not say but I say, the man thoroughly deserved the trouncing given him." Hayter's face glowered. "I'm pleased to report *that one* is no longer able to inflict his damage on the troops . . . but he *did* rise to Lieutenant-Colonel before he left, and now he's some sort of wretched Lord for a wretched northern district . . . In my most unworthy moments, I fantasize of his southern-hardened constitution falling victim to a good Orkney winter."

"If I may," Lestrade was writing as fast as his pencil would allow, "what kind of trouncing was this?"

"A thoroughly stupid one. There was the matter of a young lady involved." Hayter stopped, a brief look of pain in his eyes. "Please forgive me. It is for her sake that I will not name any names in this matter."

Lestrade nodded silently. Hayter looked relieved.

"John had a remarkable brother. I've never met anyone like him before or since. Truly brilliant man, mathematically talented, yet a bit of an artist and a natural scientist-naturalist . . . Everything he touched seemed to turn to gold like a young Midas, but unlike Midas, he had no ill consequences of his fortune. I regret there was a bit of a fragile quality to his genius. He could have borne up any hardship life itself threw upon him, but he was absolutely unforgiving of himself. I tell you, no one could possibly be as hard on that man as he was on his own soul."

"Mayn't I inquire as to his name, since we are talking of two Watsons?" Lestrade asked.

"Oh." Hayter unexpectedly looked embarrassed. "Well, this is part of it. John and his brother were so very much alike, there was an understandable but confusing mixup in the records . . . They were both registered as John H. Watson."

"How often does that happen?" Lestrade wondered.

"More often than one might think." Hayter sighed. "Our Empire might overall be wealthy, but the average man who joins the military is trying to combat poverty. I've seen entire families enlist within a few years of each other. And if I told you how many *women* try to sign up disguised as men, I'm sure you'd think my retirement was due to a mental illness." The Colonel rubbed his forehead in memory. "Their names were confusing enough, truth to tell. John Hamish Watson is the Watson you know. His brother's name was the reverse – Hamish John Watson."

"Yes, that does sound very confusing." Lestrade agreed.

"It's a common enough custom to name children after their grandparents' lines, especially if the children in question look to be the only heirs to carry on the name. If I recall my salient details, the brothers were named after their paternal and maternal grandfathers – the Hamish family and the John family. It might have been *Johns*, and they dropped the '*S*' – I know I would. Things would be confusing enough without someone thinking they were Welsh in the bargain!"

Lestrade had often been asked if his low altitude had to do with a woodscolt Cymric ancestor, so he said nothing.

"It wasn't long before the officers learned of the gifts Hamish possessed. He was quite good at what he did – and he was capable of doing anything one asked of him. Before long, he was being brought into work that was confidential in nature, but I assure you, that work was nothing but honorable. The fact that he had a brother who was so very much like him, and could mimic him quite well – Well, you might say it was a gift from Minerva for some of our Intelligence staff. Imagine having a man who can be in two places at once?"

Lestrade shuddered at the thought. "I believe I am following you, sir."

"John was the medical major, and Hamish was regular infantry. The incident with the saber was unfortunately no more than a case of mistaken identity, brought on by a certain unworthy young officer who owed his rank to family connections, and who was jealous of the attentions of the daughter of one of the officers . . . jealous enough that he selected quarrels with anyone he believed might be in competition for the lady's favor. It was in reality, *Hamish* who picked up the sword. John would have kept silent for the good of the service anyway – but add to protecting his brother – Well, I believe that he would have cut his own tongue out first before he betrayed his own kin."

"They were close then." Lestrade realized. He certainly wouldn't have felt that way about his own flesh and blood – too many of them saw *him* as a betrayer for becoming a policeman.

"As close as two brothers can be." Hayter's face had that strange look again, and then was gone.

"Correct me if I am mistaken, then. There was an incident with a jealous officer, and John Watson was identified as the person in the fight when it was in fact his brother."

"You are correct. It began as no more than warm feelings and warmer words, and then an overt challenge of skill with the gentleman's blade." Hayter sighed. "The only thing believable about that case was John's popularity with the ladies. There were Don Juans aplenty over there, and hot climates make matters even worse, but John was such an epitome of propriety that no one fear for anyone's daughter around him." Hayter chuckled under his breath. "It wasn't even those dashed good looks, either. It was the fact that he was one of the few young men who *wasn't* talking about how bloody marvelous he was. It gets quite tiresome to a young lady, who would prefer to hear about herself as the subject of conversation, you know. But every soldier dreams of rising in rank, and too often the poor girls are a captive audience to those dreams. But John . . . John simply liked to listen to people talk. He enjoyed the company of people, and people in turn enjoyed him. I'm not surprised the – Well, the jealous officer in question often reminded me of that Irish proverb – 'He who loves himself will have no rivals.'"

Lestrade shook his head. "This sounds not unlike some of the higher functions I've been forced to attend," he admitted.

"No one who *really* knew John would believe him capable of lifting any kind of blade when he was angry. John much preferred his fists in a scrum. Said you couldn't slice a man open with your hands."

"Obviously Hamish felt otherwise."

"As I said, there was fragility to his nature that counterbalanced his awesome intelligence." Hayter looked down, thinking. "John took the charge of lifting his weapon in anger instead of defense, and the trial commenced. Moriarty, who was something of the patron of the man who started the whole mess, was all for the severest punishment possible."

Lestrade sensed there was a great deal more to this story, but he held his silence.

"I believe flogging was not as harsh then as it was in the past." Hayter said suddenly. "Yet, I was glad that it was outlawed a year later. I was flogged myself once or twice, as a hot-blooded youth who felt he knew more than his seasoned superiors. There are times when the birch across the shoulders is the only way to bring reason to such a young fool as myself." Hayter's lips set. "It isn't the *physical* pain that truly bothers a man. It's the fact that *you* are the one who has to remove your shirt and stand there, not knowing when the blows will come, except for perhaps your ears are sharp enough to catch the whistle in the air, just before it strikes you. Some men can't bear the thought of that anticipation, and that is the reason for the restraints. The restraints are really to help a man save his pride, you know. If a man cannot move his hands, then he cannot betray himself further by trying to twist away or shield his back . . . ." Hayter's face had gone tired and sad in the pale light. "And of course, there are those who cannot bear the public censure of being punished in front of their peers, or the superior officers they have come to revere."

"If what you say is true, then perhaps Hamish would not have been able to bear that punishment as well as John did." Lestrade guessed cautiously.

"You have the right of it. As it was, he barely stood for his brother taking his punishment. There was no choice. If Hamish *had* stood up, then everyone would know he was working for Intelligence, and then his life wouldn't have been worth a Dari syllable to the enemy. We sent him away for his own good. The trial was very small and enclosed, and morale was at its lowest point in the men. I argued that the morale would only deteriorate further if we made the punishment public, as John was well-liked and respected by the men. Were ranks prone to the vote, I swear he would have been running the 66th on approval alone." Hayter chuckled. "I was gratified to be listened to. John had his ten strokes away from the eyes of the 66th."

"It would seem Moriarty has remembered his grudge." Lestrade ventured.

"Remembered? He'd never forget, Inspector. Moriarty is a plague upon society." Hayter abruptly stood, shoving his hands in his pockets from his emotions. "A plague," he repeated. "I swear to you, that I was not surprised to hear of John's account of his brother the Professor-Napoleon-of-Crime. Not at all. It must run in the family to be completely ignorant of what the value of life is. But why, why in god's name did a good man like Sherlock Holmes pay the price with him?"

Hayter's voice was thick was sorrow and confusion for a world that should have made more sense. Lestrade abruptly felt his throat swell up in sympathy.

"Tell me." Hayter braced himself solidly and turned to face him. "You did not need to interview me, surely? Have you spoken to John yet?"

"No. He has gone out of London on holiday with his wife," Lestrade admitted. "They were invited to the house of his wife's former employer. I had to catch the train rather than wait for the forwarding address."

"I'll give it to you." Hayter said. "They're at Mrs. Cecil Forrester's. John has it in one of his letters somewhere. You should speak to him, Inspector. If Colonel Moriarty is up to his old games, John needs every ally he can uproot to his side."

"That's quite decent of you, sir." Lestrade said, surprised.

"John saved my life." Hayter said mysteriously. "I'll always be grateful for the chance to help him." He paused, slightly rueful. "It may take some time to find that address . . . I haven't thrown any of our correspondence away, and we do communicate a lot."

"I have to leave now if I'm to catch the train back." Lestrade said reluctantly. "Can you wire it?"

"I can do better than that. I can meet you in London tomorrow and we can go up to Mrs. Forrester's in person."

"Oh, but I – " Lestrade took in the fact he was about to argue with an old military veteran who was facing a vital campaign for the sake of good, and wisely shut his mouth. "Thank you, Colonel. You're most helpful, and your assistance will no doubt be invaluable." He paused. "You have not said anything about the Chromolithograph."

"And I will not." Hayter answered. "John can explain that far better than I."

The train left almost as soon as Lestrade had paid his four-cents-per-mile fee back to Paddington Station. He grimaced and sank into the first spot that came to mind. It was all-but-empty in his car. A man snored in the darkest corner, and that was it for his companionship. This time of day, no one was going *into* London unless they had to.

*At least I'm not bringing a bag of dead squirrels with me.* Lestrade leaned his head back in the booth, closing his eyes as he thought.

Hayter's conversation had been illuminating, but there were a great many gaps in it. Even allowing for the fact that the colonel was protecting the privacy of others – and there was a *definite* protectiveness about the mysterious young lady – Lestrade felt he had only touched the surface.

The first step would be to find a way to quietly prove John Watson had not been the officer who lifted his saber in anger at this theoretical fight.

John would not thank him.

"*Close as two brothers can be.*" Hayter's strange expression came over Lestrade's memory, and the little detective groaned aloud, clapping his hand to his forehead at his stupidity.

"Twins," he groaned. "John was a *twin*. Good God, I'm a fool," he said in the failing light of the car. "Holmes is right about me." If there was an afterlife, perhaps it was the silent screaming from beyond the barrier of the grave that had inspired his thoughts this far. Lestrade yanked his notebook open and began stabbing strokes across the paper with his pencil.

*Birth certificates'll prove the relationship quickly enough – but if Hamish was working for British Intelligence, it might be difficult to prove it. Those tin-plated godlings are jealous of all information, and like very much to make documents disappear –*

-Lestrade stopped, body and thought, as illumination froze him in shock.

If Hamish was working for British Intelligence . . .

. . . By default, John had to have been working for them too.

Lestrade had never felt so stupid in his life. Nausea pushed bile up his throat as he realized the real nature of the trap Moriarty had set.

Moriarty was at the trial with Hayter. He *had* to have known about all the details.

*And he knows I can't prove John's innocence.*
*He's planning to destroy both of us.*

# NOTE

1. Lestrade has no idea just how improper a pomegranate can be to a soldier from Afghanistan.

# Chapter V – Void

"**M**ary, dearest! You look wonderful!"

John Watson, knowing from past experience that "British reserve" was a lesson Mrs. Forrester had somehow missed (at least once she got to know you), smiled broadly and took a tactical retreat on the pretense of lifting the luggage from the growler. He heard Mary gasp as Mrs. Forrester threw her arms around her. By the time he turned around, the two women were fast in their embrace.

"Oh, your colour has improved so well!" Mrs. Forrester's face was beautiful, in the way only pure kindness can be beautiful. The only lines on her face were from the gentling of love and patience. No grey appeared in her smooth auburn hair just yet – but when it did, she would wear it proudly. "Mary, I can't get stop staring at you – You look perfect!" She then contradicted her words by latching her attention to look upon Mary's husband. "John, drop that bag and come here!"

"Mrs. Forrester, you are as astonishing as ever." Watson returned her embrace as well as Mary. "How are the children?"

"Oh, as can be expected. All three are ensconced deeply in their respective schools and quite content with their lot in life." Mrs. Forrester sighed with parental tolerance. "Mary, your insistence on Elizabethan literature has quite damaged our Matthew. He has managed to memorize twelve sonnets a week to the chagrin of his instructors." She tried to look annoyed as her guests chuckled around patently false expressions of horror. "And Frances wants to know if your writings will ever be published in proper book-form for her library."

Mary hid her laugh behind her laced gloves as her husband flinched. She alone knew what he endured as an author. "But, come, you must be withered from your trip." Mrs. Forrester brushed her hands off briskly. "Mary, the East Cupola Rooms are for the two of you during your stay. Get yourselves refreshed and I shall expect you down for supper at five o'clock."

*Cupola Rooms:*

"Oh, Good Lord." John's first response to the privacy of their rooms was to perform a fair imitation of a faint on the bed. When Mary pointed this out, he groggily reminded her that it was physically impossible to faint in a backwards slant.

"You never did travel well. How is your shoulder?" She sat at his side and pressed her hand to the place in question. A groan was her answer. "What about your leg?"

"Dear heart, do not ask." John caught on to the particular quality of silence from his wife. "What are you smiling about, Mary?"

"I was just thinking of how you would press your publisher into putting your writings into book form."

"Oh, not you too." John covered his eyes with the hand that was not currently held hostage by his wife.

"Now, don't look at me that way. I wasn't saying you should. I was just *imagining* that scene in the publisher's office." Mary's smile bloomed over her face like a flower. "And on that note, perhaps you should get your rest."

"Mmm," he agreed, pulling his arm up so she could use it for a pillow. Mary stretched herself beside him and listened, eyes opened, as his breath evened out in sleep.

Thirst soon drove her to rise. That was a new change in her since carrying a child. Mary slid as gently as she could from her sleeping husband and went to the water carafe. A glance at the clock said they had at least another hour before they were expected to come down.

Mary felt quite tired herself. These spells came quickly. She should have been as exhausted as her husband, were she not so thrilled to be among the first place she called her own home. She sipped the water, cooled in its unglazed crock reflectively as a reflective mood shadowed her pale face. When John left for London, she would have to speak to Mrs. Forrester about her innocent query.

John received requests about his writing on a daily basis – along with the usual and commonplace forms of criticism and "helpful" suggestions. He shouldn't have to hear such from those who were his friends. No one else alive truly knew what writing meant to John. In the nights when the bloody desert visited him unannounced and he thrashed and muttered in a hash of languages she never understood, his only prescription was to dress and go downstairs to his writing desk. The pen kept him alive and sane while he waited for the bright light of day. No matter what he wrote about his life as a detective's chronicler, no matter how terrible and fantastic, it never compared to what stories scrolled across his eyes when he slept.

He had been honest with her during the long term of their engagement, had tried to explain that when his moods came it was no slur upon her that he had to leave. The first night had been proof enough. One look into his eyes and she knew that as bad as the horror was, *it would end here, with him.* He would not expend it upon his wife.

Those nights had not particularly lessened with time – they were forever unpredictable, and the strangest things could trigger his memory. After his return from Switzerland, new nightmares had been added, and it had not taken a great intellect or even a fair guess to know what they were about.

Mary would forever be grateful to Sherlock Holmes for several things, but her sorrow at his death was (she felt) also selfish. Mr. Holmes had been her husband's first friend and compatriot upon his ejection from the Infantry. More importantly, he had managed to be a devoutly un-interested flatmate with no probing questions on John's past. John had admitted that the one and only time he'd divined anything about his family had been over the matter of his brother's watch. John's extreme reaction had set the rules for the future: Holmes had since adopted a policy of assuming and taking for granted John for granted and would continue to do so until he was specifically informed by John himself that it would not do. What had been callous and calculation in his view of the world had been a sensitive respect in regards to John.

Sherlock Holmes had filled a bottomless void inside her husband, as neatly as a stopper holding a bottle of vitriol in place. With his death the cork was gone. John had no choice but to rebuild his life for the third time, and only one thing could exorcise the nocturnal plagues.

A pen could be a better exorcist than a drug.

# Chapter VI – A Style in the Writing

"**M**rs. Forrester, I'm afraid Mary still needs her sleep."

"That's hardly surprising, is it?" Mrs. Forrester swept her hand to the small table set in the airy library. "I shall have a tray sent up in a bit to make certain she does not miss her nourishment."

"Most kind of you." John bent to pull her chair out. She might call him by his birth-name, but *nothing* would induce him to be anything more than pleasantly formal with the woman. It was, in a way, a light game they played without effort.

"I remember those days very well. It is difficult work, bringing children into the world." Mrs. Forrester was as outspoken as anyone from the provincial Kent was reputed to be. "I see you look something like your normal self. I trust the rooms are pleasant."

"Very much so." John admitted. The butler silently poured the first of the drinks and departed with a nod of respect.

John had sometimes wondered what Mrs. Forrester's true feelings about his marriage were. It had been no secret that once her oldest daughter came of age, Mary would have been promoted from governess to paid companion. It was an honor only for the finest governesses, and there was no mistake that Mary was still missed at the household.

Kind as they were, the Forresters had been as unique in their treatment of their governess as they were in all things – a carry-over from Mr. Forrester's career traveling the world and seeing things in terms of *what worked* as opposed to *what everyone else wanted*. Lacking a social standing of peers, a teacher usually ate and lived alone when not instructing their charges. It paid enough to live on, but had the potential for wretched loneliness. They were favorite targets for the dishonorable members of the family and jealous servants in the background. Marriage was the only way out of a delicate trap – that or a sensational inheritance, which was the blatant stuff of romance novelists. In Mary's case, it had almost happened.

As much as he loved Mary, John never forgot that it was her misfortune that had allowed his marriage to the almost-heiress. Were he more of a decent man, he would have wished harder for the recovery of the Agra Treasure. The wealth would have done much to lift her station to levels he felt she deserved. And he . . . he would have remained a crippled veteran with a just-established practice and no chance for financial advancement. On his way to her with the Agra Chest, he had sunk into one of the lowest moods of his life, wondering if it were possible to return to Australia and invest in something that would give him a prayer of wealth in less than twenty years.

Mrs. Forrester was a shrewd woman, and still carried her girlhood reputation as the greatest beauty of the south with aplomb. He very much doubted she was ignorant of any of his thoughts about Mary.

"Please, John, do have another drink."

"Most kind of you, Mrs. Forrester." John capitulated. "One more shall be all I need."

The good lady took her own port and settled back into her chair. She never even blinked as a barn owl swept past the window by her elbow, although the resultant scream made John's hand spasm around his goblet. "Is it so much cooler here than in London?" she asked sympathetically.

"It is miserable." John sighed. "There are days that seem to never end. I have no idea what it will be like in August! I wager to you that soon Parliament will rise early and escape to a more forested district like this one."

His hostess shook her head. "Well, you and Mary are to stay for as long as you like. Having her back is like having one of my own children again."

"You are too kind."

"John, for goodness' sakes. Did you never have a mother to fuss over you?" As his face and hands froze, she pressed her own hands to her mouth. "Dear me, that was unforgivable. Please do forgive me anyway."

"Quite all right, Mrs. Forrester, your intentions are only good." John had recovered from the unintentional sally. "And my practice forbids me an extended vacation, but Mary would be honored to stay with you."

Mrs. Forrester leaned forward and rested her hand on John's knee, rather much like a mother or a willful older sister would. "John, she looks so well. What is your prognosis as a physician?"

John was grateful for the opening he needed. "She needs rest and relaxation if events are to reach their natural conclusion."

"Ah," she sighed. "You've done your best, I'm certain – but like it or not, Mary's heart will not let her body rest if she feels her husband is in need of attention."

"There's more to it than that, I fear." Watson took another sip of port, wishing devoutly that wine did not inspire his honesty so quickly. "The weather has made it impossible for her relaxation, and naturally it is difficult to eat. I am fortunate if she can manage something in the morning, sip on drinks all day, and have a light meal at sunset when the worst of the heat is off the walls. The regatta on the Thames was almost too much, for the level of excitement was enough to keep the entire city on a celebratory edge all night and every night!"

"That is no environment for an expecting young mother," was the verdict. Watson found himself colouring, to her low laugh. "Dear me. I seem to recall you were immune to chagrin when I first met you, John."

"Mary is a gentling effect." John could not keep the smile out of his voice. "And to be honest, I still have to remind myself – "

"That you are facing fatherhood? Mr. Forrester was much like you. He held that same wonder and puzzlement and anticipation mixed with dread and joy at the prospect of each of our children. Life truly is a miracle, John."

"It is to some." John's face darkened. "Mrs. Forrester, I confess Kent is much safer for Mary than London now." He put the nearly empty glass aside, leaning back to rub at his temples. "There are some parties present who are not pleased with my writings of late. I do not think they would hesitate to take their temper out on me."

"And you naturally want Mary out of the equation," the woman said shrewdly. "That is quite understandable, John. I've often wondered, if fifty men wished your friend dead, how many would wish the same for you?" She lifted a hand to his next words. "No, John. Mr. Holmes considered his aid to me no more than a trifle. That trifle could have easily led to a disaster in my life." Her green-grey eyes rested on him at length. "Conversely, I must assure you that what would seem to be a great indisposition is no more than a trifle on *my* part. Let me keep her here. Until the weather breaks or the danger passes, or the child chooses to grace us . . . Mary is a rare being, John. We can agree it behooves us all to shelter her from the storms against her."

John was a moment collecting his voice. "I would have done anything to prevent this, were it in my power," he said heavily.

"You are speaking of the manuscript you call 'The Final Problem'." Mrs. Forrester said confidently.

"Yes."

"I could tell when you let me read it . . . there is a style in that writing that is subtle yet different, John. It made me wonder if you were . . . well, gritting your teeth as you wrote it."

"Ha! Not far from the truth, dear lady. That was the first thing I've ever had to write against my wishes. I'm aware it shows, but I didn't know it showed so . . . baldly."

"Perhaps not to the regular reading public. But you say you wrote against your wishes?"

"Yes. Moriarty's allies were defending him most strenuously, and couple that with the fact there were too few articles dealing with the true facts of Holmes's death . . . I count four of them, including my own submission . . . Well, it stank of carp." John wished for a smoke and picked up the port glass instead, just to give his hand something to do. "I can't yet divine what the whole schematic is, Mrs. Forrester, but the business is far from done."

*Cupola Rooms:*

Mary was so sound asleep she never stirred as her husband stepped inside with the candle. Her hair spilled down her shoulders like dark honey and brushed the smooth lines of her throat and collarbone. She had either forgotten to take out her gold hoops or was simply too tired. They gleamed in the tiny pinpoint of light.

*She* is *tired*, he thought with a mixture of guilt at their travel by coach and relief that it was over with. But if he looked closely, he could see the soft glow of a woman who was expecting a child. And he *did* look closely as he prepared for bed. Then, he paused in the act of setting the candle down. He shook his head with a wondering smile, silent, and kept watching her.

By degrees, Mary felt her husband's presence. She opened her eyes slowly. He was sitting at her side, the glow of a single candle throwing light into the shadows of his open shirt.

"You're wearing your James face, dear," she murmured sleepily.

"Am I? I wasn't aware of it." His teeth reflected the candle in his smile. "I feel I *must* watch you while you sleep, Mary. It is almost the only time where I can find you stationary."

"You make me sound like one of those perpetual motion machines your scientist friends are always trying to discover so they can make themselves rich."

"Not at all. But you have a need for more peace and quiet now than you ever have. Surely you can't deny it."

"I shan't deny it. What would be the point?" Mary propped herself up on her elbow and the couple regarded each other in the soft silence of deep feelings.

John wordlessly reached out to cup the side of her face in his large hand. "Can you stay here when I return to London?" he asked huskily.

"I know you'll worry about me much less while I'm in the care of our formidable Mrs. Forrester." Mary's laugh sounded as husky as her husband's question. "Don't look so, my dear. This is yet another step we must take."

"Steps we must take apart." He was calm enough in his voice, but his eyes were deep.

43

"We will still take them together." Mary reached up to cover his hand. "These steps are being taken for our son."

"So certain?" He teased her as always over her foresight.

"Always," Mary teased back.

Another long silence. The candle burned to a flaw in the wick and guttered, the light creating movement over their faces. Neither moved, both comfortable with silence. He could see the weaving of her cotton nightdress, the small flowers she embroidered into the trim. Nothing was as deep and bright as her eyes.

"What is it, John?"

"A foolishness."

"Then tell me," she urged.

"I miss you already," he confessed.

"I won't try to convince you of the illogic of that," Mary's hand slipped from his to rest at the back of his neck. "Seeing as how we feel alike. But I must remind us both not to let our time together go to waste." She pressed her hand down gently, and he lowered his head until their lips touched. Her other arm slipped up, and she felt him smile against her lips as her hands locked around him as securely as a padlock. She pulled her weight against his side – a shameless use of his old wound – and they were lying inside each other's arms.

"Are you quite certain?" John's voice was decidedly strained.

"John, Mrs. Forrester is hardly my first exposure to remarkable women and their advice." Mary pulled her head back just enough to drink in the sight of him as she found a shirt-button. "Without being as blunt as either of them, I believe we both benefited from a childhood in the tropics."

*Paddington Station, London:*

Even London slowed down sometime after midnight. Lestrade put his feet off the platform and whistled for the first cab that would have him. He fell, more than climbed, into the seat and gave his directions to home. He blinked. When he did, the driver was pulling to a stop.

Clea opened the door from the inside as he was puzzling out how to fit the key into the lock. "Geoffrey, you're worn to the bone!"

Lestrade was not too tired to marvel at his luck in marriage as she pulled his coat off and hung it up. With an arm around him she drew him upstairs to the landing, whispering not to wake up the boys, and did he want anything to eat?

"I'm too tired to eat, dear." Lestrade smiled, leaning his head on top of hers – how a woman who was small enough for him to dwarf her had managed to produce two such strapping sons was a wonder between them both. "It's just as well. I was offered a bag of squirrels today."

"If you come home with anything furry, they'd better be bald and cooked." Clea tilted up to give him a kiss. "If you're too tired to eat, then you must be sure to make up for it in the morning."

"Certainly." He paused to give her an awkward, one-armed hug as he fumbled with his much-wilted collar. Clea *tsk'd* and made quick work of the job, then to his cuffs. "I'll have to be up at six if I'm to get back on the train by seven," he groaned softly.

"Wouldn't've been cheaper to find a hotel somewhere?" Clea wondered. She usually was very deliberate and choosy in the times she accused him of not thinking clearly. For now, her dark blue eyes were only curious.

"I was invited to spend the night with the Colonel, but I couldn't bring myself to do it," Lestrade confessed. "It will be another full day out – I'll send a wire if I'm trapped out of home again."

Clea rolled her eyes as she shook her head and neatly stacked his sweat-filthy collar and cuffs by the bedside for tomorrow's wash. "Merciful stars, I hope Scotland Yard appreciates the man I married. How did I ever be so lucky?"

Lestrade leaned his head on her shoulder. "If I recall right, you proposed to me."

"That's because it was Leap Day, you grand fool!" Clea said fondly. "That's the only time a woman may propose to a man, and I wasn't about to wait another four years!" [1]

"*I* could have." Lestrade pointed out. "Because I didn't know what I was missing."

Clea struggled not to laugh too loudly. "Had you known, would you have proposed?"

"As soon as I figured a way around your brothers." Lestrade let go with great reluctance and took the hot washcloth she'd wrung out for him. Train soot came off his neck like a day in Wales.

"Oh? Which brothers are you talking about?" Clea asked in a fairly dangerous tone of voice.

Her husband hesitated, and then went for another soak in the washbowl. "Clea, it hardly matters if it was one-third or all six. You are *still* the only sister they have."

"It's hardly my fault the men ran strong in the family." Clea sniffed.

"Still do," he muttered, not quite out of her hearing.

She dropped his cufflinks into the solution-bowl in order to smack him on the top of the head. Soot came off. "Good Lord. That's it. You're getting a proper scrub before you stretch out on my clean sheets,

45

Geoffrey." At his groan she started to smack him again, but experience reminded her not to. "Unless you want to sleep on the floor under the horse-blanket." Clea's horror descended when a thoughtful look crossed his face. "Oh, no you don't! That was a rhetorical question!"

"I wouldn't mind," he protested as she stood, grabbed his arm and dragged him to his feet. "Honestly."

"I would!" Clea exclaimed. "March with me, Inspector!" Her sharp ears caught a thread of a weary mutter. "You *won't* drown if you fall asleep in the tub. I'll be sure it won't happen – or are you going to try to tell me you're the only man on the globe that can wash his own back?"

## NOTE

1.  Because Leap Year Day technically did not exist for centuries in Great Britain, February 29th was seen as a day for correcting wrongs – in this case, the fact that only men had the right of proposal. The law that permits women to propose to men has been in existence since 1288.

# Chapter VII – A Matter of Slander

*Paddington Station, London:*

Colonel Hayter looked dismayingly fresh and capable as he slid in front of Lestrade on the platform, paid for their tickets (without asking the Inspector if he could), and tossed a single overnighter and a burlap into the spot by the window. Lestrade followed suit more slowly. His night had been far too short for much sleep.

"You don't look like you've had any rest, Inspector," Hayter embarrassed him with his observation. "Have you been working the night?"

"It feels like it." Lestrade said reluctantly. "I'm pleased you are looking well."

Hayter brushed that off and made himself comfortable. "For an old campaigner, it is nothing. Were you able to learn anything more about Moriarty?"

"On such a short notice – no. He has his own clubs, and keeps to them." Lestrade found the back of the booth extremely comfortable and closed his eyes for a moment as the train lurched onto the main tracks. "I am beginning to think he was somewhat estranged from his late, unlamented brother, though . . . they did not travel in the same social circles."

"Odd enough." Hayter grunted. "It is not the professor that I knew. I can only say I am unsurprised that he turned out to be as cankerous as his brother." Hayter steepled his fingers in a thinking motion. "A pity Moriarty is such a common name. I am prone to enough paranoia."

Lestrade had to chuckle at the thought. There were enough Moriartys in the Empire to populate a small fiefdom.

"At any rate, I accomplished very little before my wife bade me remember that most human beings need a certain percentage of their life to be at rest." Lestrade stared out the passing view as clusters of trees and grass replaced houses and buildings. "And cleaner than the moment they were born into," he added under his breath.

"I sent a wire to Mrs. Forrester when I found the address." Hayter had pulled out his watch and was cleaning it with easy strokes. "They'll be expecting both of us, but Mrs. Forrester – and Mrs. Watson, I should hope – believes you have a bit of a medical conundrum on a case and you needed some discreet opinions on the matter."

Lestrade felt a knot loosen inside his chest. "Most convenient, Colonel. And you can explain your presence by a long-standing invitation to Mrs. Forrester's?" Lestrade in this case was not apologizing for his curiosity. Among his particular social status, it would be beyond the pale of boldness to drop in so quickly and so presumptuously.

Hayter's waxed moustaches bristled with a suppressed laugh. "I was quite impressed with the Widow Forrester at Watson's wedding," he commented. "And it is also the first time I put eyes upon you, to be truthful. Not that I was completely sure of it at the time. You didn't arrive for the first part of the ceremony."

"I was working that day." Lestrade confessed.

"Just how many of you plainclothesmen were there?" Hayter wondered. "I had been quite proud of myself – preening, even – for routing the 66th and the Fusiliers together who could attend, but I'm convinced Scotland Yard out showed us!" He still sounded slightly put out by the fact.

"How many?" Lestrade paused to think. "We all tried to show up at one time or another. It was a decent enough mark of respect. Dr. Watson had done us a fair turn in the past, and it wouldn't have been decent to overlook that."

"So you regard him without Sherlock Holmes?" Hayter pounced.

Lestrade frowned slightly. There was something underlying the Colonel's pleasant tone that felt deep and hidden. "I first met Sherlock Holmes some years before I met Dr. Watson," he began to explain. "But Dr. Watson was the first of the two that I actually *knew*. And his work at the hospital, his proximity to the station, *and* his private practice ensured we would cross paths on a regular basis." Lestrade mentally reviewed the Colonel's question. "I'm aware that Dr. Watson's name is usually sounded *after* the name of Sherlock Holmes. But that only happened in the Yard when the two were together, and that only because it was Holmes's nature to be out in the foreground, while Dr. Watson chose to pull back and exist in the aft."

Hayter's face cleared – slightly. "John made observation, long ago, that if he was to truly watch the play unfold, he must do it from the front row and not the stage itself." He went back to cleaning his watch.

"A neat touch." Lestrade offered. "I don't think I've ever heard him described in such a correct manner."

"Well, he has a natural horror of being the focus of anyone's attention." Hayter passed off that rather peculiar comment absently, and moved to the polishing of his lens. "There's a freedom in being ignored. Watson shirks no responsibility, but he does treasure his freedoms." His mustache rippled with a faint laugh. "I'm convinced that's what made

Holmes such a successful room-mate of his," he confessed. "They fit like jigsaw pieces – tit-for-tat. Watson always gave the impression that the world could see him as it chose – and if it was wrong in its judgment, it was hardly *his* fault. Holmes, however, felt and said that what you did wasn't as important as what the world *thought* you did."

"I remember Holmes saying that in the past," Lestrade mused. "I still can't reconcile those words with how I think of him."

"Holmes was that very rare creature, a logical philosopher. I daresay it would take our lifetimes to cipher him out." Hayter blew on the crystal of his watch and held it up to the sunlight with a critical scowl.

"Well, there had to be more to him than that statement, or Watson would have never tolerated him." Lestrade said firmly. "Not for even two days."

"It is a question that demands a conjectural answer." Hayter agreed, pleasant again now that he had eradicated a minuscule speck of dust off his watch.

*Kent:*

"*John!*" Colonel Hayter promptly disavowed another image of veteran propriety by clasping a surprised and pleased Watson to his chest. "And you've gained weight! Who would have dreamed?" Still grinning, he held the shorter man at arms' length, his teeth flashing white. Lestrade suddenly thought that those flashing teeth would not look at all assuring to someone he was angry with.

"Colonel Hayter!" Watson remained the more diffident of the two – Lestrade knew just how he felt. Hayter was beginning to remind him of a seasonal storm – calm between squalls. "To what do we owe this surprise?"

"I have not forgotten the broad invitation your lovely wife's employer once extended to me." Hayter's face colored as the lady in question came down the stairs. "And here she is. How do *you* do, Madam?"

"I do quite well, thank you." Mrs. Forrester smiled and lifted her hand to his, where it was promptly and fervently kissed. Lestrade forced himself to re-evaluate Hayter's bachelor status. He and Watson slid a look to each other. "I have not seen you since the wedding."

"Has it been so long?"

"Long? Colonel Hayter, these two children are barely married at all!" Mrs. Forrester indicated Mary as the young woman turned a deep red to be so categorized. Watson's reaction was merely resigned.

"Ah, but look at them." Hayter swept his long arm to the young couple as they joined each other. "One would get the impression they'd

49

been married fresh out of school." Hayter beamed, immune to the knowledge that the Watsons were feeling decidedly under the wire. "And they'll be married until the next Jubilee, if there's any justice in the world."

Mrs. Forrester had discovered Lestrade. "You must be the Inspector." She turned, neatly deflecting Hayter's attention, and producing her hand. "How do you do, Mr. Lestrade. Or is '*Mister*' a proper form of address?"

"That is fine, Mrs. Forrester." Lestrade felt the full effect of the woman's eyes – like a slash of foxfire in a moonless night – and was proud of recovering from the full force of her personality so quickly. Perhaps his exposure to Hayter had an ossifying effect. It crossed his mind to wonder what kind of man the Mr. Cecil Forrester was, to have been married to someone like this. "At your service."

"Not at all. I understand you were plucked out of your usual territory by business." She stepped backward now that the introductions were done – much to Lestrade's relief. "We shall leave you then to your work, but we hope you may stay for noon-tide."

"Thank you, Mrs. Forrester. You are most kind."

"I adore the manners of our young men." Mrs. Forrester announced to a smiling Colonel Hayter.

*Library Rooms:*

"Lestrade," Watson had a touch of long-suffering tolerance in his voice that the Yard normally associated with Sherlock Holmes and hypochondriacs. "So you and the Colonel have met?"

Lestrade took a deep breath. "W-well." He pondered on where to begin, then caught the look in Watson's eye. They began laughing at the same time. "Oh, good Lord. Was *that* your *commanding officer?*"

"Part of the time during my Afghani term," Watson said, once his breath was recollected. He pulled his handkerchief out of his sleeve and wiped his eyes. "I highly recommend him for a young man's first experience with larger-than-life characters." The doctor tried very hard to look serious. "Am I to assume from the burlap bag he carried, mulligatawny will be on the menu in the near future?"

"That or American Burgoo." Lestrade tried not to look apprehensive. He paused to wipe the sweat off his brow. It wasn't even lunch-time, and the heat was crawling into the walls.

"I enjoy the Colonel's company." Watson said firmly. "But when he has his active moods, no one can match his energy." He stuffed his hands in his pockets, a moment he would never adopt around women. Lestrade never could make up his mind if the man was restrained or deliberate. "So this is a case," he said slowly. "How may I help you?"

50

"Dispelling a matter of slander." Lestrade again produced Moriarty's package.

# Chapter VIII – Men Have Done Worse

Watson's face was anything but what Lestrade had imagined. "I *had* wondered," he said as if to himself.

Lestrade felt sweat prickle out of his face and neck. "John," he murmured, "can you explain this to me?"

Watson set his lips tight. Lestrade again loathed the circumstances that had led to this point. "It was Moriarty, wasn't it?" Watson startled him. "He came to see me not so very long ago . . . over a month . . . right after I shared the manuscript of 'The Final Problem' with a few people. He must have heard . . . that I'd written down the truth of what occurred . . . ." The doctor let the image drop to the desk on its own weight and sank down into one of the overstuffed horse-hair couches by the window. "For Heaven's sake, take that jacket off before you collapse from heat prostration, Inspector . . . Since his visit, I've been preparing myself for every conceivable and not-so-conceivable possibility in his desire for petty revenge."

"Lestrade sighed. "Yes, it was Colonel Moriarty," he admitted. "Not that I'm convinced it could be called *petty* revenge."

"Well, I'm surprised at him. It would seem his brother inherited the greater bulk of intelligence as well as brains." Watson stroked his mustache once, musing. "The simple truth is, that is not me in that lithograph."

Lestrade looked at the lithograph, then back at Watson. "If you'll forgive me, the resemblance is astonishing. The *only* thing that doesn't scream 'John H. Watson' to me is but a small thing and – " He stopped, hesitating.

Watson's lips twitched, although he was being very good about his self-control. "Go on, Inspector," he urged.

"Well . . . the eyes." Lestrade indicated the expression. "There's a . . . I suppose an emptiness to the expression, and if you'll forgive me for being so bold, but I can't imagine for one moment *you'd* be looking that vulnerable. You'd be more like the man who is walking erect – ready to die before you let your face be so open in such a revealing way."

Watson made a soft noise, and it sounded so much like Bradstreet in a contemplative mood that the smaller man wondered if this was a Northern mannerism. "The man walking erect *was* dying when that image was captured." He barely noted Lestrade's loss of colour. "A bullet entered his back while he was bent over a fallen cavalryman. Not enough to bleed his life out all at once . . . No, it took longer than that. He vowed to see his companion to safety if it was his last power on earth." The dark brown eyes lowered to the black space at the empty fireplace. "And it was."

Lestrade swallowed, feeling cold against the warm weather. "If that man with the head-bandages is not you, how would you know this?"

"The man was my brother." Watson said simply. "And his expression is such, because being exposed to the harsh desert sun had damaged his eyes. A concussion of the battle had left him unconscious but with his eyes opened to the sky. He was dazzled . . . all but blind. While I was wounded in the left shoulder, he was in the right." Something very strange slipped across the doctor's eyes for a moment, yet was gone before Lestrade was even certain it existed.

"I am sorry." Lestrade said simply. "But your brother *did* survive?"

"If one can call it that." Watson's voice was muffled. "He was not long for this world after."

Lestrade wanted to ask if his brother had ever regained the use of his eyes before death . . . but decided he did not need to know that badly.

"John . . . I am very, very sorry." What a dearth of adequacy that was. "You were close, then."

Watson said nothing, but his eyes spoke volumes.

*Great sorrows cannot speak.* Lestrade remembered the Donne quote vividly. His thoughts were knotted beyond repair with the conflict in his emotions.

Watson took the moment to do something with his hands. He rose and rang the bell. The maid must not have been far. She appeared almost instantly and was requested for something cooling to drink in the hot weather.

"That can't be the entire affair," Watson said quietly when they were again alone. "The Colonel surely had more than *this* to attack me with."

Lestrade flushed awkwardly. "Yes, but I do not feel comfortable with speaking to you on such a personal matter."

"You have no choice." Watson pointed out. "I doubt he chose you at random, you know."

"No, I do know." Lestrade made a basket of his fingers and rested them on his knee. "I'm sure he chose me deliberately."

"I'm more than 'sure,' Inspector." Watson had rose and was pouring the tea glasses. "I consider myself an innocent when it comes to the actual networks of crime, but I *do* know human nature, and I am certain gossip, innuendo, and chatter exists among the polite societies of the criminal mind as much as it does in say . . . Buckingham Palace during a full moon." A snort floated up from behind him, and he chuckled sadly. "Holmes never made any mistake in his observations with the Yard. Gregson is the smartest, but Lestrade is the best of professionals. There was a distinction, and he never failed to note it."

"There are times when I wonder what in the world he was talking about." Lestrade's dry fingertips took the cool moisture of the glass greedily. He took a long drink, feeling the dust wash down his parched throat.

Watson suddenly laughed. "He often inspired that feeling in me."

"Yes. Well. The fact is, this is probably a trap on both of us – " Lestrade caught the expression in Watson's eyes. "In fact, we can dispense with the *probably*. Holmes may have called us fools with justification, but to deny this as a fact would be *insane*. Insane I am not."

Watson breathed out his nose and let his head fall back. "Very well. Since we are forced to play his childish game by the rules he has set down, we may as well make up some rules of our own." There was a grim, set look to his mouth that held unspoken promises for Moriarty. "What did he tell you, pray?"

"He said that he was the Colonel Moriarty at Maiwand, to begin with." Lestrade listed the first point by holding a finger up.

"There were *two* Moriartys at Maiwand." Watson scoffed. "One was a Lieutenant-Colonel, but that's a small distinction, I'm sure." His voice was laced with irony. "There were also quite a few Watsons, if one wants to split hairs."

"He also accused you of being . . . Well, flogged before the battle for . . . not performing your duties." Lestrade knew without a doubt Watson would never lift a hand to him – Watson was too conscious of man's inhumanity to man. That did not remove the fact that he was no doubt inflicting a deeper, invisible hurt on the other man. "He gave me this copy of the actual report . . . and it did say that a Surgeon-Major John H. Watson was reprimanded by corporeal punishment for inviting a fracas with his dress saber."

Watson merely looked puzzled at first. He was quiet for so long it began to make Lestrade nervous.

"It's been a long time since I read that report," he said, as if to himself. "May I have a moment to look at it?"

Lestrade naturally expected Watson to make such a request. He waited. Watson opened the papers with a silent delicacy of touch, his eyes already hooded in concentration. Lestrade honestly didn't know how Holmes could read thoughts out of a person's expression – a studious look was a studious look.

Watson read quickly – the contents were not unfamiliar to him, Lestrade realized with a sick sensation.

"I noted no inconsistencies from the original version." Watson finally re-stacked the loose pages and tucked them neatly back in the envelope.

"Can you tell me anything?" Lestrade knew he was almost pleading, but he didn't see a choice.

Watson closed his eyes for a moment. "I can't tell you *everything*," he said gently. "There is still a mandate of silence to protect the innocent parties in this case . . . What has Colonel Hayter already told you?"

"That it was your brother Hamish who picked up the saber while impersonating you, and you took the blame for it."

"'Took the blame.'" Watson repeated bitterly. "I suppose that's something I must forever live with." He rose to his feet in a new energy, glass in his hands as he looked out the window. Colonel Hayter was walking, arm in arm, with Mrs. Forrester and Mary Watson across the greensward. "I didn't really have a choice, Inspector. Please understand when I give my word, I intend to keep it. My loyalty to the Crown is only superseded by my loyalty to my Hippocratic Oath." He took a long drink without saying anything for a moment. "I loved him like any man could love his own brother, but we were always firm believers in picking up our own messes. It was a debacle and no mistake."

"Men have done worse to protect those they love." Lestrade reminded him.

"And they should not." Watson was still speaking in that bitter voice. "My brother was working to defeat a corruption in the army. That corruption went throughout the ranks, and up *all* the levels. We were also in a dangerous part of the world, where too many times a commander's rule was the only law. If a man were to be wrongly executed for a crime, it would be two weeks on foot before that crime would be reported – and by then, its importance has faded from remarkable and urgent to . . . to the commonplace of the 'What's done is done'". Watson took another drink. "He should not have forgotten such a fact. It could have meant the death of him – it almost *was* the death of him!" An anger Lestrade had never once seen on Watson's normally restrained face was gone. "It *led* to the death of him!"

The doctor turned halfway to look at the seated Inspector. The easy grace he normally carried in himself was gone. Memories were not favorable to this man, yet he would soldier his way through them.

"At that time, Hamish was pretending to be recuperating from a recurrence of malaria. It was a common enough malady, especially for men who have been in India. That gave him enough reason to lie low, but one night there was word that two of his marks were nearby. He persuaded me to switch uniforms and roles and went to the makeshift Officer's Den in my role – " He caught Lestrade's puzzlement. "The Den was a nickname caught up by the men who have been in India. It was sort of an informal club and meeting-place, although the dress code was *anything* but informal. I took his place in the camp cot, but it was all done against my better judgment." Watson's fingers clenched around the glass as though he would like nothing more than to break it.

Lestrade pulled his hip flask out and wordlessly poured a jigger into Watson's tea. Watson lifted an eyebrow at him, but the dangerous black mood lifted from his eyes and was replaced by a tint of irony.

"I should have never allowed him to go to that place," he said firmly. "We were much alike, but while he was the smarter man, *I* was the one who could hold my drink. When they thought they were looking at John Hamish, the 'tender naturally placed my usual order in front of him. Naturally he drank it. And then he drank another. Tensions were running rampant. Battle was less than a week away, and we all knew it would be a terrible thing. Officers were already half-blind in their cups, but you know how it is – as long as you give the *appearance* of being all right, then everything *must* be." Watson sipped his new drink reflectively. "I can't say I was surprised when he was apprehended for being in a fight. I daresay he never even knew about the law against the use of the medical saber. It wouldn't have applied to him."

"If he was apprehended," Lestrade wondered, "how was it the two of you kept up the pretense?"

"Simple enough. Propriety allowed him the visit of his brother and his commanding officer . . . We switched our uniforms quickly enough and Hamish was sent to the eastern side. For all that had gone wrong, the information he'd collected that night had been useful enough. The eastern side was where his targets were being transferred and he had to be there. To make sure there was less confusion, he combed his hair in a different pattern than I normally did, and gave himself a different shape of the moustache . . . by the time I was receiving my ten strokes he was well-established on the line."

"Is there anyone you can go to for help in this?" Lestrade asked desperately. "Anyone at all? Doesn't – didn't – Holmes have connections with the government?"

"None that I would go to." Watson said with a deathly quiet knell in his voice. "I've spoken too much already, Inspector. The more this comes out, the worse it will become. There are people that still deserve protection from this scandal."

"How can that be?" Lestrade demanded. "You wouldn't have chosen to take blows meant for your brother, and yet you will place yourself at risk for this?"

"I had no choice then, and I have no choice now." Watson told him.

"Damn!" Lestrade slapped his hands on his thighs in frustration. "Watson – John, for the love of God! What is so important that you're still keeping quiet?"

Watson's eyes were anguished. "Geoffrey, it's not my secret, and yet I am trapped with it."

Lestrade stopped, feeling bile claw up his throat. He stared at Watson, lost for words.

"First of all, Inspector, you're being watched as much as I am. I have a feeling that there's much more to this than meets the eye . . . Why not simply go to the papers with this evidence?" Watson shook his head as if to himself. "Why not launch a large campaign of accusations that will make all the dailies temporarily rich?"

"Perhaps Moriarty has his own events he does not want known."

"If he favors his brother in any way, then he must be as sick in his soul as the professor was." Watson rubbed his jaw.

"I'm thinking you should perhaps stay here a while." Lestrade ventured carefully. "Away from London. A house of women is naturally well-guarded on the part of the staff."

"I cannot." Watson admitted. "I have closed my practice for a few days. Mary had to be brought out of London. The hot weather is unhealthy for her . . . ." He lowered his eyes. "Mrs. Forrester has been kind enough to insist on her presence." The doctor passed a hand over his eyes. "I will return in a few days. I'll worry about that moment when it happens."

Lestrade's thoughts had already slipped backwards, to that initial feeling of unease. "John . . . why are you calling and acting as if this nightmare is *petty revenge*?"

"My own conceit, I'm certain." Watson said stiffly. "I've never held a cause for revenge. It is all petty to me." He took another drink. "Anger I can fathom, but not hatred. It is not one of the logical emotions."

"Forgive me, but I wasn't aware there were any logical emotions," Lestrade admitted with a lifted eyebrow.

Watson, unexpectedly, smiled just a bit. "They are if their effect is logical."

"I'm afraid I'm still in the dark then. Give me a few years to think about that before I demand an explanation."

Watson chuffed. "Agreed."

Both men fell into silence. It was an easy excuse to watch the women walk across the lawn with Hayter, examining the tiny plots of herb and flower among the butterflies.

"Revenge is a confession of pain," Watson spoke so softly Lestrade barely heard him. "A Latin proverb . . . so true, and yet from the same part of the world that gave birth to the Mafiosi."

"You said Hayter was your commanding officer for part of the Afghani Campaign. Was *he* your commander when you switched uniforms with Hamish?"

Watson flinched slightly. "That comes a little close to the mark, Geoffrey. I would prefer not to answer that."

Lestrade breathed slowly and quietly through his nose. "Dr. Watson, were this anyone else in the world, even were it Sherlock Holmes, I would not believe them. Don't get me wrong. Holmes had no compunction in lying or deceiving me if it meant the end result was a captured villain. But you are different. I believe you. It simply isn't in your nature to let someone else take the wrong end of the stick. You do realize your inability to answer the questions I feel most important . . . makes me wonder just how corrupt this matter was, and how far it went."

Watson had been looking at the ground directly outside the window at Lestrade's words. He looked up then, eyes steadfast and calm.

"I hope you never find out," was his answer. "For your sake, for your peace of mind, and for optimism you may yet possess in human nature. I hope you do not find out."

"Is there anything you *can* tell me?" Lestrade leveled the bar flat-out to the doctor.

Watson finished his glass, thinking hard. Lestrade barely breathed as a mixture of emotions slipped over his face, as intangible as fish just under the waves.

"I will tell you two things." Watson said at last. "The first one is only from what I heard as a soldier. I cannot vouchsafe for its accuracy."

"Go on." Lestrade encouraged.

"Colonel Moriarty is not a man one plays chess with." Watson said unexpectedly. "He is clever, and careful, and he never makes a single move of importance unless he has two other pieces to back him up."

Lestrade exhaled. "Interesting." Men played chess the way they played life. It was no doubt one of the reasons why Holmes had never played at all.

"The other . . . ." Watson set his glass down and absently re-tightened the loose cuff on his left sleeve. "The other is only my own suspicion. I can't prove my feeling on this." He looked up, but Lestrade said nothing. "Moriarty may have been one of the people my brother was looking for. I have no proof. I have no way of finding proof. But if he were . . . Well, it would make this entire mess all the easier to fathom."

"You have given me much to think about." Lestrade said quietly. The tension still hummed in the doctor's body, making his movements unusually stiff and awkward. Lestrade had never seen him such, not even when they were under fire by criminals in London, or when he had been asked to identify the remains of a mass murder off East End.

*Well, no, of course not,* he reminded himself. *All those only had his life at stake. Whatever is going on, there are* other *lives at stake and he's trying to protect them.*

# Chapter IX – A Slap of the Glove

*"When the swords flash let no idea of love, piety,*
*or even the face of your fathers move you."*
– Julius Caesar

*Kent Estate:*

Lestrade was still searching for a way to tactfully press Watson for information – even a broad clue – when they saw the strollers were slowly turning 'round and heading back to the Manor. As a man, they fortified themselves with the last of the tea, squared their shoulders, and departed. By the time they were outside and down the steps, the doctor's countenance was back to its usual pleasant self.

Colonel Hayter pretended everything was perfectly normal as they all met up by the wisteria vines. Lestrade did not miss the split second that passed between the soldiers and was amazed the women could ignore it. Clea wouldn't have . . . but then, Clea had grown up in the middle of the lion's den known as Lancashire Cotton Mill Separatists. [1]

"I'll be taking a quick ride to town to send my wires back to my estate," Hayter announced. "May I trouble you gentlemen for any messages?"

"No, but I would accompany you back to the station." Lestrade answered. "I should be going home tonight."

"Oh, wouldn't you prefer to stay?" Mrs. Forrester inquired with a decent honesty that quite flabbergasted the Inspector. "Both of you have already traveled so far to get to my estate."

Lestrade rolled several possibilities in his mind, but the usual "Oh, I couldn't impose!" would affect the hostess about as well as someone tossing an expired rugby ball into a club field *after* the bets had been placed. "Mrs. Forrester, I promised my wife I would *at least* send her notice if I was unable to return tonight." And for the sake of his own pride, he added, "I have friends at the nearby inn and I had hopes of greeting them."

Watson glanced over, as if he was admiring Lestrade's ability to escape the bell-jar of Hayter's affections.

"I will go to the station after supper. You can surely stay that much longer with us." Colonel Hayter voiced his sentiments just as Lestrade captured a dreadful premonition that was soon justified: "I had shot extra squirrels for the occasion."

"I have a lovely bottle of Comet Wine and I've been needing an excuse to open it up." Mrs. Forrester added to the bribe. At her words, Hayter's expression briefly wore a Biblical covetousness.

Mrs. Watson's smile was warm and gentle as she returned to her husband's side, and natural they did look together. Content with being taken for granted, at ease in the sidelines, they were a perfect match for each other as they simply enjoyed the company of others. Lestrade was reminded of the earlier observation and had to agree. John and Mary looked as though they had been married for years, and would always be together.

*Upstairs Library Suite:*

"I thought the Colonel would come up *before* dinner?" Lestrade was adding "fresh water" to his growing list of things to be grateful for. He sighed out as the wet cloth steamed sweat off the back of his neck.

Watson sighed with a most patient expression. "With a lovely widow in need of entertainment?" He stared at a rather large painting of the late Mr. Forrester, mostly done in the aggressive yellows of the Indian sun. "I hope this isn't an unfortunate development . . . ."

"You don't regret their meeting?" Lestrade was all prepared to be nervous at his (however accidental) part in said meeting between Bachelor and Widow.

"Not at all . . . It's just . . . ." Watson's eyebrows crimped together. "Would it ever occur to you to introduce a typhoon to a waterspout?"

"Ah." Lestrade coughed. It took no length of imagination to conjure the probabilities.

Clea had often (and volubly) praised the fact that she was retiring where her husband was forward, and *vice-versa*. He, in turn, would retort that there was precious little for him to be forward to, what with the superlative method Mr. Cheatham had employed in the upbringing of his only daughter. Clea would always laugh, and tease him, but she would be pleased as she joked.

With the older couple in the schematic, Lestrade found himself at a loss to imagine either Mrs. Forrester or the Colonel as anything but a force of nature. He hoped devoutly Clea would not age along those lines. She was enough of a tigress as it was, and he was still nurturing his semi-impractical hope of living long enough to retire with her.

Watson threw himself back on the horsehair divan and managed not to slide right off and onto the carpet. "Well, how are the boys?" he asked with his eyes closed. "Have they recovered from the cough yet?"

"Yes, well enough, but their second teeth are coming in, and that seems to make them irritable."

"I'd say they have trouble getting to sleep, though." Watson noted.

"Mmm. Running a sporadic temperature, that makes them fretful and anxious. I'm afraid I feel deservedly guilty for being away."

Watson opened one eye – unnerving talent, that, and paused to stretch. "A fever with teething means they're pulling calcium from their skeletons to create their new teeth. See if a little boiled custard in the evenings would take care of it."

"I'll add that to the wire." Lestrade said fervently. "Do you always do that?"

"Do what?"

"Pull your pharmacopeia out of the ordinary."

"*Certainly not.* I'd lose my respect as a physician." Watson answered in a voice drier than the roofing-slate on the Manor. "The overall reverence for a medical man depends on his ability to be abreast of all the obscure, convoluted, bewildering and exotic substances that can be administered by methods subcutaneous, oral, or Heaven forbid, moxibustion." [2] He lifted his palms up in apology. "There seems to be a universal reverence for the exotic while familiarity breeds contempt."

"Sounds like Parliament." Lestrade marveled. "I always knew I made the right decision by joining law *enforcement.*"

Watson grunted. "I have nothing but respect for the law . . . but I would rather not live in it."

Lestrade felt a strange lump in his throat. "We always felt some envy over the two of you about that."

"Hmm? About what?"

Lestrade wasn't sure he could make Watson understand. "Well, unlike those of us at the Yard, you could pick and choose your cases. It's not like we could." He shrugged awkwardly. "And there were plenty of times we felt Holmes was turning a blind eye to the *law* in order to commit *justice.*"

Even now, Watson had mixed feelings about talking about that very thing. He wondered if he would ever be reconciled at the some of the things he had done with Holmes.

"John, you're a million miles away."

Watson slowly pulled himself out of his thoughts. "Forgive me, Lestrade. It was not intentional."

"I'm aware of that." The little man was favoring him with the kind of expression Watson had often bestowed upon Holmes – Why Lestrade was giving it at *him*, he had no idea.

"Lestrade, is there something on your mind besides the fact that you're being held hostage by upper-class kindness?"

Lestrade had to laugh at the aptness of the observation. "Well, if I may, Doctor . . . for my own personal edification, mind you . . . ." Lestrade cleared his throat. "I was speaking to Colonel Hayter the other day and I'm not sure if I inadvertently caused him embarrassment or not . . . perhaps you could explain it."

"Explain what, do you mean?"

"Is there some kind of, well, *overture* about pomegranates that escapes the usual public eye?"

"*Pomegranates*?" Watson turned as scarlet as an Army jacket. "*Inspector*? What brought you on *that* topic?"

"To tell you the truth, I am not at all certain." Lestrade scratched his ear. "It was something the Colonel said yesterday."

"Go on." Watson encouraged, his beet-red tint about to stabilize.

"I was asking him about your dress saber," Lestrade reiterated, "and he said that for all you cared about it, you would have used it to peel a pomegranate, and then he – well, he turned the same shade of scarlet you're wearing right now."

Watson coughed into his handkerchief. He kept his face there for nearly a full minute. Perhaps he would have recovered sooner, but every time he lifted his gaze he took in Lestrade's bewildered expression and was rendered speechless all over again. Lestrade finally sat down and picked up a book of poetry to leaf through while Watson recovered his equilibrium.

"There's a . . . ." Watson said in a strangled voice. "*Ahem*." He cleared his throat. "It carries a symbolic significance in Afghanistan . . . for the . . . ah . . . imagined resemblance to a woman's breast . . . ." Lestrade hadn't thought Watson could get any redder than he already was, but he was wrong. "It is a topic of many poems and songs of a suggestive nature . . . and . . . ah . . . how to . . . ah . . . 'get to the treasure' of a willing woman . . . ."

"Among the *Muslims*?" Lestrade couldn't believe it, yet the dew on Watson's brow did not look to be inspired by the *outside* temperature. "I thought they kept their women under lock and key!"

"Outside they do live very sheltered lives, wrapped up in yards of cotton and silk." Watson agreed. "But hot climes in turn inspire hot blood – they were just as quick to cut up a British soldier with their knives as the men. We were always a puzzle to them, actually. They theorized we English must spend more time building fires to keep warm than enjoying the earth's bounty." Despite the years past, the doctor still managed to sound a bit disgruntled at being criticized for narrow-mindedness. 'Peeling a pomegranate' was a line in a song the women sang when they tell the men to cut open their collar to get at – Oh, good Heavens, do you mind if we stop here?" he asked desperately.

"Not at all." Lestrade took a gulp of wine off the carafe-table. "Not at all. I'm going to change the subject now . . . ."

"There you are." Mary pushed the door open. "I've found them!" She paused and took in the spectacle. "John, I think you were in the sun too much!"

*Western Tea-Room*

Dinner had been enjoyed. Mary and John had bidden Lestrade good night and retired early, for the heat of the day was still glowing in Mary's pale face and John's limp had suddenly manifested itself, just as the barometer began a slip dip to a forewarning rain. Hayter returned alone, commenting that Lestrade certainly had good connections if he could pick a place like the Medway Colt – He planned to visit it again before he regretfully parted ways with Mrs. Forrester's hospitality.

The "old couple" regarded each other across the silver and damask in a silence that comes only from knowing experience. Between them, as if in unifying force, rested a slender bottle of wine brewed from exemplary grapes during the year of the comet, 1845.

"I'm happy for them." Mrs. Forrester opened the topic as well as the bottle of wine.

"Hmm." The Colonel tilted his head as he reached over to pour her glass. "I'd harbored hopes for that boy for years."

Mrs. Forrester chuckled. "He's hardly a *boy*, Colonel."

"My dear, I speak in the relative span of years. I am old enough to be his father. That makes him a boy . . . ." The Colonel's face twisted at some private thought, a sad one. "John was born old," he said suddenly.

"That type is usually far too serious." Mrs. Forrester protested. "John's hardly that sort of man."

"You didn't know him in the military." The Colonel wrapped fingers like iron hooks around the thin rim-gilded glass before him. "He had a terrible burden back then, looking out for his brother. It had been much easier for him when they hadn't been stationed together, but . . . they were and oh well."

"I imagine he would have worried a lot less if he didn't have a brother to look out for." Mrs. Forrester answered sensibly.

"Hamish was too brilliant," Hayter said brusquely. "I confess, I preferred John. Most of us did. John was Hamish's – well . . . his *translator*. Hamish was rendered human through John. It was easy enough to fathom their dynamic. I'm sure John knew even from infancy there was no point in competing with Hamish in any way. There was no sense in even trying. He would always be the second-best compared to the first-born. That didn't mean he didn't make an effort to be his own man, it was just . . . more difficult."

"John never mentions his family." Mrs. Forrester said just a shade primly.

"I daresay it's too difficult." Hayter rumbled. "And here I've made Hamish sound like some kind of villain . . . He wasn't, I assure you." He puffed his shoulders out. "My dear, I'm making a mess of things."

"No, I daresay a bit of Comet Wine will straighten your thoughts out." Mrs. Forrester had pulled a slender flower from its vase and was neatly pinning it to her throat.

"Now that is fair enough." Hayter looked into the depth of his own cup. "Afghanistan was so much more terrible than India . . . ," he said as if to himself.

"Was Mary mistaken? She had said you had met John in Afghanistan."

"Very true, Madame . . . but we had both been in India before the desert." Hayter looked every bit his years in that moment. "My dear Mrs. Forrester, there are wars, and there are wars . . . India was a different Universe from that of Afghanistan." He leaned back in his chair. After a certain passage of years and no other company, there was no point in stiff propriety.

"Colonel," Mrs. Forrester said with perfect calm, "if your feelings are in conflict, I can only ask you to think of the foremost thought in your mind and speak along its dimensions."

Hayter smiled. "Perhaps someday I may be able to speak of you of red mangrove swamps and the maneater that was the terror of the rivers. I fear if I tried now, my ability to describe the wild otters and the lean tigers would fall short of reality. That was not how I met John, but it was how I first heard of him, and it led to our meeting in Afghanistan." He sighed under his mustache and swirled the wine in the glass. "Forgive me for that."

*Cupola Rooms:*

"No, I have no idea," Watson confessed. "Only the basic rule, that the tendency increases with each tendency – I daresay someone is trying to create an equation on it somewhere."

Mary only shrugged. "It's all right, John." She had divested herself from her strict clothing and was now staring at her reflection in the oblong mirror on its stand. As she regarded, her husband came up behind her and rested his arms on her shoulder. John, typically, did not look at himself. A mirror was no more than a tool to be used for grooming and shaving. He merely looked down at his wife and kneaded the flesh between his fingers and her bones.

It was easy to feel herself beautiful and perfect under his regard.

"When we are gone," he murmured, "speak to Mrs. Forrester about your concerns. The woman is a limitless fountain of knowledge."

She smiled up at him as he found a particularly stiff muscle. "Would it worry you to have two at once?"

"Ah," his face wavered. "I don't think I would be *worried*, per se. We'd certainly be living on much less sleep!"

"I can't imagine what it would be like." Mary said gently. "I spent so much of my life alone . . . The idea of someone always being there . . . ." She was still amazed at the thought.

"Would we be the parents of twins," John spoke very slowly, "I would encourage them to follow their individual pursuits as much as possible. Even if it stretched our finances to the ending-point. There are few ironies greater than being a twin, Mary. They are defined as unique *because* of their plurality."

She laughed at his light joke. "We're frightening ourselves, aren't we. This is counting one's eggs before they hatch – Oh, goodness." Mary turned bright red as John threw back his head. Quicker than thought, she slapped her palm over his mouth. "Don't you dare laugh!" she hissed, her voice trembling with suppressed emotion. "John H. Watson, if you think I am naturally skilled in that form of low wit, I – " Her lips were quivering too hard to keep talking. John managed to obey his wife, but there were tears in his eyes. He lifted his hands in surrender.

"I *swear* we'll keep this to ourselves," he vowed, face sober, eyes glistening.

"Oh, all right." Mary muffled. "Go ahead and laugh. You'll rupture something if you don't."

*Scotland Yard:*

Gregson held the door open for Bradstreet, carefully looked to make sure no one else was following, shut the door with the utmost care, and then whirled on the ball of his foot, eyes narrowed to slits. "Have you completely lost your mind?" were the first words out of his mouth.

"That remains to be seen." Lestrade admitted. "The good news is we'll know the answer very soon."

"This is a *bourach*."

66

"I'll ask you what that means later, Bradstreet." Lestrade leaned back in his chair, rubbing deeply into his eyeballs. "Right now I'll settle for a guess that involves 'hideous mess'?"

"Right on the pound," Bradstreet admitted. He stood, arms folded across his chest, the Yard's one-man version of Hadrian's Wall. "What do you have to say for yourself before we read about your career sacrifice in *The Times*?"

"I don't have anything to say." Lestrade sighed. "I'm just . . . clearing the air."

"Sherlock Holmes died to keep this kind of thing out of London!" Gregson growled. "One martyr is quite enough, Lestrade!"

"I don't plan on being anyone's martyr!" Lestrade snapped back.

"Could'ha fooled us." Gregson jabbed. "One Scotland Yard Inspector is not going to take on the British Army and expect to come out of it wholecloth!" Gregson poked the air in front of Lestrade's nose with a thick finger. "You go up against the Army, you need your own bloody army to do it with!"

"You really are angry," Lestrade marveled.

"Damn!" Gregson swore. "Lestrade, *try* to use your head! Army. *Army*. Army. That is, by definition, a rotating body comprised of people who have been taught to obey orders, and to kill if that is what the orders require! You know full well that the soldiers who return that can't re-adjust to civilian life aren't sent to prisons or sanitariums where they need to be – They get *promoted* and sent off on god-awful missions that no one ever hears about! Moriarty couldn't have risen to the rank of Colonel without being aware of any of this, and you know what his *family* is like! He's probably sucked evil out of his mother's breast! *You are mad to take this on without any help!*"

"Is there anyone here who has a question about the letter I sent?" Lestrade asked desperately.

"Only I'm wondering why you haven't asked Patterson to this little *soiree*," Gregson chipped in. "He's the bird what brought down the Professor Moriarty Gang! Wouldn't he be interested in this too?"

"There's a reason why Patterson is on extended vacation." Lestrade snapped. "I grant you he did a splendid job, which would have only been possible to an isolationist with few friends and no family at all. That was what was required to bring the Professor down and it still took Holmes to do it. *But this is Moriarty only in name*. This is *Colonel* Moriarty's affair, and he decided in his wisdom that I would be a perfect foil for his work."

Bradstreet pulled a chair up by the door and sat down, hard. "Well he must have a gang or two at his own disposal," he commented. "No one's ever heard of him in our civilian ranks."

"You know how the military works." Gregson pointed out. "It might as well be another country – or worse, they *are* the country, and *we're* just the foreign-soil authorities, hanging about at their gates and begging for handouts. They keep to themselves and they work to themselves. Any crime occurs, they deal with it or bury it – and they tend to bury it first, rather than let the word leak out."

"*Ungh* . . . What did you find out? Anything?"

Bradstreet breathed through his teeth. "Government Intelligence wouldn't *have* to be involved to make a man's papers vanish in Scotland! And looking for a single Watson is like . . . Well, looking for a single rock halfway up a cliff." He rubbed his thumb over his chin. "Records are execrable up North," he admitted. "You have multiple names, sons and brothers given the same name, children named after parents, grandparents, great-grandparents . . . Watsons have been around since Middle English, but we're talking over seven different ways to spell it, thirteen names associated with the family, and I counted *sixty-six* septs in the clan alone!" He paused to let that sink in. "Wyatt really was a popular name for a while . . . Over in Moray, two-hundred-twenty-five out of three-hundred people in the village were named '*Watt*' so you can guess for yourself how many "Watsons" followed after – and they don't even have a tartan." [3]

Gregson said a word no one had ever heard from his lips.

"Oh, this gets *better*." Bradstreet promised. "Assuming our Watson is telling the truth, and the given names are inherited surnames, John and Hamish are about two of the most common names in half of Scotland, *and they are very common surnames*. The blending of the Hamish and the John with the Watson clan – I did have a *bit* of luck there. In Edinburgh. In fact, Edinburgh is the very *first* place where the name came up. 1392. Now here's something to chew on: Edinburgh is also where the James (that's the English version of Hamish) Watson line *vanishes* in 1818." He spread his fingers. "*Gone*. A couple of plagues, some warfare, judicious thefts of children for the workhouses, and four-hundred years of genealogy simply melt like the snow."

"In other words, we're going to have a real mucking time figuring out anything through family records."

"But if we poke around the *military records*, I guarantee you the penny to the pound that someone is going to let the Colonel know about it!" Bradstreet wearily pulled his lunch leftovers out of his pocket and began eating cold beef tongue and horseradish. "And I wouldn't trust this Colonel Hayter, either. He's protecting someone as much as Watson!"

"What are the odds of some kind of military scandal, abroad, making its way back to the papers in London?" Gregson was thinking hard, his eyes half-shut. That particular cool, if not callous, tone was in his voice and boded ill for someone who would choose to work against his wishes.

"I'd say it would depend. Once in a while, something leaked out during the Second War, but it couldn't possibly be a fair representation for what really happened." Lestrade was thinking too.

"This is about as fishy as a day in Billingsgate." Gregson slapped his hands on Lestrade's desk. "Look, it's clear to a blind man Moriarty is trying to use Scotland Yard to do his filthy work. *Why is that?* Why isn't he going through the natural, logical channels among the military secret agents? It must be something *he* wants to take advantage of, and he alone. No one else." He glowered. "You know, I'm beginning to think I owe Watson an apology. I used to rant at how we looked stupid next to Holmes, but Moriarty must believe we *are* stupid to pull this kind of a stunt."

"So you're going to play the daft act?" Bradstreet shrugged. "I use it all the time. It works beautifully, especially if you break sticks while you're talking."

"Don't discount military *arrogance*." Lestrade warned. "Moriarty clearly sees himself above us. I felt like I was a butler under inspection the whole time he was here. If so much of his world and his thinking are within the boundaries of war, then he could be as blind to us as we are to him."

"Which means there's a chance one of us would let something accidentally slip . . . With any luck it will be Moriarty, and not one of us." Gregson snapped. "But for now, he's slapped Lestrade with the glove, and it's Lestrade's turn to respond. What are you going to do?"

"First of all, I'm going to ask you to stay on the alert. For now I'm concentrating on this matter and I'd be stupid to think I could solve this by myself." Lestrade scowled at the paperweight on his desk. It had some kind of uninspiring motto about dealing with adversity. "I'll be speaking with Colonel Moriarty tonight. I doubt it will be pleasant, but I'll be sure to let all of you know what happens."

"Where's Watson?" Bradstreet asked suddenly.

"He's back at his practice. I'm visiting him as soon as I'm done here . . . I had a few thoughts in my head on the train back, and I need to see if there's anything to them." Lestrade felt a headache coming on. It was probably just the heat. He hoped.

# NOTES

1. Lancashire is in the northwest of England, and separatists still exist today, although not to the extent as they did in Lestrade's time. Lestrade privately thinks it has something to do with the drinking water, which is close to the Irish Sea. It is without a doubt a very complicated, diverse, potentially quarrelsome place to claim home. Lestrade has no plans to retire there, unless of course, he lives to witness the years of his forgetfulness.
2. Not an exclusively Chinese therapy. The Irish and Scots were practicing it for centuries.
3. Nor did they until our modern times.

# Chapter X – Any Meaning at Atll

London was still as hot as ever, but Watson remained unaffected by the scalding temperatures. Ninety degrees heat was really *negligible* compared to India – in the swamps one might believe the air itself were on fire during the monsoon. While he hadn't spent much of his life there – barely a blink – it yet remained one of his more vivid recollections.

Ballarat's mythical *bunyips* had been enough of a thrill to a young boy seeing the Smallest Continent. Swamp tigers in the sub-continent hadn't been that much of a difference when he was a grown man.

Absorbed in his thoughts (which were how lucky Londoners were to be free of clouds of mosquitoes), he smiled to himself as he slipped the keys in their locks and opened the doors. Anstruther had left a note, good man. He read it to learn that the patients' projects for that day (an entire family) had decided a trip to the Serpentine would better suit their health. Watson had to agree with that sentiment. There was a chance of a cooling breeze on the open water. He had every faith they would return to see him – or some other poor physician – before fall.

His house practically rattled without the presence of Mary – or Ivy, who could rattle even if she wrapped herself in down and bearskins. He set his bags down quickly, flipped the shingle out, and began opening a few judicious windows. Mary's roses were blocking some of the dust off the street. Not the original purpose she had planted them for, but he was glad for anything that would afford her lungs some small protection.

Several minutes later he was seated by the half-open window at his consulting room, poring over the week's schedules while tea leaves steeped in a sunlit glass jar. If Mary knew the sacrilege he was inflicting upon her prize Congee . . . well it was just as well she was with Mrs. Forrester.

Alone, thoughts of that kind-yet-inscrutable woman sent a shadow over his face. Mrs. Forrester shared some kind of history with Mary, not dissimilar to the kind of history he had shared with Holmes. It was difficult to pin down, like seizing smoke, but the relationship between employer and employee was too deep and affectionate to be within the bounds of propriety in the society of the *ton*. It was a deep closeness, protectiveness on both sides.

Mary had never *once* asked him probing questions about his unquestionable risks with Holmes. He had to give her that same courtesy. Still, there was that foolish part of his nature that wished he did know more about the past the women shared.

*If it was your business, she would have told you – and* before *your marriage*! he reminded himself sternly. His fingers wrapped around his favorite ink-pen and he began drafting up a list of the supplies he would need by the end of the month. A low knock at the door startled him. He twisted back in his chair to peer at the door and recognized Lestrade through the dusty glass. "The door's open!" He called and, a few moments later, the Inspector was pulling his hat off his sweating face with relief.

"How are the boys?" Watson asked by way of greeting.

"They seem to be pulling out of their teeth – thank God." No priest ever prayed as heartfully as a parent. "I see you're settling in to your bachelor lifestyle for a bit."

Watson rolled his eyes to the ceiling. "If I wanted to be a *bachelor*, I would have rented a room at Hayter's and promptly bade my sanity farewell." He capped his inkwell as his guest snorted his amusement.

"I noticed there were some peculiarities he had that reminded me of Holmes."

"Lestrade, if you need to smirk, don't hold it back. It would be unhealthy to bottle that amount of emotion in." He returned his pen to its stand. "Hayter, alas, is quite easily amused by the various and sundry. His hobbies are in accordance with his tastes, and he lives far enough away from his neighbors that he needs never worry about their complaining if he suddenly desires to set off powder-charges in his cannon or go fox-hunting in the dead of night."

Lestrade paused. "He has *cannon*?"

"*Several*. He captured them in battle . . . Don't ask me how he got them home. [1] I think you need special permission for that kind of thing, be unrelated to any insurrectionists, and pay exorbitant shipping fees." Watson was sympathetic to the Inspector's expression. "Also, I think the Government has first-call to captured cannon metal, as that is what is usually melted down and re-cast into our soldier's medals of valour."

Lestrade sighed. "That is all quite fascinating, in a murky and disturbing kind of way, but I'm afraid I am here for one more bit of business."

"I thought as much." Watson answered without rancor. "How may I help you?"

"May I see your dress saber?"

Watson blinked. Lestrade realized he had managed to surprise him. "I have no reason to deny you that request," he said slowly, "but forgive me for sounding a little bewildered."

"I understand." Lestrade lifted his hands. "Doctor, simply think of this as another example of my bulldog tenacity. I must turn over every stone in my path, and to tell the truth, I know very little of dress sabers, save for a few that were involved in past cases in most unpleasant ways."

Watson made a horrible face as he got to his feet. "There are better ways of committing murder, I can tell you." He fished for the ring of keys on the wall.

"Oh? Is the metal cheap or something?"

"Well, not always . . . I mean, one gets what one pays for, after all . . . but sabers aren't the most efficient way of committing murder, Inspector."

"I'm not certain I understand what you're saying." He followed the doctor up the narrow stairs, both men feeling the press of heat increase the closer they reached the attic.

"Murder weapons are, by nature, weapons that are simply for killing. Sabers were designed for self-defense as much as mayhem. One can *block* with them as well as cut." Watson scowled at the rustiness of the lock. "Speaking of cheap metal," he muttered under his breath.

Lestrade turned that revelation over in his mind. "You are saying as a doctor you could only use the saber for blocking?"

"Well, no, that's a common misunderstanding. If I wanted to, I certainly could. One hand on the saber, and the other hand wrapped around my Adams – there is no law against my *shooting* the enemy in combat." He lifted a darkly ironic eyebrow. "If someone is trying to kill me, I may use the saber however I see fit." The lock yielded with a cast-iron grunt. "And I fully plan to, should I ever be forced to do so."

Both men winced at the wall of heat that rolled over them. The cause was clear. The attic, like so many buildings, had been designed in mind for servants' quarters and as such, had been fitted with large windows (being cheaper than bringing gas lamps in). The shutters had slipped on their latches and the sunlight had been permitted to flow inside without hindrance. Watson hurriedly stepped to the window under the eve and yanked it open. "Good *Heavens*." He breathed out. "Just a moment . . . it's all in this trunk." He moved quickly, putting one hand down on the lid of the trunk to brace himself before he dropped down to his good knee. A shriek of wood rubbed together and he was pulling an oil-cloth wrapped bundle out of the trunk.

Lestrade took the saber with a tinge of guilt. "I believe I'm running out of questions at this point, Doctor, but I still have a few more."

Watson looked curious. "Ask away." He folded his arm over the rim, not getting back up unless he had to. Lestrade had often seen him in such a pose while guarding and treating a fallen man on the ground.

"Did you ever use this saber in combat?"

Watson's dark eyes flickered as realization dawned. "I believe I know what you're asking, Lestrade." He pointed at the bundle with his left hand. "I can assure you, I never used that saber in combat."

"That is good enough for me." Lestrade answered. "I shall try to return your personal property as soon as possible."

Watson only shrugged. "It's not as if I'll have call to use it again." He tried to speak lightly, but Lestrade had heard such jokes before. One out of eight men in Scotland Yard had been in the military in some capacity. Given a choice, most of them would return to it if it were only possible.

Watson listened to the plodding tread of the Inspector's soles going down the stairs, and then the creak of the door as it shut after. Alone in the stifling attic, lit only by the glare of the windows, he felt crowded with the memories inside the trunk.

Pandora's Box had no horrors compared to what a person could lock up of their own volition.

He made himself look down at the trunk's remaining contents. They were all cloth-shrouded like his saber – a box of dead remains buried like the past. He had a scrapbook in the very bottom, holding all the Berkshires and Fusiliers. If he were to open it up, it would not be to relive that past, but to look for the faces of the dead.

And there would never be a short supply on death. When it came down to it, it was the living who were in the minority. Why people didn't appreciate that fact more was a wonder.

Ordinary thoughts against extraordinary times. The doctor rose slowly, feeling the blood flow through his bad leg in reluctance. He would write a letter to his wife tonight. Life was for the living, and he needed to reaffirm that living more than ever. Mary joked of being in exile, but it was no more a joke than his light comment about using his saber. Even now, he was embarrassed for saying those words, but Lestrade looked as though he had understood.

Life was for the living. He had to remind himself of that every day. The hot, sun-molten attic was a far cry from the Pleistocene chill of Reichenbach Falls, but it was there underneath his skin, and no amount of sun would drive out that coldness he still felt.

*Holmes is dead because he faced Moriarty alone.*

*Holmes is dead because he would not let me stay with him.*

Reichenbach. Maiwand. Two insensate chess-boards of the world where war was fought and only one side could win.

*Holmes was never able to face Mary when we came back injured from our cases. He put me aside for her sake.*

He was relieved to be alone with his thoughts. He knew he needed to keep working through his feelings if he were to survive them. Burial of thought was far more dangerous than burying memories in dusty trunks.

If Holmes's death was to have any meaning at all, he had to respect the words written inside his silver smoking-case. Holmes had been close to quitting the world, his incredible genius weary of searching for a worthy opponent. He had been searching all his life, and with Watson, he had been temporarily distracted. A whetstone for his intellect . . . but that intellect had grown sharper and sharper and still there were not enough enemies for his challenge. Holmes had needed something to defeat. More, he needed something *worthy* to defeat.

Watson couldn't begin to imagine the kind of hell his friend had been trapped in – a hell not even of his own making, but of Nature's. What reason was there in the creation of someone who possessed mental powers so high he was, to all purposes, an anomaly? Watson had never believed in such things before. It was simple decency to paint everyone with the same brush, to give all the same boundaries for good and evil. And for a time, Holmes had been as much like other men as he was capable of.

Holmes had adapted to the terrain of the ordinary well as he could, but Reichenbach had been the ending point from Baker Street's beginning. Watson could not have stayed with him forever. Not once he realized there was someone else out there besides Holmes who was interested in John Watson as John Watson. While he never believed in telepathy, there were times when Holmes and Mary had demonstrated a wordless communication in his presence – God only knew what they were talking about without words, but he knew he had been the subject every time. Neither combative nor competitive, there had been a sameness in the two people closest to his heart, and that, he knew, was why Holmes had decoyed him on that false case. Holmes had regard for few men and even fewer women, and his regard for Mary was selfless enough that he would not leave her a widow if it were in his power to do so.

"You know, Holmes" Watson said aloud, "You were right, and I can't blame you for what you did, but I am still angry." He sighed, feeling old and tired. "Angry that I did not see your thoughts as usual. Angry for trusting you enough that you wouldn't mislead me, even though you have so many times. I could have lived in mistrust of you, Holmes. God knows I had enough reason to. It was because you never mislead me out of malice, but for my own good . . . or someone else's good."

He had said it. He felt the better for it, although he knew enough not to petition any ghosts to listen. Holmes would have never consigned himself to a nebulous half-world the restless dead were alleged to inhabit.

Mary's tea leaves would be ready now. Watson carefully closed the lid on the trunk, leaving the lock open, and made his way downstairs to write to his wife.

## NOTE

1.  Captured cannons were used by the British to cast into medals that commemorated victories or significant battles. Maiwand, which had been anything but a defeat, had five medals but Watson qualified for only two of them, the Bronze Star of Kandahar, and the Afghan War Medal. Many veterans wore these two together.

# Chapter XI – The Lines of War

"**I** received your letter." Colonel Moriarty announced as he pulled his large hat off his head. Bradstreet, Gregson, and MacDonald lounged in the back of the small office with small cups of coffee and biscuits, grabbing a quick meal before returning to work. "I trust your investigations were fruitful?"

"Oh, one might say that." Lestrade decided not to stand. "We came across some interesting evidence when we searched Dr. Watson's house the other day." He did not mistake the sudden leap of something eager and vampiric in the other's eyes.

"Did you?" Moriarty's voice hushed.

"You said Dr. Watson was in an incident involving a saber." Lestrade reached under his desk and pulled out a sword in a scabbard. "Would this be the kind of military saber being referred to in the trial?"

Moriarty's face flushed. "Yes," he said stonily, and his hands twitched. *JHW* was inscribed on the plate of the scabbard, along with the single star of a Major. "I am certain that is Watson's scabbard."

"Really?" Lestrade looked puzzled. "It seems very ordinary to me."

"It has a Major's star. The *JHW* is obviously for John H. Watson."

"*Hmm.*" Lestrade made a thoughtful noise. "I see. Well, if you are absolutely positive this is Dr. Watson's dress saber . . . ."

"I would swear to it." Moriarty said excitedly.

"Oh . . . ." Lestrade paused. "Well, if you are certain . . . ."

"Of course I am certain!" The Colonel snapped.

Lestrade twisted his head back to look at Gregson. "Well, that settles that. I'm very sorry, Gregson. I suppose you'll have to look harder to pin something down on our dear doctor."

"Hang it." Gregson made a face of disappointment that would have been believable only to those who didn't know him.

Moriarty caught on in increments. "What do you mean by that?" He half rose out of his chair, broad muscles seeming to expand under his coat. "What tricks are you trying to pull?"

"Oh." Lestrade blinked. "I'm *sorry*, Colonel. The investigation has hit a dead end, I'm afraid we'll have to drop our pursuit of Dr. Watson for now." He held the Colonel's corpse-coloured eyes and did not quite smile. "Now that you *positively identified* the saber as belonging to Dr. Watson."

"Explain yourself, Inspector." Moriarty's face looked anything but assuring. A cold calm had descended like a slow frost upon his face.

Inspector MacDonald took a half step forward. "Allow me to introduce myself, Colonel Moriarty. My name is Inspector MacDonald, and I – and Inspector Bradstreet here – are the first persons Scotland Yard consults in the matter of bladed weapons." His big, bearded head bobbed like a large Yule Goat, and he took the saber out of Lestrade's grip, holding it aloft.

"A very nice saber." Bradstreet admired. "I regret I've seen my fair share of them inside men, but it has led me to become something of an expert on the subject . . . Inspector Lestrade came to us for our professional opinion as soon as Dr. Watson's saber was discovered in his house. Something strange about it struck us almost instantly . . . ."

MacDonald drew the saber out of its scabbard, and held it horizontally so the lights would reflect off the smooth metal. "This saber," he said calmly, "was *never* in any kind of conflict. There're no scratches, dents, or flaws in this metal that would be the result of any kind of skirmish with another saber, nor is there any sign of the polishing required that would blur or hide such marks." He shrugged, but a smirk crept out.

"We're very sorry." Inspector MacDonald commented. "Not that we'll drop the case, sir, but for now events seem to be at an impasse, and it really is impossible for us to continue without any further information. It's counter-productive to go any further without delving into military records, and you know how difficult *that* can be."

"Yes, of course." Lestrade blinked, struck by the pleasant thought. "Colonel, would *you* have anything to add to this case? We would assuredly welcome it."

Colonel Moriarty's face had become as readable as a mountain of blue shale. "You think to mock me." he accused without tone, without lifting his voice, without any real display of anger or disappointment. "I halfway expected something of this nature, and I confess you have not failed me." His large head slipped to one side, branding the Inspectors with his fungoid eyes. "You have not won," he said simply. "You are men of the law, and you have passed your own little tests. I, however, am a man of war, and a man of the Queen's Army. We are two very different forces."

"I would regret the thought that we would be opposing each other, Colonel." Lestrade felt easier for addressing the vicious man by his title rather than 'Sir'. "It is clear you are trying to accomplish a subtle means, and we see such things on a weekly basis here at the Yard. But as men of the law, we can only be men of the facts. It is true we make our share of mistakes and then some . . . but we are defined by our limitations as much as you are."

"It would be strange indeed to think that my army would be in disagreement with *your* army, Inspector Lestrade." Moriarty said gently.

"Not at all." Lestrade's voice slipped into a deep mode. "Scotland Yard takes its duties most seriously, sir, and we stand behind our reputations. I vow, none of us would imagine that someone would come to us with . . . a fictitious or frivolous case . . . ." He smiled to take the venom out of his words. "Do stay in touch with us, Colonel. We welcome the opportunity to assist active members of Her Majesty's Armed Forces."

For the first time, Moriarty's lips softened above his granite chin. "You have gained my respect at last." He surprised the little man before him as he stood, and even doffed his hat. "On that I bid you a good day."

The Colonel walked out of Scotland Yard imperiously, as if he was above or unable to notice something so petty as the fact that every man present, from plainclothed to uniformed, had stopped dead in their tracks and was watching him in thoughtful, cold silence as he descended the steps to his private cab.

*Lestrade's Office:*

Gregson gnawed on his thumbnail before quietly shutting the door to Lestrade's office. "I believe," he said softly, "the lines have just been drawn."

"I'm afraid it is a bit more personal than that." Lestrade had risen to his feet, trembling from an hour of restrained tension. He circled around his desk as Bradstreet and MacDonald peered to see what had taken his attention. He bent and picked up the object the Colonel had dropped on his way out.

The Colonel's glove.

"Surprisingly subtle," Bradstreet murmured. "Lestrade, you *do* carry your gun with you at all times, do you not?"

*Kensington Practice:*

> . . . *Of course, Mrs. Laurister sends her regards. I have often wondered if she makes a point of her weekly constitutionals* because *she so enjoys your company. In your absence, my dear, she has moved from a nervous hypochondriac to a focused, charity-driven woman. I rather wonder who the real woman is under the façade she must wear for London. Mr. Laurister seems not the worse for wear*
> . . . .

Evening was settling over Kensington in stages. Watson fancied the worst edge of the heat was beginning to ease away. Eighty-five degrees would feel cool in comparison.

His pen hesitated over the paper, and he looked up to the slanting golden sun as it splashed against the struggling roses Mary had so determinedly cultivated against the bricks. The ink threatened to pull under the tip and into the soft fibers of the paper. The doctor stirred himself and continued:

> . . . but you ask me not of these things. I promised I would explain to you, and I am. It is simply difficult for me to speak of, and while writing is an easier channel for my feelings, my dearest, I still must work up my nerve. This then, is my attempt.
>
> In response to your question: Yes, I believe England would have waged war with Afghanistan no matter what. I know you have seen the chromolithographs of that land, read the various writings on the rare flora, seen her peculiar fauna. I don't know how much you have read, but I do know that I have often come across a book with your silk thread used as a mark between the pages, and naturally I look to see where you are in case the thread falls out. India gave us a common bond long before we ever met, and I am grateful that it gave you some small frame of reference in your remarkable ability to understand me.
>
> Mary, the Crimea and India conflicts only led to Afghanistan. So many of us went from the tropical jungle to the high desert because generals who had forgotten war thought one blistering clime was the same as the other, and they thought that because Afghanistan was between Russia and India we would adapt as well. But you have seen the emptiness of the Afghani deserts, the small clusters of palm trees and the withered cypress trees that must have borne leaves when the Romans were complaining of the Israelites. The land has shaped its people for certain. They have been forced by hardship to fight in the only way they know how, and that is to win at any cost. They have precious little to lose, for it has never been a wealthy land.
>
> And England never openly wished for its sparse resources. It said it only wanted the land itself. Control of Afghanistan meant control of two of the three trade routes for the Silk Road. One of the roads was Kabul itself, connecting

*India with China. I honestly cannot tell you why they call it the "Silk Road", for silk was the least part of the reason. Anything that can be bought has passed through those invisible gates. In my short years as a soldier, I witnessed the trade of spices, tea, gold, silver, waterfalls of precious gemstones, dye, salt, and yes, even slaves. Being called a barbarian by slave-masters is a unique experience that I do not care to dwell on.*

*You have asked, but forgive me in this. I cannot tell you of Maiwand itself. Allow me to talk of the differences between the two sides . . . We had the Martini rifles, and they had the poorer Sniders. They could simply ride down the slopes, hit us hard, and run back to the safety of their ledges while we moved the slower, had baggage and supplies to protect, and of course, many of us wore bright red. I will not say more. It is enough to be a veteran of the Crown's greatest humiliation.*

*Maiwand taught us that force of will cannot win a battle. It can come very close, and it can spur a dear victory . . . but it cannot win by itself . . . .*

The doctor watched the tremor begin in his hands and he put his pen away in silent defeat. He sat, face in his hands by the window with his eyes closed. London was so quiet in the Kensington district. Without the sounds of the train or the cabbies, Afghanistan was no further from him than the touch of the sun burning into his hair and clothing.

And no more surmountable than the chasm it had left inside him.

Men died every day, and without any reason at all – not even with the benefit of a poor reason. He was at a loss to explain it, but that was how it was. Perhaps Holmes would have been able to untangle the Gordian problem, for he had been the philosopher for the two of them – an oft-cynical, disparaging philosopher to be sure, but he had only *dismissed* the softer emotions – he had not *denied* them. And for all his scorn for emotions, he had not blindly insisted on a cold "blood for blood" justice. Watson could not think of a single person that had been forced into murder that Holmes had not felt some sympathy or pity for.

Still waters ran deep.

He lifted his head, eyes still closed as he thought. By now Lestrade would have drawn his do-not-cross line before Moriarty. As to what would result . . . he did not know. He trusted the Inspector, knew that Lestrade was aware that this Moriarty was playing a game no less vicious than placing two animals in a pit together. Between Lestrade's inflexible sense of duty and Watson's equally inflexible honour, there would be few good outcomes.

He took a deep, shuddering breath and held it for nearly a minute.

They always marveled at his ability to ignore the blistering heat of summer. They wouldn't if they knew he felt the coldest inside himself, the warmer the sun burned his skin.

*I have to trust Lestrade*, he reminded himself. He deserves that.

He picked up his pen again.

*My dearest Mary,*

*Afghanistan is a jealous land. I said in the top of this letter that The Empire desired the land of Afghanistan . . . I could speak to you for hours of the treasures it hides under its stony soils. I honestly believe pearls and coral are the only gems not native to the miner's tools. There were sapphires, quartz, aquamarines, emeralds, rubies, lapis lazuli, tourmaline, garnets, topaz, and gems of colours and tints I have never seen before or since.*

*Those gemstones, I believe, are a trap to the unwary, for this apparent wealth gives its own people no profit. It is a sad fact that the Afghani make no more than the poorest pittance for all their labours. Only the poorer stones reach their markets. The finer grades go on to the markets of the world. When I was in India, the officers spoke of their personal treasures of tea and spices. When I was in the desert, it was the hushed talk of gems that hovered around the men of power.*

*Yet if you pore over the newspapers, the war records, and the fantastic books written about the Second Afghan War – or even the First – would you come across mention of these gems? Precious few words exist of those precious gems. Were the gems part of the reason why we marched to our deaths? I ask myself that question in the days when I can think about the war at all. Over and over we were told the land was needed. That can mean more than one thing, can it not? The land includes what is in the land.*

*In the end, my answers exist without proof, for there is no point in speaking of my feelings. The only ones who would know would be my own comrades, and so many of them ended their lives in the sands.*

*There you have it. Your husband is a romantic, but not where jewelry is concerned, I fear. I share the wonder of a stone's beauty, but when it comes to its true value, I fear Holmes echoed my feelings perfectly in that wretched carbuncle affair. Regard for the inanimate can only lead to idolatry. I cannot see a gemstone without thinking of the price in life, and the price that continues to be paid throughout the world.*

*Your Mrs. Laurister once said you deserved gems for your birthday, and you laughed when I responded you deserved far more than that. I was not joking. You deserve more of your roses, the climbing vines that throw the heat off the building in the summer, and the small violets that thrive in the cool windows of winter. You are so much a creature of life and light, you would never be properly suited with the cold and superficial value of a stone.*

*I remain as always,*
*Your loving husband*

*John*

*Quoting from* "The Adventure of the Blue Carbuncle"

*When the commissionaire had gone, Holmes took up the stone and held it against the light. "It's a bonny thing," said he. "Just see how it glints and sparkles. Of course it is a nucleus and focus of crime. Every good stone is. They are the devil's pet baits. In the larger and older jewels every facet may stand for a bloody deed. This stone is not yet twenty years old. It was found in the banks of the Amoy River in southern China and is remarkable in having every characteristic of the carbuncle, save that it is blue in shade instead of ruby red. In spite of its youth, it has already a sinister history. There have been two murders, a vitriol-throwing, a suicide, and several robberies brought about for the sake of this forty-grain weight of crystallized charcoal. Who would think that so pretty a toy would be a purveyor to the gallows and the prison?"*

# Chapter XII – Bellweather:
# A Foreshadowing

*Colonel Hayter's Estate:*

The end of the month brought the relief of rain. It began with great subtlety, with clouds no smaller than the hands of Judean prophets at the blue ridge of mountains to the north, but they sank down with infinite patience against the green of the outlying lands circling London. It looked much like a thin, silvering curtain as it rinsed the heat out of the land.

Colonel Hayter watched the march of the elements from the stone tiles of his palazzo. He was beginning to feel the slight stirrings of his age. Not a common observation for a man of his personality and vigour. Still, his back was as straight as ever, taking the growing years off his spine and the phantom aches of long-ago wounds. His very skin felt alive and tingling as the damp air pressed against his soul. It made him thankful for the warmth of his wool-blended coat.

The small trap was unsheltered against the rain, but swift, and the passenger jumped down quickly, his single bag following. With a quick murmur the driver turned the trap about and trotted back the way they had came, back to the main road that led to the train station. The passenger paused for a moment, watching, no doubt engraving the sight in his memory before he began walking across the estate.

Hayter would never mistake John Watson for anyone else. The Army had lost a good man with the price of a Jezail. He walked across the glittering emerald greensward with less of the old military starch, but never civilian calm.

*The young men are now fathers,* Hayter smiled, surprised at the pain in his throat. *The age I was when I was treading the mangrove swamps in search of tigers. God willing, John will not make the mistakes I did – Let him make his own.*

John grinned, his teeth gleaming under the darkening sky and he scaled the steps with an eager spring. The two men clasped their hands in old warmth. John's overheated body radiated curls of steam from his damp coat.

"A sight for sore eyes, as ever, John." Hayter clapped the shorter man on both shoulders. "Come in before the damp leaks into your bones. If my old wound is acting up, surely yours is singing along with it."

84

"That depends," Watson retorted. "Which old wounds are we referring to?"

Hayter laughed again. "Inside, lad. There's a mug of new cider, and our names are engraved on't in silver!"

"That sounds like the answer to a prayer," John pulled his coat and hat off in the same movement, hanging them in the foyer's rack before the scandalized old butler could beat him to it.

They settled slowly before the low fire kindled against the damp. Hayter mulled the cider himself using the iron tongs set by the mantle. Several minutes passed as they passed through the pleasantries. But the iron of manners meant less to a military man's sense of efficiency, so they did not spend much time on the inconsequential.

"Thank you again for the book," Watson wrapped it up. "I was most pleased – and surprised. I had no idea there was such a thing as a manual to hand-algebra."

"I confess I don't know how I lived without it all these years." Hayter held his cup under his nose and breathed in, momentarily blissful at the sweet perfume. "Did it hold your attention then?"

"Very much so. It was very similar in its methods to what I was taught as a boy. The use of the zero was quite useful."

"Quick, man, how would you display thirty-seven times two?"

Watson set down his mug and lifted both hands, his fingers bending in a numerical pattern. Hayter laughed.

"How goes our friends at Scotland Yard?" The Colonel asked, his voice tactful.

"Lestrade is incorruptible." Watson spoke with unique frankness. "But I worry for his family if this case involves him any deeper." He ran his fingers over the sweating cup. "I . . . gave him some of the information he needed. It remains to be seen how deeply he will pursue this case." He took another drink, needing the moment to collect his thoughts. "He never asked to see my brother's saber," he added, barely audible.

Hayter flinched. "If he sees your brother's sword, that might very well be the end of it."

"Then we shall have to be ready." Watson only shrugged. It was not the response of the man of action he was known for. It was the gesture of a man who was nearly tired to death.

"Moriarty has a gift for spoiling lives," Hayter observed bitterly. He had found his box of cigarillos and held the open lid to his protégé. "I've grown careless, my boy. After all these years passed and nothing came about with his ghoulish machinations . . . ." Simply speaking of the topic was painful. The fire's crackle gradually overwhelmed the conversation.

"What could we have done differently?" Watson asked. It was always that question. A question Hayter could not answer. Try as he might, there were no answers.

"I can't answer that, John. But we all did our best to stop that cancerous business from spreading back home with us." Hayter puffed slowly as he spoke. "The problem with cancer: Does one surgically remove it, or seal it off?"

"I am often asked that question in the line of my work." Watson's brown eyes were dark as cavern pools. "My patients ask me, what do *I* want them to do when *they* have cancer." He sipped slowly. "As a medical man, I must tell them that surgery is the only guarantee. But so many people would rather court their own deaths by choosing treatments that sacrifice nothing of their body . . . A man I knew . . . he died a few months ago. He had a cancer in his arm. In the lymph. We could have just cut it out of him, quickly, before it spread. But he could not bear the thought of people looking at his unwhole arm. I . . . can't understand any of it." He sighed. "Sealing off an evil is not the same as sealing off a cancer in a human body. Eventually, the human cancer comes back."

"I have done many things I have disdained for the good of the Crown." Hayter lifted his mug in a toast. "For the good of my men. For the good of others. We have sacrificed of ourselves to stop Moriarty's greed, John. My honour is satisfied that we did what we must. But I have never more regretted involving you and your brother."

"That was not your choice," John answered, just as steadily. "You could never have stymied Moriarty's smugglers without our help."

"Yes. *I know*. But the two of you went beyond what I asked for, John. *Yes, I know,* I *didn't* know what I was asking at the time, but – Look what it cost you both: Your health, your sense of pride . . . ." Hayter's gaze did not waver, but his eyes brimmed with bright water. "Those who loved you. You were fortunate, John. Mary came into your life and I felt your happiness as deeply as my own. But there was no Mary for your brother. No return of hope for he. I mourn that as deeply."

"None of this was your fault!" Watson had stood without seeming to move. "Matthew! In God's name! You saw a terrible thing that would have ruined the honour of every man in the War, and you took the steps needed to stop it!"

They squared off before the fire, older man and younger man, taller and shorter, with ghosts hanging out of their eyes.

"What would you have told our superiors?" Watson pressed. "*What?* Could you have told them everything, or would you have been able to stop at the surface? Could you have merely confined it to the smuggling? Or would you have had to tell them our own men were in direct communications with the enemy, smuggling contraband back to England? Could you have told them *how* the smuggling was taking place? Would you have been prepared for *that* consequence?"

Hayter's face twisted in pain. "Of course not." He rubbed his face for a moment, and the silence of the fire again overwhelmed the room. "But I am still sorry, John. I am still . . . sorry."

"You paid your own price." Watson answered heavily. "Was it not your daughter my brother loved?"

"A daughter I will never see again. I knew that when she married Moriarty's foul manikin." Hayter tried to laugh at the odds of fate. He sat down instead. "The fortunes of war, John. The fortunes of war . . . ." He was ashamed of the tears that unmanned his confession, but it would have been deeper cowardice to pretend otherwise. "Can we contain it?" he wondered. "Can we contain this cancer?"

John knelt on his good leg, resting his hand on Hayter's shoulder. The Colonel was an old man now, exposed in the light of heavy truths. For all they had spoken of, John felt the deepest sorrow at the sight of a good man beaten.

"We do what we must," he said simply. "No one has ever needed to explain your duty, Colonel. You always knew it." He took a risk and gripped the tight shoulder. "I would have done it again, you know that. The cost we suffered would be nothing compared to the cost of this getting out."

Hayter took a deep breath that vibrated his bones. He was a moment collecting himself, and then it was to offer a weak smile. "Strange. We shall see then, shall we?"

"Yes." Watson met his gaze. "I will go to Mrs. Forrester's and see to Mary. But I am returning here. We shall see what develops."

After picking the locks on the tradesman's entrance and the door to the attic, Lestrade was really quite surprised to see the trunk had not been sealed shut.

He set the dark lantern to his side, his skin prickling in the stuffy gloom of the attic. Outside, the rain was rinsing the detritus of summer off the roof-tiles. He put his lockpick-kit back in his pocket next to his gun.

A year ago he would have never contemplated breaking and entering, even for the greater good. The *law* was the greater good, not some malleable concept of benevolent anarchy. But he was trapped between the pull of strong forces: There was a definite sense of losing time, as if an hourglass had burst in his hands and now the sand was slipping through his fingers. Moriarty's silent and not-so-silent declaration. The look on John Watson's face.

This whole pretense of proving John Watson had been remiss in his duties, a liar for sensationalist journalism, had been nothing more than a foul test. Lestrade had congratulated himself for not – quite – falling for it, but it was afterwards, when he'd made his way home to dinner with his family that the full horror had struck him.

The test was not over.

Moriarty was a military man.

A military man commits to reconnaissance *before* he actually attacks.

Lestrade had concentrated on the apparent target of Moriarty's ire: John Watson, the man who had openly incurred his wrath by speaking out against the whitewash of the dead professor Holmes had died for.

Surrounded by the warmth of his family, knowing he could take shelter in it at the end of every day, the realization had struck him. *Family. Shelter.*

*There had been two John H. Watsons.* Two men, wearing the same face, given the same name by mistake. It happens more often than one might think? Hayter's casual comment had been thrown in, almost out of nowhere, and it was true enough, Lestrade was sure. But . . .

*But . . . .*

If there was one thing Lestrade had learned from his association with John Watson, it was that honest men could make the most skillful dissemblers. They were used to being credible in the eyes of others. Colonel Hayter's similarities to Watson had not gone unnoticed.

The British soldier was always stationed in family units. It was part of what made them a unique army. There was always a neighbor, a relative, a friend to be a part of the battle, to automatically watch out for each other and knit in an unstoppable force.

John Watson had been sent to India as part of the Northumberland Fusiliers.

For some reason, he had been transferred to the Berkshires in short order.

No mention of Hamish being transferred with him, so by default he had to think Hamish had been in the Berkshires *first*. So. Which twin, he wondered, had been enlisted under the name of *John H. Watson, Berkshires, first?*

"Still a fool, you are, Lestrade," the detective murmured under the fall of the rain.

His fingers sank into lifeless canvas-wrapped bundles, seeking with his fingers to be as invasive as possible for this wretched business. John was being used. Hayter was being used. He was being used. By sheer mathematical logic, he had to believe that Moriarty's plans went much deeper than the cold manipulation of three men.

Something long and hard pressed back against his touch. He scrabbled, ensuring of its shape, and eased it out. The ties were simple square knots, and fell apart easily. It was another saber, much like the first. *JHW* was cut into the plate.

Lestrade's hands shook as he pulled the handle. The blade parted from the scabbard with a low hiss, as if threatening him for trespass. Lestrade knew he deserved it.

By the open panel of the dark lantern, the metal sword gleamed back at him. Gouged, pitted, scratched . . . and brutally etched in a spidery track of symbols and runes anyone with Celtic roots would recognize. Lestrade stared, his eyes round.

"John," he whispered. "What are you involved in?"

*West Station*

The Colonel watched the rain batter the practice yard. Inside the barracks, the men were warm and dry, laughing over their evening rations and daydreaming about where they would go to further the glory of the British Empire. They were still young, still ignorant of the forces that pulled against them. They had no idea, yet, that Nature was an enemy too.

The rain reminded him thinly of the hidden curtain that absorbed so much of enemy activity in India. There had been nothing like that in Afghanistan. What rains that fell were by nature as punishing as the rocky lands. Afghani rain had only been good for diluting blood.

He turned his back to the window and drew the curtain. If he could see out, an enemy could see in. With that settled, he returned to his chess table by the fire. One of his spoils from the campaigns. It was a fine set of carved camel bone, set with delicate silver filigree and very small but tasteful semiprecious gemstones.

He picked up the rook and regarded it thoughtfully. The Watsons had always struck him as being rooks – straight lines were their forte, after all. It amused him to think that such a people, capable of the highest degree of manners and all the useless fripperies society required, nonetheless lived their lives with their eyes facing front.

It still disgruntled him that he had to deal with the least intelligent brother. Hamish had stuck him as one who would coldly calculate the odds and recognize futility. John, however, had that ridiculous breed of loyalty that mothers and schoolmasters tried to instill into their sons at birth.

Still, he would have to do. Sherlock Holmes was dead. No one else was left alive who could discern the entire disgrace of Afghanistan. Once Moriarty had been satisfied that his brother's murderer had perished with him, he had initiated his first steps to coup his brother's work.

If only Moran had not been prepared for him.

From Colonel to Colonel, Moriarty would remain bitter at his brother for choosing that mongrel example of Iberian nobility over himself. He had been every bit as good a tactician as Moran – but Moran had a taste for killing that made Moriarty impatient and disdainful. In his more enlightened moments, he told himself that it was just as well his brother had deputized Moran, who hadn't thought it beneath him to assassinate. He had enjoyed being told he could hunt the masses and bring back another trophy.

Colonel Moriarty felt he was made of better stuff.

He set the rook down, then picked up a Knight. Hayter was either a Knight, or a bishop – neither moved in forward lines. Hayter's unexpected cleverness at stymieing Moriarty's smuggling ring had been as unexpected as a diagonal blow. From a tactical viewpoint, it had been satisfying to realize the puffer had been capable of any subtlety. Choosing the Watsons as his weapons had been another excellent display. Moriarty had endured fools for so long he actually rather admired old Hayter.

But Hayter was no longer on the board. His ability to do much of anything had ended with his retirement – a retirement Moriarty had gently persuaded by arranging the marriage of one of his favorite men to Hayter's beloved daughter – and that had been only the beginning. It was as beautifully done as dropping poison in a well. The heartbroken man had left the military and resumed his bachelor ways, mourning the loss of his only child and his failure to protect his flesh and blood.

In all this, that left that little Inspector. Moriarty was still disgruntled at having to employ a tradesman, but it was fitting that the pawn was the smallest, simplest piece in the set, valued only by its numbers. A pawn was not worth much in the game, but the game needed at least one.

# Chapter XIII – A Nightmare Path: Among the Rocks

*By that foul water, black from its very source,*
*We found a nightmare path among the rocks*
*And followed the dark stream along its course*
*– Dante:* The Inferno

His breath steamed the damp air of the small hut despite the blaze of a small fire. He watched in clinical concern, knowing his temperature was rising steadily.

Long experience had taught him he made a terrible self-physician. Here there was no choice. He could either trust to his own discretion or be wiser.

The question was . . . was his fever high enough to interfere with his thinking? Was this letter a mistake?

He felt it was not. His feelings had been wrong before. His feelings were not regulated by his brain. The two sabotaged each other as much as possible.

Just a simple letter. Heart and mind were in agreement on only one thing: Do not undo what has been won at such a high price.

Almost.

The pen simply stopped moving, poised upon the soft-woven linen paper sent beneath. The fingers wrapped around the pen were unable to command.

After a time, the instrument was withdrawn and returned, not without regret, to its place under the lid of the traveling-desk. He sighed, and it turned into a shudder as he realized the narrow path he was on. He had been about to commit himself to paper, to physical traces. What, then, if his fever worsened and he was left without control? What would happen to the words he had written and left behind?

Rain, steady and without remorse, continued to pat down upon the old hut. He listened to it for an unknown length, not thinking, not able to think. The sound of the water against the thick thatch of the structure, designed to last for eighty years, was unique. It struck the thatch at an angle, breaking the force of its impact, and rolled off with little friction.

In the Alps, records of avalanche victims are kept for as long as it takes. Sometimes they are found in a day. A week. A month. But the papers go back decades, a century, and multiple centuries. This village had just finished the burial of a citizen, lost five-hundred years ago, unearthed from the melting ice two weeks ago. His identity had been made based on the scars on his head – the hairs had worn off centuries ago – and his hammerhead thumbs.

*The black mood is upon you.* He heard his own voice speak to him, but it was a strange voice. It had stopped sounding like *his* throat long ago, and donned the inflections and soft accents that Watson kept. *It is upon you. What will you do?*

*What can I do?*

He rose to his feet and went to the low fire that smouldered in the pit below the short chimney. Here they still hung fitches of bacon in the throat to cure, and buried their breakfast in the coals to cook overnight while they slept, heat creating nourishment while the heavy frost settled outside, crackling against the oiled parchment of the window. This place was too cold for glass windows.

Here they still grew hens-and-chickens on the thatch, to provide healing salve against burns, and to repel the gods of thunder who might burn their lives to ash.

Here they threw nets into the air and caught small songbirds, creatures who knew only music, and wrung their necks for the evening's soup. He had paid for the life of a kingfisher yesterday. It had no song that his violinist' ears understood, but its bright eyes had reminded him of something he had tried to forget. The shepherds accepted his bribe with tact and dignity. They did not understand why someone would remove a hard-earned mouthful of food, but they did understand the desire to see something live.

They understood that, in this harsh land, where the small cattle wore hides over a quarter-inch thick, a coat earned from the bitter cold that owned the land, and where life was short and sharp and sweet as the cheeses curing in the sunless shelters away from the winds.

Here they wore the same grass clothing as their ancestors did in the days of Bronze, knew berries as their only source of sugar.

He thought of Watson in moments like these, and no other. He would have loved to wallow in this strange world, sampled the oddness and differences the way another would have tasted a truffle. He could see him now, in his mind, telling the shepherds stories of the particular bogeyman of his Northumbrian homeland, the Brown Man, who wore grass clothing like these shepherds, but who would tear to pieces anyone cruel enough to hunt for sport. They would have liked Watson. They understood a man who could spin stories for hours without repeating himself, and yet possess the ability to sit in silence for days if that was what was required of him.

They would have *resonated* with him. Even now, he could imagine the battered shepherds sitting around the smoking fire with him, passing over the leather flask of pink liquor brewed from the thumbnail-sized wild strawberries, and asking his opinion of the state of the world. They would have listened to his stories about the Blue Hag of his homeland, who was heralded by the winter herons, and struck the killing frost into the ground with her staff. How she raged against each spring by throwing her staff under a holly tree, which was why it never grew anything underneath its shade. How she shrank into a lonely grey stone to wait for autumn's return. The killing merciless cold was never far from these men. They would have understood the bitterness of spirits born before their time to last over the millennia, past immigrants and the Roman conquerors who attacked both their peoples, past armies of elephants and madmen, to these times now.

Watson loved life in all its strangeness, its colours, its flavours, and its pains, which were as vital as its pleasures in the experience. But himself? *He* had never known that kind of love. It galled him as deeply as a burr under a limb. Reminded him of his handicap. His love had rested in the *problem* of life itself. The way a geologist loved the flaw of the stone that yielded so much information. He had always pulled back, pondering, and plaguing himself with the love of minutiae, unable to believe that entire cases could not be solved if only *one* particular clue would not be found.

Oh, for how much longer would it rain?

He had woken to its tap. He had existed to its song. He had slept with it, dreamed of it, and woke to it, and it always returned to the roar of the falls.

And the screaming of a man left in its bottom.

In such times, bound by helplessness, he experienced a hatred of his own brother, and a hatred of himself.

How could he have known he would have missed London so much?

He had always loved that city. He had been drawn to it as much as it had drawn his brother. As it had drawn Watson. So many people within such a small space guaranteed possibilities. With Mycroft it had simply meant the government. With Watson . . . anonymity. A way to be forgotten when he could not bear the regard of another person's.

With him . . . with him it had promised the interesting crimes attracted by said oblivion in the masses.

*You are ill*, his mind thought coldly. For some reason it sounded less like Watson and more like Lewis Carroll: *You are ill, Father William . . .*

.

His own observations were useless. He knew he was burning with fever. He knew the sweat stood out in his brow and smudged the clean

93

white weave of the linen paper. He knew it was a harsh sign and not one for encouragement. He knew that the ague settling into his bones would compel him to draw, shuddering, under the blankets at arm's length by the fire. With any luck his guide would miss his presence tomorrow evening and come looking.

It meant so little compared to the real truth: That he was ill and alone and the only one he could trust with his life was back in London, safe, with his wife and the promise of a child.

He would not envy Watson for finding happiness in London.

But happiness was something he could never define easily. Like art, he knew it when faced with it. He associated Watson with happiness.

Sebastian Moran.

John Clay.

. . . and the third man. Ephemeral. Unknown. Traces of him in the Tyroleans. A cohort of Moriarty. A peer of some sort. Perhaps even a partner, who had vast connections and wealth while Moriarty supplied the men and the means.

The names winked at him, moved before his tired eyes in the firelight. They traveled with him, were his companions even more than his own thoughts, for they were ghosts that could emerge at a moment's notice.

A man who fled, was proven dead, would be hard to trace. An expensive man. Who would spend money to pay for the pursuit of a wasp across an open field? And yet, they felt they could. Their arrogance would be astonishing were it not so disturbing. More than once, he sensed a test in this exile, as if they themselves could not call themselves his Master until they were able to prove it.

The world was changing. Here, at the top of the world, he could step back and sense a rumbling variance. The taste of something he had not seen in a very long time.

*Brother Mine, were it not for the sake of the world, I would not be your eyes and ears now.* He found another blanket folded for a pillow and wrapped it about his shoulders. *Had there been a time when I would have relished such a challenge? What would be left after such a test?* He could not imagine surviving this – it went against all logic and reason. One person could not make such a difference when so many large, powerful people were working against his goals.

*If War is to come, will any of us survive?*

The thought sickened his fever-wracked mind. He had no need to conjure powers of imagination why he must stay on this nightmare path. He need only to glimpse backward to a day that still lived fresh behind his eyes.

*You have been in Afghanistan, I presume . . .*

A man returning from Hell will carry pieces of it back with him. It had revealed itself in the flat dullness of the brown eyes – more black than brown – and an underlying fear as if he could not quite believe the enemy was gone and he was on home soil. Just a simple deduction, a way to break the ice, and the dull ice had melted by degrees, until they belonged to a living man again.

He had been gratified at the man's honest admiration in his abilities. It had been like standing in the sunlight after years of enduring amused contempt of his "peers" who treated him as nothing more than a carnivale attraction *unless they needed something of him* . . . Here in Watson's eyes he remembered *why* it had been so important to be a detective. Why he had wanted to do more than see the world, but translate it for others.

He thought of the War threatening, and the thought of more Watsons stumbling lost through the streets of their home . . . or never going home at all.

*He will enlist, if they need him. He will not let another man face a bullet if he can be there with them. His wife and son will have to wait for his return, not knowing if the enemy will take mercy on a doctor . . . or there will be half-a-hundred different ways to die . . . Enemy, the foolishness of an ally . . . or simple disease, like the one who visits me now.*

He shivered suddenly, cold inside and burning out.

*If only war was for those who deserved it. Not the small players on the field. And their small sons . . . .*

He closed his eyes. The firelight was now too bright to his sensitive eyes. There was nothing to do now, but to accept what was happening, and wait, trapped inside his mind with what-ifs.

*Watson, be safe. There are giants in this world, playing their so-called Great Games when there is only a Childish one. Like it or not, my skill has brought about their notice and they are compelling me to play my own part in this. The Giants care nothing for the small ones at their feet, and yet it is because of the small ones that I am here.*

How many more times would the Great Game be played? Was it not enough that the good, decent men of the world – the Watsons – came back broken and betrayed if they came back at all? He knew his friend had never returned to the place of his birth after Afghanistan – as if his shame had been too much to bear or the loss of his innocence too sharp. The endless nights doled on in Baker Street when he could not sleep and he had to sit at his desk and write out his thoughts – the nightmares that left him screaming at night for those left behind, and the simple knowing that his world was altered beyond its ability to retract.

Holmes had not realized the beauty of the equation until years later. He had known Watson's whetstone-nature had given him a renewed sense of purpose in his work. But it had taken longer to realize *he* had given *Watson* a purpose to live that was just as necessary. For all that he lived in peacetime, for all that the Army sent him home, Watson could not stop living like a soldier. His decent nature would not permit him to live in any way but to be prepared for *whatever wars would come.*

Come what may, veterans across the world were sitting with their own thoughts, reading the news between the lines of the paper, and hearing the unspoken words in debates and speeches. They knew what Holmes had needed to learn: The fires of war, once lit, are never extinguished. They only die down to embers, and wait for the winds to fan them again.

But, if Holmes and his brother managed to do their part, perhaps these veterans would stand their silent watch in vain.

The Great Detective, the world called him. Not a name he would call himself. He shivered deep inside his blanket and inside himself. He had never dreamed his life would be dedicated to detecting such as *this*.

# Chapter XIV – The Narrow Path

*Kent:*

The soft weave of the paper rubbed against the whorls of Mary's fingerprints as she held up the telegram in her left hand – her right hand was too worn by sewing to feel the gentle lines of rag paper. Against the delicate morning light, her face never looked more like a flower. "*The Bloom of Health*" would have been named after Mary.

Mrs. Forrester was polite if forward (albeit she lived in Kent for a reason, and that was because her speech was irretrievably blunt for most her peers). The woman's gentle face, still in possession of its lively spark, regarded Mary over the table.

"Is it good news, then?" she asked as though she already knew.

Mary lowered her gaze out of habit and good manners. "Yes, it is," she heard herself say softly. She knew her eyes were shining. 'John will be here tomorrow-eve."

"I am glad to hear of it," Mrs. Forrester said gently. "He shall be glad of your continued good health."

Mary hesitated at that moment, her blue eyes on the fine work of the tatted tablecloth.

"My dear Mary, whatever is the matter?"

"I don't know," Mary confessed. "I confess, I feel a bit worried . . . ." Her gaze lowered even further, beyond the table and somewhat on the floor.

The older woman's eyes were sad. She leaned over the tea-table and touched the smaller, smoother hand. "Dear Mary," her voice was throaty. "I want you to be happy, my girl. God knows, you deserve to be happy."

"I am happy!" Mary protested. "Very much." She beamed suddenly. "Do I not have you to thank, however indirectly, for my John?"

"I had no control over the way he fell head-over-heels when he saw you." The widow's eyes sparkled with a patent strain of mischief. "I didn't even know of him at the time."

"Well, know or not, the damage was done!" Mary laughed. "I went to Mr. Holmes for my inheritance, and I returned with a husband! A more than fair arrangement, if you must know."

"Some might argue that a woman needed wealth more than a husband." Mrs. Forrester was a devout suffragist, but she did not subscribe whole-cloth to every sentence that came from their lips. It lead to another reason for her staying out of London.

"A source of wealth that was rooted in betrayal, thievery, and murder," Mary pointed out. "When the treasure was lost, it was a clean start for the both of us."

"I'm afraid you're too sensible for most of *this* world, my girl." The older woman held the younger one's small hand tightly. She shook her head slightly, eyes wry and mouth amused. "Recovering the Agra Treasure was a slim hope, but the odds of you finding someone like John were close to a miracle."

Clea Lestrade swore suddenly, using one of the riper Lancashire expressions that had slid through the barriers of family, upbringing, parents, tutors, headmasters, and six beleaguered nuns at the Sacred Heart Finishing School for Young Ladies. She was in the act of throwing her much-abused ledger into the wall when her husband's arms came about from behind her.

"One of these days, you'll do that when I'm not in a fine mood, and you'll be sorry," she warned. "And so will I, for causing harm to one of Scotland Yard's finest!"

"We can both be sorry together," He bent down to breathe in the scent of the kitchen in her blue-black hair. "Making the boys their favourite again?"

"I don't know about you, Inspector, but it pleases me to punch that they beg for meals that cost almost nothing to cook." Clea's dish in question was potatoes in thyme-oil. In order to cut down on the mad levels of heat that pounded into London, the dish would be roasted over the fire-pit in the landlady's garden. London would never lack for available scrapwood.

"They have their mother's cooking to thank for that," he said into her ear. "Bank account giving you trouble again?"

"The usual. Turning the balance over to the Church at the end . . . They thought there was a mistake in the totals."

"*You*, make a mistake in the totals?" Geoffrey lifted a droll eyebrow. "I daresay you haven't made a mistake in mathematics since you stopped confusing the letter '*O*' for the *zero*."

"Why *thank* you." Clea pulled away and leaned into the marinade to check on its contents. "Well, it's a new clerk. I'll just turn the whole blessed book over to him in the morning. He can see for himself what the answers are. You're home early," she observed. "Are you finishing up your day in the office?"

"For what it's worth," he said in an ironic tone. "I wasn't getting much done over at the Main. Gregson and Hopkins are caught up in a confidence job involving elderly citizens, and it's got them into a most contagious mood . . . When I walked in this morning I had the urge to go find something more productive and safer to do . . . like juggle angry cats." He rubbed his hand into the back of his neck. "I'm going to take a glass upstairs," he sighed. "Let me know if you need anything."

"Just make sure you've got plenty of air," Clea warned him. "I'm not having you faint over your books because you forgot to open a window!"

"Yes, mum," He slipped a quick kiss on her cheek before she could slap him with her cup-towel.

"As bad as your own boys," she muttered into the atmosphere that he'd just inhabited.

He tromped back down the staircase a moment later. "Have you seen my Gaelic dictionary?"

"Check Martin's corner." Clea rolled her eyes. "And while you're at it, see if he's walked off with my calligraphy pens again."

"Pens, right," he muttered under his breath. "At least we know what to get him for his birthday . . . ."

John returned to Mrs. Forrester's, weary and bleached of life as a bone cast upon the beach. Yet, he smiled to see his wife and in the security of the house, held out his arms and drew her to him. When he smiled, his entire face followed, and warmed Mary from the very depth of her psyche. She found her own answering, and she drew herself into the wide circle of his arms gratefully. Her ear caught the warm thrum of his heart underneath the blanket of skin and tissue and rib. How he loved to touch her hair. It was often a joke between them.

"You shall be weary from your train, John." Mrs. Forrester announced as though there could be no possible alternative. "Tend yourself upstairs. Mary will see that you can rest before dinner tonight."

"You are too kind, Mrs. Forrester." His reward was a friendly sort of glare as the widow bustled herself out.

"How was the Colonel?" Mary asked.

"Well as usual. Putting up a good enough show to hide his loneliness." John sighed.

"I don't see how such a gregarious man can be lonely." Mary shook her head.

"It's one of the oldest stories in the book, sweetheart." John had his back to her while he tried in vain to make his stiff collar cooperate in the humidity. "He was estranged from his daughter when she married a man he disapproved of. Both parties are quite too stubborn to admit to their mistakes." It was the usual story about Hayter, and John was so used to recounting it he half-believed it himself.

"How terrible." Mary shook her head.

John now fumbled with his tie in the mirror, having given up on his collar and its need to be completely replaced. Mary stifled a chuckle at the horror in his face as he realized he had somehow been clumsy enough to wrap the cloth around his finger in a knot. She reached up and deftly corrected the damage.

"My Master-at-arms would have flogged me for that," John murmured with a dry smile. "He always felt that if we could assemble our rifles in the moonless dark, we could attend to our uniforms with the same degree of efficiency." Telling falsehoods usually betrayed himself somewhere. *I must try to remember not to knot my neck-ties while spreading slander . . . .*

"You're out of practice," Mary pointed out reasonably. "You've had a wife to help you for too long." She straightened up to kiss him. "I think I need to loosen my stays again."

"That's good news," he said. "Don't worry about it."

"I think *you're* doing the worrying, John. I've seen you wear your serious 'James' face a great deal lately."

"I'm told that is a common symptom." He bent slightly to give her a kiss. "Now, I'll have you know I did find the thread you were asking for, but it's been put on a back-list. You shall have it by the end of next week."

"Well, I suppose I don't have the right to be too disappointed."

"What are you sewing that requires *so much* blue and green and yellow and pink?"

"The gowns, of course." Mary tapped his nose with a finger. "Since we don't know if we're to have a son or a daughter, I'm decorating the hems in a floral garden style. I've finished the Christening Gown and cap and boots, and everything else you can think of."

"Everything but the naming." John smiled. "I'm sorry to say I've been no help with you there."

"What is there to worry about the names?" Mary wondered. "If it is a girl, we name her Margaret, and if it's a boy . . . What do you want to name him?"

"Arthur." John answered without a pause.

Mary, however, did pause. "Arthur?" She repeated. "Why Arthur?"

"It's your father's name." John pointed out reasonably, "And I've always liked it myself. We can always tell people it's my horrible romantic streak talking."

"You have managed to surprise me," Mary took his hand. "I would think you would choose another name."

He hesitated at last, and the flicker of pain lit, brief as a spark. "We can always decide on the middle name later," was his only response.

100

She understood. She always understood. She smiled to prove it. "I like Arthur."

Clea Lestrade paused in the doorway and tapped her knuckles on the door-frame. The brief rains of the week were only a memory now. London was starting to steam in its own juices.

Geoffrey never even heard her. He was bent over his desk, frowning as if in the spasms of a headache, with a long sheet of paper and charcoal-rubbings spread over the top. She knew without looking he had been taking copious notes from the battered Gaelic dictionary spread open and broken-spined at his elbow. Someday, she would find him here slumped over with heat prostration, and he wouldn't even know it!

She felt the sweat prickle her skin as she rapped again.

Geoffrey looked up, startled, his eyes slightly vague and turned-inward as his thoughts were slow to release him to the outer world. "Oh."

"It's supper-time. The boys ate their share and are washing up in the tub." Clea snorted slightly "Well, let me correct that: They're *in* the tub, I felt it would be cruel to make them sit in hot water in this heat."

"You won't get Nicholas out," Geoffrey warned. "He'll stay there till he shrivels."

"At least I'd know where he is." Clea chuckled lightly.

"Too true." Indoors and after-hours, he unbent enough to remove his collar and cuffs, loosened his tie, and began clearing the space off his desk. Clea returned a few minutes later with a still-warm romertopf and two mugs from the cellar.

"I haven't seen you wear this much of a worried look since . . . ." Clea sighed and went ahead and said it. "Since this last February, when you were fretting about an upcoming, supposedly *ordinary* case that turned into you and two Constables getting shanghaied by pirates on the wrong side of the English Channel." [1]

Geoffrey winced slightly. "Well it taught me not to make a living as a fortune-teller." He drizzled grain mustard over his portion and passed the rest to Clea. "And for the record, they were smugglers, not pirates, and we weren't *shanghaied*, we were held hostage so the rest of the gang could escape!"

"What in the world is the distinction?" Clea wanted to know.

"If you're *shanghaied*, you're put to work on the ship. Being put to work is the whole reason for being shanghaied in the first place." The detective mentally inventoried the conversation. Not even Watson could make half of Clea's Amazonian thought-processes believable to the public. For someone who could no doubt man the defenses and muster the troops in time of war, she was strangely ignorant of any education that would be gleaned from sensationalist literature.

"Well . . . you were hostages," Clea began.

"Yes . . . ."

"Didn't that mean you were working, in a way?"

"In that context . . . possibly. *Must* you always find the difficult questions?"

"I'm sorry, dear. I have remarkably little experience with such things."

"Thank the Merciful Heavens for that." Geoffrey breathed. "I don't think I could clean up after the mess." Clea, practical child of Lancashire that she was, never went anywhere without a knife under her apron. On special occasions, she carried a two-shooter in her pocket. "I think it made everything the worse because none of us knew that while *we* were fighting for our lives, Holmes was in Switzerland fighting for *his* life."

"You never talk about that."

"I never know what to say." Troubled as he was, ignoring his wife's cooking was unforgivable. They ate in silence for a few moments, while the occasional splash and giggle floated up the stairwell.

"It was . . . I honestly don't know how to describe the man, Clea. I *don't*. Lord knows I've tried. Back in the beginning, it was easier for us to keep a working relationship. I could consult him whenever I needed help, and he always gave as good as he got. I'll admit, a lot of what I visited him for, was what he kept in his head. He had all his facts stored up like a library, and *he* had the time to go off and research for days on end. I never had that luxury."

"No, I can't imagine you ever did." Clea agreed. Time was the worst enemy for a policeman.

"Once he got famous, though . . . and I *know* he would have gotten notorious without Dr. Watson's help. He just made certain the fame was positive and not destructive . . . that's when we got at loggerheads. I couldn't ask him for help like I used to. It made me look like I didn't know what I was doing, and it never felt good to know *he* was on the opposite side of the case! And then when all was said and done, after getting raked over the coals with every third statement that came out of his mouth . . . he'd just . . . blow it all off and tell me I could have all the credit. As if it made up for everything."

Clea could see that her husband still winced at particularly vivid memories.

"He never understood that I *couldn't* leave his name out of the reports." Geoffrey finished softly. "He just . . . *I don't know*. He was brilliant in all other things, but in this . . . If I'd done as he wanted, the word would have gotten out that I'd been covering up my own inadequacies." He took a drink of beer – late in life, his wife had finally gotten him to appreciate bitters. "He drove me half to Bedlam every time I saw him, and there were days when I prayed there'd be something I could arrest him on, just to create a sense of balance . . . but more often than not, there'd be justice at the end of the day when he was involved. I can't resent him for that. But the last time I got too chummy with him, word got out. After that, I made certain we kept our working relationship to the blunt and antagonistic." He shrugged upwards. 'I'm at a loss to explain it, Clea. How could someone be so intelligent – how can someone who can map your whereabouts for the past three days by looking at your shoelace, be so *ignorant* of police procedures when he was *working with the police*?"

"Geoffrey, I'm sure I don't know." Clea shrugged back. "But you said more than once in my hearing that he was much easier to work with once he took up rooms with the doctor."

"Believe me, Clea, Sherlock Holmes *before* he moved to Baker Street was not a man who inspired trust."

"And you miss him."

"Yes."

Clea was quiet for a moment, thinking of what she could say that would be the right thing. Her husband had almost no friends outside the parameters of his work – it was simply how he was. It made relating to him interesting at times.

"This new case you're on . . . you're wishing you had a Mr. Holmes?"

Geoffrey exhaled wearily, his eyes tired. "I'd take him back, arrogance and all right now, because there was *one* thing he could do that I never could. He could move *through* the parameters of the law. I'm trapped in them, tight as a train on its tracks."

## NOTE

1    See *The Moon-Cursers*.

# Chapter XV – Cave of the Dead Druid

Three hours later, Lestrade's headache had gone from annoying to *grim*. Clea found him his head resting in his arms on the desk and promptly thought the worst.

After she found a pulse and *he* found a scolding, she further compounded her authority by marching him downstairs to the little garden in the back of the building. For all its flaws, the house was the first to be cast in shadow in warm weather. He sank into the wooden bench and stared with one eye at a milky-looking liquid she produced in a stein.

"What is *that?*" He asked – quite reasonably. While she'd never tranquilized him unknowingly – yet – he would never, *ever*, put it past her.

"Ginger-water with treacle," she retorted. "You need it."

"Is there something for a headache in there?"

"*Yes,*" she said firmly.

There was no doubting that tone of voice. He sipped it in silence as she took her seat next to him on the bench. The cool blue shadows of the building lengthened by degrees and somehow, a small breeze blew in from the narrow alleyway.

"Is there anything I can do that would help?" Clea asked. Blunt though she was (Lestrade had a brief horror imagining her in the same room with Mrs. Forrester. She was bad enough with Hazel Bradstreet), she was also considerate.

"Not unless you can help me decipher Gaelic Ogham," he said without hope.

She turned that over. "That's the alphabet the Scot-Irish used?"

"Yes. I'm trying to . . . decipher a message in Ogham, and the problem is I don't know which direction I should read it. Up, down, left, right . . . It can go any direction, and is the message in the symbolic language or the syllabic?" He rubbed his aching head. "I'll give you a clue. The letter *A* in our language started out, ages ago, as the symbol for an ox. In the Ogham alphabet, do I read the marks to read the letter *A*, or *ox*?"

"That sounds like a terrible job! No wonder you wished for Mr. Holmes!"

"I'm wishing for him very devoutly right now," he said softly. *Because this involves his best friend, and Holmes would turn this entire island over and sink it in the Irish Sea if Watson needed help.*

Adding to his usual (and quite familiar) sense of inferiority, Lestrade knew Holmes had the connexions of the higher class, family, and prestige Lestrade was utterly lacking. John Watson was in danger. It didn't take even a man of *average* smarts like him to know *that*. But . . . as a police detective his sway was minimal, useful only as long as he employed the symbol of his office, and only for as long as he kept the authority granted to him. One word from a single supervisor, and that would come to a crashing halt.

*Couldn't there be an ally from the old days?* Lestrade's head throbbed anew at the possibility. *Couldn't there be someone who would be willing to help him after all the help Holmes gave them?* Holmes had been treaty to everything and everyone imaginable, from the figurative cabbages to kings. Wouldn't *someone* be willing to offer him aid?

More to the point: Why was Watson so open to the aid of a police inspector who had very, very little authority in the grand scheme of things, rather than applying to one of these silent giants that surely owned to a sense of obligation?

There was only one reasonable answer to that question, and he didn't like it.

Clea held his hand, hot as the weather was, and they rested quietly. Mrs. Collins had sprinkled water over the small patches of herb and spice plants, and in the last goldenrod glow of the day, everything gleamed like diamonds. Oregano hung heavy lavender-tinted bloomheads and a thick sprawl of Clea's rosemary curled like a green spiky octopus against a slowly-spreading carpet of thyme. A flock of wrens tended to the insects buzzing about the small beds.

"We need to think about bringing your hens soon." He tried to bring his mind back down to the family dynamic.

Clea smiled. "They're safe enough at the Charity, at least for now," she chuckled. "My biggest problem is with the new tweenys . . . They see anything edible as something that *should* be thrown into a soup-pot."

"I don't think its illegal to sell rat, so long as people know what it is . . . ." He got a smack for his troubles. 'I seem to recall, when we were hit by the ice-storm and couldn't go two streets without putting our lives lightly, all you could do was fret about the state of your flock." He blinked and rubbed gingerly at his head. "The pain's gone," he said in wonder. "What kind of anodyne was that? I couldn't taste a thing."

"Sometimes the heat itself brings about a pain in the head." Clea told him. 'In which case, treacle's got nearly everything you need to replace the strain."

"All these years, I thought it was just my trying to get my treacley brain to work!"

105

"Enough," Clea said fondly. "When you're self-critical to this extent, I *know* you need to get some rest. However," she poked him in the shoulder, "you'll get your best rest once you get London scrubbed off you."

"I have nothing to say in defense of your statement," he smiled, but there was a weary, defeated slant to it she didn't like.

Lestrade woke up from the heat. Clea was sound asleep. She possibly thought this was a climactic picnic after a morning with an eight-hundred-degree bake oven. He slid out of the bed as quietly as possible and went for water.

He paused at the boys' bedroom. Martin usually had a hard time sleeping at night. He was nocturnal by nature, capable of existing on very little rest. He was quiet this one time, perhaps worn out by the temperature of the bedroom. Their one window had slid down on its runners. He silently pulled the window back up. A faint breath of breeze drifted across his face. Nicholas rolled over. He was the younger by a year but about to outstrip Martin in size. Cheatham blood. Their father shook his head at the strangeness of life. Martin took after the Potier side, as he did. Nicholas took after the Cheathams. No one who bore the name of Lestrade actually *looked* like a Lestrade.

Just as well. When it came to family, one appeared to take as much bad with the good, and he wasn't quite ready to reconcile himself to the rest of his ancestry.

He turned the lamp down at his desk and returned to the task at hand. A roll of soft paper stretched across the desk, held down by two books and a paperweight. In the centre rested a dark grey rubbing of a military saber scarred and wounded by a ladder of distinctive Gaelic letters.

Lestrade had not actually carried Watson's saber out of the attic. He'd settled for a soft-paper rubbing to collect the engravings on the metal. So far, that was the one and only thing he was proud of accomplishing. The quondam major would have noticed something, he was certain.

If he hadn't arranged this . . . .

Watson was still military to his core. He carried his handkerchief in his sleeve and tended to his own boots. More than once, Lestrade had popped by to visit to find the doctor sewing up his own coat with the same neat precision required of a man on campaign. He allowed Mary or that poor maid to take over for him when he was too tired to do it himself (but considering Ivy's habit of butchering shoe-leather, Lestrade couldn't blame him).

Was it like *Watson* to go through the trouble of unlocking the attic, unlocking the trunk, and loaning Lestrade the saber he showed to Moriarty

. . . and then just casually, carelessly "forgetting" to lock both trunk and door after him?

*Not bloody likely. Not bloody likely at all. He's trying to ask for help in a way that doesn't interfere with an old promise.*

Time and again, Lestrade had encountered this sort of problem in his line of work. There would always be people who could not unbend their rigid codes of conduct and honour, even when their very lives were in jeopardy. Watson's low, soft-spoken statement said it all: *I made a promise.* But what promise? Was it for the sake of the dead brother? One couldn't harm the dead. Only their memory.

*And that's why Newgate is full to the brim of honest men. Because they've hung themselves on their own honour, and the dishonest men have let them.*

And that all left it to Lestrade to figure it out. Watson was clearly misplaced in his trust, that was certain. He was so out of depth on this he might as well give up on ever seeing the sunshine again.

The detective sighed and felt the familiar throb in his temples. Back to the translation of whatever earth-shattering message was left on this sword.

It was a sadistic sort of genius that would write a code no one else could fathom – it might as well be Egyptian Hieroglyphs for all the sense he could glean out of his Gaelic dictionary.

*Give me enough time, and I can figure out what you're saying.* Lestrade's observation to Bradstreet's teasing phrase in Gaelic had returned to haunt him years later. Lestrade *did* know a fair bit of the Gaelic – the *spoken* versions. He'd learned on the street and on his feet. He didn't have the skill for the written word.

Ogham, for all its flexibility (so flexible, Lestrade felt it was nearly useless and no wonder it was confined to mnemonic devices on lonely tombstones in the middle of windswept barrens), was based on a very narrow definition of rules.

### UIAMS DREUG

*Ui-A-M-S* broke down to a complete string of nonsense if one looked at the symbol meaning of the Ogham letters: Elbow-elm-neck-willow.

*DREUG* would translate symbolically to something even worse: Oak-Red-Eaidhadh (an unknown word)-earth-field.

Total rot, unless John's brother was as sadistic a genius as the late lamented Sherlock Holmes. (John Watson had intimated his brother had been of a similar bend of mind . . . or perhaps "slant" was a better

107

description?) Lestrade toyed for a moment with the look on the man's face if Holmes'd been given this thing to sort out.

But, string the letters back together . . . .

*Uiams* meant *cave*. It was Scot-Gaelic, not Irish, so Lestrade felt he could be mostly assured on this translation. He wasn't certain he should be totally trusting this dictionary. It was literal to a fault and didn't seem to understand there was such a thing as context in its definitions.

*Dreug* was even worse of a headache than the first word. It was short for *Druidhe-eng*. It meant *"Death of a Druid."*

Put that together, and one got quite a string of almost-nonsense: *Cave of the Dead Druid*? *Dead Druid's Cave*? Which one was it? Was it a pun? Was it a riddle hidden inside a riddle?

Pulling out the massive index of place-names in Scotland, there was no such locale on the map. There were plenty of places known as *Weems*, or *Wymes*, or similar spellings, which was the modern evolution of *Uiams*. There was even a castle of that name. But no caves on the index fit any such description.

Leaving Scotland and going for Great Britain itself, and it was all still fruitless.

That left a narrow spectrum of possibilities:

> *1) Hamish Watson was referring to a place that did not exist in the records Lestrade had.*
> *2) Hamish Watson was referring to a place that only a few people would know about. Twins were notorious for having their own language, their own code-phrases and understanding. In which case:*
> *3) There was never such a place as Cave of the Dead Druid. It was all a secret code name.*

*Don't think of the infinite. Stick to what your eyes tell you,* he thought. It was easier that way. He wiped a sudden flush of sweat off his face.

*John is asking for help,* he reminded himself. He still didn't know why *he* was the one being asked, because God knew, he didn't even have cleverness on his side. If anyone knew how limited *his* imagination was, it was Sherlock Holmes's flat-mate! Of all the times Holmes had scolded, berated, taunted, and scalded him for not being able to think off the tracks, he'd done it with Watson standing right there.

For some reason, Watson had some bizarre, misplaced, optimistic faith in him. Faith that he could hammer his way through a secret code, written by a dead man, during a war that had so few survivors that there was no point in even asking them for aid, regarding hostile enemy territory that would be impossible to visit, and under the angry enmity of the brother of the worst criminal London had ever seen.

Just . . . *Marvelous*.

# Chapter XVI – Councils
# Before War

*Paddington:*

While the Inspectors all knew where their comrades lived, Hopkins had never before set foot at Lestrade's domicile. He was not even very familiar with this portion of London, but he relied on his memory to keep from getting lost as he wended through the new knot of travelers on their way to-or-from Paddington Station.

"I can go if you're busy," Gregson had offered, buried up to his collar-bone in a loose jumble of what had been someone else's reports from years ago . . . and Hopkins had honestly contemplated taking that offer. In the end, he had refused. Still, the closer he got to the doorway of his address, the less calm he felt.

Early morning heat was rising against the kerb as the street-washer's traces evaporated to the canopy of London. For all its brightness in such weather, London would always have a bit of grime attached to it. Sometimes it gave Hopkins the urge to find a fire-pump and wash down the trees so they would look as green as they ought.

Nothing for it now. He braced himself and squared his shoulders, rapping on the front door briskly. It opened almost instantly, which jarred him out of his usual composure. An elderly woman with a face strangely smooth for her years blinked up at him and he smiled reassuringly.

"May I help you, young sir?" She asked softly. Her accent was smooth and cultivated, the way the very high-class servants were taught. Hopkins had a feeling she hadn't been *taught*, though. There was a natural ease about her, and he suspected there was mettle in that backbone – she was Lestrade's landlady, after all. He couldn't imagine anything less than a plate-iron dragon.

"I beg your pardon, Madam." He touched his hatbrim and for good measure, pulled it off while he pulled out his badge. "Inspector Hopkins from Scotland Yard. I'm here to see Mr. Lestrade."

She absorbed that politely, appeared to come to a decision, and stepped aside. "He's out in the garden," the woman announced. "Shall I bring you a cup?"

*A cup of what?* "I . . . yes, please. That would be most appreciated." Hopkins decided. He no longer knew what to do with his hat now that it was off. Mrs. Collins took the matter out of his hands – literally – and before he knew it, his hat was hanging on a hook next to what had to be Lestrade's Derby.

"Right this way, young sir." The landlady began walking through the narrow hallway. Hopkins paid close attention as he followed – once he'd begun employing the methods Holmes had laid out, it was damned impossible to *stop*. The result was, he felt more observant, but more scatterbrained than before when he was a sergeant rising in the ranks.

A thin wooden door, obviously hung up during the warm months, was pressed open and Hopkins stepped into a small world of choking growth. He blinked, pausing in his step, and wondered what the actual colour of the brick walls were behind the . . .

. . . instead of the ubiquitous ivy, German Hops crawled up, rough papery leaves greedy for the heat of the sun. The lime-green papery fruits, looking nothing more than small pine cones, dusted pale gold pollen onto the stone walkway at his feet. Clumps of cooking herbs and spices appeared to be doing their best to leap out of the containers in which they were confined. A sweet odour hung in the air like grapes, but for the life of him, he couldn't see *anything* like a grapevine. The largest rosemary clump he'd ever seen in his life burst out of an old whisky-barrel in the middle of the courtyard, brimming with tiny flowers as blue as October on the coast. A pole thrust in the barrel holding a small sundial. At the opposite side of the yard stood a marching line of gooseberry trees and the smallest, knottiest dwarf apples imaginable.

*Am I still in London?* Hopkins wasn't the least bit ashamed that his mouth was hanging open.

"She never gets tired of that."

The familiar voice hammered home the reason for his being there. Hopkins conducted a maneuver that resembled whirling like a Dervish while simultaneously jumping out of his skin. In a slim corner of shade Lestrade was seated at a small plank table, a traveling-desk before him with a tin pitcher and a single tall tin cup.

Hopkins experienced another shock, as somewhere along the line, Lestrade had impressed him as being the sort of man who would wear nothing less than evening formals up until ten minutes before bedtime. That was ridiculous of course, but without backup proof . . .

The older man was conceding to the returning heat of the city by wearing a light summer suit, but his jacket was off and his waistcoat was half-buttoned. His sleeves were rolled up to the elbows. Hopkins felt strangely relieved that he still had his watch hanging off its chain. But his hair was far from the usual proper slicked-back-with-lime. It was depending carelessly in a flick from the left to the right, as if doing a full job had just been not-worth-the-bother than morning.

"I . . . ." Hopkins tried to think of something to say.

Lestrade was smiling very slightly. "Mrs. Collins pretends otherwise, but she's sunk enough pride in her garden to be charged for Biblical Covetousness. Nothing pleases her more than to lead newcomers to her courtyard, and then bask in their reaction." He looked himself throughout the sweep of brick, stone, and living sculpture. "She's been working on this for nearly fifty years, they say. I can well believe it."

"It's . . . ." Hopkins quite forgot his nerves in his wonder. "I've never seen anything like this outside the Royal Gardens."

"Thank you, Mr. Hopkins." Mrs. Collins re-emerged from behind him and neatly set down a fresh pitcher that looked to be the twin of the dewed one by Lestrade's sleeve. The promised cup followed. "Luncheon will be in a few hours if you care to stay."

"I . . . I can't promise to stay, Mrs. Collins." Hopkins said hastily. "I'm sorry."

"Have a seat." Lestrade lifted his dark eyebrows. "Is the news so bad?"

Hopkins cleared his throat. "Well . . . you know that Gregson and I were collaborating on that confidence job with those senior citizens."

Lestrade poured out their glasses. "I know it put both of you in quite the mood," he said dryly.

Hopkins felt himself blush to his roots. So much for their having a private discussion in Gregson's office with the door shut. "It's turning out to be a difficult case," he answered bluntly. "And it may have gone deeper than just confidence."

"Go on." Lestrade encouraged.

Hopkins took a deep breath. "You know what the records are like . . . even before half the Universe was packed up and moved to New Scotland Yard . . . Piles of papers and folders and whatnots." Lestrade nodded, both rueful and slightly ashamed. "It looks like some of the files that would have helped us in the case were part of what went up during the Fenian Bombing."

Lestrade grimaced. "That was several years ago . . . ." He tapped his fingertips against his glass. "I can believe it, though. The worst of the damage was right by the Chief's office . . . ." He frowned. "If the files were there, then they would have had *something* to do with the Irish."

"Yes, sir. Traveling Irish, to begin with." Hopkins picked up his own glass. It was already sweating on the outside from the heat. *I can't believe Lestrade's walking around without a collar and tie . . . Well, this is his home and he is on his weekend . . .* He took a sip of a pale-coloured tea that tasted of flowers. "There was a mix-up with the Tinkler Folk, and – "

112

"I remember." Lestrade had his eyes closed, concentrating. "The deceased in question had passed on some of his clothing, and his family went into a righteous panic. Accused the tribe of stealing the clothes and small effects."

"Was there anything else besides small effects and clothing?" Hopkins wondered eagerly.

"I need to think about it," Lestrade murmured. "It will come to me. It was during the winter months . . . ." His eyes opened, wryly. "It seems to me there was *something* they thought valuable in some way . . . ." A distant look softened the normally sharp brown eyes. "Something . . . odd . . . ." A frown drew his brows up. "And you think this strangeness about an Irish tribe is connected to a *confidence scheme with elderly citizens?*" He couldn't help the confusion in his voice. "So many years later?"

Hopkins shrugged helplessly. Something of his private anguish must have shown then, because so far Lestrade wasn't acting like the tetchy, short-tempered and prickly Inspector he'd heard about through his meteoric rise in the ranks.

"Inspector, no one else in the Yard within the past forty years has such a . . . rapport with the Walking People. If there's a connexion, we'll have to rely on your memory and your assistance."

He was confused when the older man appeared to flinch at his words.

"Is something wrong, Mr. Lestrade?" Hopkins was uneasy anew.

"It's best not to call them that, Hopkins." Lestrade spoke slowly, and Hopkins somehow knew without proof that the older man was not answering his question. "*Lucht siúil* or Tinkers . . . but *Walking People* isn't really what they call themselves." He forced a smile. 'I know you're too much a gentleman to call them 'Pikeys' or 'Knackers'."

The door swept open, and a tiny woman adorned with blue-black hair piled up in a pile of French braid sped out with a cutting-basket under her arm. "On business?" She smiled at both the men, and deep blue eyes twinkled. "I'm just trimming the verge for the stew tonight. I can come back later if it's private."

"No, not at all, Clea." Lestrade's face softened from its strange and troubling expression. For a moment, he looked years younger. He flipped his wrist in a good-natured gesture and she moved to a small hedgerow of parsley about to bloom.

Unfortunately for the tactical maneuver, the moment gave Hopkins the chance he needed to press. "Mr. Lestrade," the young man began, "please, believe me, if I said something to offend – "

"No. No." Lestrade lifted both hands up, trying to be placatory and advisory at the same time. "You just . . . inadvertently spurred a memory I hadn't expected. That's all." He rubbed his chin, eyes throwing

113

downward as he thought. "I'll have to go back and dig out my journals," he said at last. "How quickly do you need this?"

"Oh, it can wait a few days." Hopkins assured him quickly. "Gregson is still interviewing his victims of the confidence scheme."

"What exactly am I looking for?" Lestrade mused. "The details of the alleged theft?"

"That . . . and anything like it that came up at about that time." Hopkins sighed. "Gregson said there was something about that case that . . . paralleled something he'd picked up about the confidence scheme." He blushed slightly and hid it in his drink. "He isn't quite sure what he's looking for just yet, but he says there's something amiss about the whole thing – more amiss than the idea of swindling old folks out of what little pence they have."

"That's amiss *enough*," Lestrade admitted. "Off the top of my head, all I can think of, the alleged theft of clothing was a farce of confusion. First of all, the Tinkers were confused for the actual Gipsies . . . and while most people can't tell them apart, believe you me, they're as different as night and day if you ask them." Lestrade had closed his eyes again. "The clothing . . . it was all about the clothing, for some reason . . . ." He gnawed on his lip. "Gipsies won't touch a dead man's property," he said slowly. "I think that was part of it. Yes, I'm sure that was part of it . . . ." He tapped his fingers on the table, a metronome to his thinking.

Hopkins felt a stir of hope, finally. "Is it possible to speak with them?"

"Er . . . ." Lestrade looked a bit leery. "I'd have to find them first. This is a big island, and they travel outside of it a bit. They spent half the year in France their last time out . . . ."

"What about records? Can Scotland Yard track them through traveling records?"

Lestrade laughed, but softly and without malice. "The tribe you want is comprised of one of the Dooley septs. The Dooleys are the absolute oldest name among the Folk in existence. Whenever they want to travel, they're not about to use their real name, so they won't be Dooleys, unless of course, they're pretending to be Dooleys from *another* tribe . . . Hopkins, honestly, we won't get our answers there!"

Hopkins looked crestfallen.

"Hopkins, for Heaven's sake. This isn't like you. The man I know by reputation isn't emotional or excitable, not by a long chalk." To do him credit, Lestrade looked concerned, not angry.

"Forgive me." Hopkins took a deep breath. "It's just that . . . this *is* emotional." He looked down at his hands. "I don't mind admitting, there are times when I wonder if I wasn't promoted too quickly. This is something I feel out of my depth with."

"Bosh." Lestrade finally opened the bottle on his temper. "They knew you had it in you. They just waited until you got enough basic experience under your belt." He leaned back in his wooden chair, arms folded over his chest. Hard-looking muscles moved over long bones. Despite the twenty-two years' difference between them, Hopkins had the instinct that Lestrade could mop the floor with his face if he wanted to. "What's got you so worried?"

"Gregson and I are working on this case together because of the overlap." Hopkins explained. "Gregson's been working on organized crime, and it's beginning to look as though someone quite clever and cold is behind this scheme of Old-Timers. I was involved because of the poor old people themselves. It was my case, but I was glad to open it to Gregson once it was clear how large it was."

"Good Lord." Lestrade winced. "*More* organized crime . . . or at least a small family at work." He leaned forward, picking up his drink again. "And here I thought London was getting crowded because we've got an extra million or so people in it now . . . ." That last was said under his breath. He set his empty cup down with relief. "I'll need some time to get through my personal notes, but I can surely find something. Not that I'm telling you it's what you need."

"I know you've got a full caseload," Hopkins said humbly, "but we could use you." The young man looked down at his wrists, finding a great deal of interest in his cufflinks.

"I'll see what I can do." He smiled then, because Hopkins looked like he needed some sort of reassurance. "But this is hardly my case. There's no point in arguing seniority from years ago. I think it's still a long shot."

"It's all we have at the moment," Hopkins said, breathing his relief. "Thank you."

Lestrade watched the door shut behind the young man. He was quiet for so long that his wife gave up pretense of giving him privacy and returned to his side.

"You have a look on your face, and that's a fact," she stated.

"That," Lestrade said slowly, "is the future of Scotland Yard." He struggled to express what he was feeling, when he wasn't completely certain it would make sense. "His generation will have a great deal more freedoms and protections that ours ever had." He put his ink-pen back inside the writing-desk and began busying himself with shutting everything up. "There's at least twenty nonsensical laws he'll never have to deal with, thank God, and better pay . . . ."

"You don't sound jealous, dear, but you don't sound happy either."

"I'm not. I'm honestly worried." He tilted his head backwards to look upside-down at his wife. She put her basket down and rested her hands on his shoulders, patiently kneading the hard knots that always lived there. "Suicides are going up again among the men. The discipline's getting harsher. There's some men now that I swear to you are no better than the criminals they're arresting. Frankly, Clea, the best thing to happen to New Scotland Yard happened back in March when they consolidated the Lost Property Office with the Carriage Office!" He snorted. "That's it! Ever since the Bow Street Strike, I've barely seen Roger. And then . . . ."

She watched as her husband shook his head. "They're wanting me to remember something that happened years ago . . . Hopkins is young enough to be my *son*. He has no frame of reference to anything that went on before 1882. I've been in the CID almost forty years. It won't be much longer they'll ask for my retirement."

His voice was flat and devoid. Despite the baked heat of the bricks, Clea shivered from a chill.

"Does it bother you that you haven't promoted higher than Inspector?" She hated herself for asking, but still . . . He had tried very hard to discourage her back in the hectic months of their courtship. A dead-end career had been one of his salvos. Another one had been his patient reminder of their age difference. As even her brothers had known Clea was "born old", that hadn't bothered anyone but himself.

"The largest reason why I was never promoted," her husband said slowly, "is due to a combination of reasons that emerged in 1877 . . . Things only made themselves worse with my familiarity with undesirables like the Tinkers. They've needed my help often enough. It looks like I'll be giving it again." He picked up the pencil he'd been using for first-drafts and studied it as if it had suddenly become unfamiliar and dangerous. "They're asking for my help, using notes from a period in my life I'd rather not think about . . . and at the same time, I'm trying to help Dr. Watson with *his* case." He slowly rose to his feet, turned around and faced her. "Clea, if I did retire soon . . . would you be surprised?"

*West Station*

Colonel Moriarty picked up one of the chess pieces at his table and studied it.

116

# Chapter XVII – Gathering of Minds

*If I did retire soon . . . Would you be surprised?*

Clea Lestrade had been expecting such words from her husband for some time . . . since whatever business had been pulling him into the case he was in now.

For a moment she simply looked up at him. She liked having a husband who *wasn't* tall as a shipmast. It saved her neck. He was truly concerned about what she thought. Clea took in the lines about his face she was certain hadn't been there before 1891. (Small wonder. She was certain she owed her first grey hairs to that year.) – and the darkness of those eyes. Thank god the boys had his eyes. He didn't need lenses, even when reading. She was getting nearsighted, though his Gipsy friends insisted it was nothing a cup of their special teas wouldn't cure. Clea had a robust palate, but drinking something that tasted like summer hay was the end of her tolerance.

At arm's length, she didn't need help to see him. She reached up to brush a forelock to the side, smiling as she did so.

"You're no good to us if you're miserable," she reminded him. "If I'm to imagine you as anything other than a policeman, you'll have to give me time to think about it . . . a lot of time."

He relaxed slightly, to her private relief. She'd used the word "policeman" rather than "Inspector" deliberately. The broader word was safer. It reminded him of his profession, not his rank.

"It's up to you when you retire," Clea said at last. He wanted *some* sort of response from her. "If I feel as though the work is getting too much, be assured I'll tell you."

That conjured a light smile. 'I'm sure you will," he teased.

"You *are* aware you married a future fussy old woman." Clea's heels let her kiss him with minimal effort.

"Does that mean I'll be a curmudgeon?"

"Why should just one of us embarrass the boys?" Clea pointed out. Finally – he laughed. "But, seriously, Geoffrey. Do you want me to visit Father at a better time?"

"Not at all." He answered without doubt. "I'm sure he's missing you three."

"You do know he's grown to like you too."

He did not quite roll his eyes upward, but there was that general impression. "So long as he doesn't demonstrate any more wrestling moves."

To be fair, Clea *tried* not to react. She wound up snorting in his shirt-front. "Geoffrey Lestrade, you are . . . incorrigible."

He laughed under his breath. "No, go on to your *Tad.*" Try as he might, there were *some* words that just could not be corrected by the proper English grammar. He worked so hard not to be anything less than acceptable when he was at work, but when he was at home, things slipped out. It was one of his more endearing traits.

"Go on to your *Tad*," he held her at arm's length, fondly, though she knew he was already missing her. "They haven't seen you in too long. It would also do the three of you good to get out of the worst of the fogs."

"I won't argue with you there, but one of these days, you'll have to join us on vacation," Clea warned with a gentle smile.

"I daresay it won't be long." Her husband smiled.

*Kent:*

"*Where* did you go?" John had no difficulties with being flabbergasted. That Mary and Mrs. Forrester had an unusually amicable relationship, he knew. That both women had a streak of independence and unpredictability – that too.

He might have known the combination would have led to some recklessness.

"St. Mary Hoo." Mary smiled. "We've gone there before, John."

*I heard you, dearest,* John thought. *Hoo is Old English for Peninsula. Peninsula means coast. Coast means mosquitoes. Mosquitoes mean illness* . . . Aloud: "I'm merely surprised, that's all. The air of Kent must agree with you."

"I confess it does at the moment." Mary confessed. "But I wanted to see the little chapel, and it is such a beautiful place. I made sketches that I shall show you some time when you're too paralyzed with boredom to attempt to escape." Her smile was delighted, and worried as John was, he was grateful to see a spark of Mary's old spirit return. The heat of London had truly drained her.

"Why don't you show me now?" He asked gallantly. "After all, I'm in a mood to sit down for a bit, and you may need me in a paralyzing mood later on for something else."

Mary laughed, her fingers curling into his. "We went to Allhallows," she began. "I always thought it was a lovely name. It's such a small place,

John. I don't think there were even three-hundred people in the Parish . . .
."

"The Town was named Allhallows because of the All Saints Church, isn't it?" John tried to remember as his wife tugged him to an easy chair.

"Yes, the chancel was heavily restored – heavily. You should see it sometime, John. It's a beautiful, dignified architecture of flint and stone, and a lead roof – I daresay they needn't worry about lead thieves over there." Mary smiled as John chuckled at that. "And we went to Yanlet Creek and looked for Roman artifacts after!"

"Really!" Now there was something John would have enjoyed. "Did you find anything?"

"Well, I found *something*, but I don't know what it is." Mary took her cue like a true artiste of the stage. Her hand swept from her reticule to John's open hand. Startled, John felt the weight of it tug his hand down. He opened his fingers and peered at what was resting in his palm.

"Good Lord," he said.

Mary was smiling, but this was about as close as "beside herself with glee" as John had seen her since learning she was expecting. "Can you think of what it could be?" she wondered.

John turned the small object over in his hands, several times. "Mary, I believe you've found an atlatl tip!" He ran his fingertip down the end of the small stone barb. "The nocks were cut into the ends to ensure speedy delivery through the air." He tugged on his mouth thoughtfully. "I've no idea how it got there, but it looks like the assembled weapon at the Museum."

"Well, you should have it." Mary said proudly. "An apology for not taking you with us, although I'm certain you would have been less than stimulated at our examination of the flower-garden around the Chapel."

John's laugh was full this time. "You may be right, dearest." Trying not to smile made it worse. His worry – and annoyance – had melted. Mary looked so *healthy* now. Which reminded him: "Where is our gracious hostess?"

"I'm afraid one of my former charges got into a bit of trouble with the Headmaster." Mary confessed. "She wouldn't permit me to attend. Claiming of course that my presence would cause death by utter mortification."

"Being seen out of trouble by one's own mother is enough of a humiliation." John agreed. "Which one was it? The youngest?"

"John, that's telling tales out of school. Suffice to say, it was nothing I ever taught!"

"I would never dream of such a contemplation." John rose and pulled her to her feet by her hands. "Are you so certain you're ready to return to London?"

"I miss my roses, John," Mary said in a way that quite broke his heart. "And my little garden in the back. And, I miss *you*."

"This is only temporary," John did his best to look firm, but he feared he only came off as being ineffectually stern. "A few days, no more. I mislike what the fogs can do to your constitution."

"I have no choice but to take care of myself," Mary answered, "As you are quite aware, *Doctor*."

"Very well, you win," he sighed, but his protest was feeble. He had missed her too. They hadn't known each other all their lives, and yet it felt that way at times. Being without Mary was a purgatory sensation. "But once the rains strike, you're coming back here."

"The rains will come very soon." Mary said with a low sadness. She loved the warmth of the harvest season. The chill, gray rains of London she could forgive, but the loss of her tiny rose-beds made her sad every time.

The evening lamps were under inspection as Hopkins returned to Gregson's office, pulling his hat off with relief as he did so. Sweat stuck to his forehead and he sighed as he carefully hung up the head-wear on the wall-hook.

Slender, well-dressed, neat. The gesture reminded him so much of Lestrade that Gregson was hard put to keep his smile to himself. It was easy to do with a mountain of paperwork between them.

"He says he'll start on it. I told him we wouldn't actually need anything for a few more days yet." Hopkins regarded the man-made mountain doubtfully.

"Good of you to say so, but you know Lestrade thinks on-time is late." Gregson riffled a stack of files as if they were large playing cards and passed them over. "We'll have to make up a summary of this case for his perusal too."

"Thank you." Hopkins sank to the guest chair and frowned as he began searching for scraps and clues. "I'm still appalled at how many deaths were in London that year. This is going to aggravate our search."

"Too right. Nothing like a four-month fog to make a distraction!" Gregson shuddered at the thought. "Lestrade was put out of commission for a bit, if I recall. But he had that case that I think involves this one."

"He was on medical leave?" Hopkins wondered. "Was it the fog?"

"It certainly wasn't because they needed extra staff at the Palace . . . ." Gregson found some worthless paper and balled them up, tossing them

120

over Hopkins' shoulder for the waste can. "Yes . . . he started getting ill. The fog settled in his lungs and he went on half-pay . . . for a while it looked like he'd be going to the marble orchard, but he pulled through. Those Gipsies is what did it, actually. He did 'em a favour, and their witch doctor fixed him up somehow. I'm sure it saved his life, but it was *years* before he got his colouring back." Gregson was completely unaware of his fascinated audience. "Looked ill and peaky up until his marriage."

"That sounds like something too fanciful for the *Strand*." Hopkins pointed out. "Helping people isn't how the public sees Gipsies."

Gregson laughed. "Their cure involved a lot of tincture of a certain plant my mum called 'pukeweed'. I suppose Lestrade felt he had nothing left to lose by that point . . . but he picked up this habit of drinking their horrible tea after, and once in a while he'll pull up a cup of something that smells like cough syrup, says he has to take it to keep his lungs clear."

Hopkins had nearly spasmed at the knowledge that there was a drink *Gregson* called horrible. There was a reason why all the young Inspectors were told they had to get a cup from Gregson's teapot when they first promoted. It was like "crossing the line", but Hopkins felt the thick brew was hardly less inhumane than getting tarred and tossed into the cold Atlantic. He shuddered at the thought.

"I still don't quite know what to say around him," Hopkins said at last. It was his candor that endeared him to his colleagues. It was against his nature not to speak his mind, even if it could get him in trouble. "I feel like an apology is in order but there's never been a time where I could approach the subject."

Gregson shrugged. "That's up to you, you know. I doubt it would make a difference to him either way. He's been in the Force for decades. He isn't going to waste his time with what-ifs."

"Still," Hopkins persisted. "All that aside, I'm not sure he wants any of us to get close to him on a case."

"That's because of Moriarty." Gregson answered bluntly. "Until we can pin him on *something*, Lestrade is going to be one of that man's primary targets."

*Paddington Street:*

Lestrade flicked his injured hand in the air and, since he was alone, swore. This time the stubborn lock gave way and the trunk opened. He pulled the weighted lid back and sighed, resigned to the loss of his day in such an enterprise.

So many years ago! He hoped this was the right trunk!

121

Journal by journal, each submission was entombed into a trunk and normally, never taken out again. Daily records were all well and good, but paper and pen was a fairly cheap way of getting things off one's chest at the end of a rough day. Unfortunately, records were lost. Records were *stolen*. Absent records meant a dearth of proof, but at least a man would have a memory at his disposal.

Clea never asked about his strange habit, but then, she probably thought it was just one of those absurd hobbies policemen kept.

1884 . . . 1882 . . . 1870 . . . Lestrade vowed to line the books up in proper order when he was done. 1882 again . . . another '82 . . . *that* had been an interesting year . . . almost as interesting as the 83-84 months that comprised their somewhat hectic courtship . . . He paused as his fingers touched that memory-ledger in question, and despite himself, lifted it up to the sunlight.

Life was strange and its paths almost treacherously surprising. If a ball-gazer had told him running across slippery London roof-tops in pursuit of a half-mad lead thief would bring him to marriage, he would have suggested the closest and cheapest cab to Bedlam. It *still* didn't seem real. Bearing in mind what he *looked* like after sliding over those filthy roofs, it was a wonder Clea hadn't dealt with her first view of him in a more negative and colourful manner.

He opened up the journal to the day in question:

> *Two days before Autumn. My closest friend nearly killed me today. Not deliberately, or even accidentally, but through the laws of physics. Any more protests about his "large bones" are going to be met with the scorn they deserve. I feel like my arms have been ripped out of their sockets. Sixteen-and-a-half stone, my eye. He's well over two hundredweight if he's a peppercorn!*

Lestrade laughed softly to himself. There was nothing wrong with his memory of that day. Bradstreet hanging off the two-storey gutter and yelling at him to hurry up and pull, damn it, was amusing *after* the fact. When it happened, it was just simply terrifying for both.

A few more paragraphs of this tirade aside, and Clea entered the scene:

> *Of all the times to look like I've been attacked by a gang of sooty boys. I cannot believe the LR's new proprietress didn't run me off. She would have been within her rights. I'm sure I was frightening off the customers.*

Little did he – or anyone else – know, Clea Cheatham was about as immune to fear as a statue was immune to fashion.

Lestrade hesitated, reluctantly thinking of the piles of mass he had left to sort through. Hopkins. Gregson.

A few days, Hopkins had said. Perhaps he hadn't meant it, though? He was clearly placatory. Lestrade breathed through his nose, wishing devoutly he had the measure of the young man. He'd become so . . . *timid* around him. What the devil was his reputation turning into? And he'd been that way since spring . . . since Lestrade's hardscrabble return from the Channels and Sherlock Holmes's death . . . .

*Oh.*

Lestrade blinked as the epiphany washed over him. Hopkins had been one of Sherlock Holmes's very rare, exclusive "protégés." While "worshipful" was far too strong a word for the way Hopkins had looked upon the detective, the fact was that Hopkins was treated in a downright avuncular fashion by Holmes. In Holmes, the young and fresh-minted Inspector had finally found an outlet for his bright, flexible mind. In Hopkins, Holmes appeared to believe that the Yard was finally improving from its usual level of idiocy and conventionalism.

Gregson and Hopkins working together. Two of the *very* few men on the Force that never really got the rough side of Holmes's tongue.

Unlike Lestrade. He'd lost track of the number of times Holmes had disparaged his abilities by the time 1881 had rolled around. With time, Holmes had only seemed to get worse, as if he was trying to force *some* sort of specific response out of him – a response Lestrade still didn't understand. "Imbecile" seemed to be his favourite appellation, but there were *plenty* of other words at his disposal. Some of them made Lestrade glad he owned three dictionaries.

*Hopkins is worried about how I feel about working with him?* Lestrade was troubled by the realization. Had he ever *done* anything to give the man the impression he'd be against him? Lestrade didn't *think* so – he'd never thought about it before, and Hopkins hardly ever moved in his circles.

*If Hopkins has a reason for this impression, I'll have to mend it. And quickly.* Lestrade realized his mind had veered off into space. He was sitting on the floor by the trunk, back against the bed with his wedding finger marking the spot on the page. *If only there was such a thing as a spirit-level for relationships . . . .*

He sighed, defeated again. He should have caught on to this a long time ago. *All right. Don't press it. Don't hurry up with your evidence . . . Give him the few days he allotted you.*

# Chapter XVIII – The Language
# of Art

*Little Venice:*

"**W**ell, Clea?"

Clea Marie's mind stumbled at her father's voice. "I'm sorry, Da, I wasn't paying attention . . . ."

"I didn't say anything," Charles Cheatham pointed out. "I was merely hoping you would speak about whatever it is that troubles you."

Like many daughters, Clea Marie Lestrade *née* Cheatham admired her father. It was hard not to. Despite age and blindness, he remained physically fit and healthy for his years.

For the last ten of those years, his impressive physique and snow white hair and beard had led to his comparison of the popular image of Old Father Thames (without the garbage floating in his beard). Finally, someone had broken down and decided to use him as a model. The brave person in question was Clea's most amicable sister-in-law Elizabeth Cheatham *née* Harris, who was currently surrounding Charles Cheatham with several hundred pencil, charcoal, chalk, and oil pastel sketches.

Most of them were on the floor. Clea guessed they were the failures of artistic translation.

While she was thinking of how to respond, Elizabeth looked up from her table-easel, eyes blinking lightly in the cool north light of the sun-room. Little more than a large cupola, the light was watery and blue-tinted, adding to the illusion of water and mystery.

"I can leave, if you wish," she offered kindly. "I'm sure Mr. Cheatham is growing weary of his inaction by now."

Charles Cheatham chuckled deep in his chest. His blind eyes, white as his snowy hair and beard, were disconcerting to everyone who didn't know him. Bare to his waist and wearing bronze Celtic jewelry that appeared to be a blend of Neptune and Nodens, he was without a doubt a fearsome sight. Rather than endure the usual Classical Myth association with mer-men, Elizabeth had scorned the notion of her father-in-law in a giant fishtail, and ingeniously sewed up a long length of layered stiff silk of a shade somewhere between grey Atlantic and blue-green of the river. With some deliberate manipulation, the effect was as if Charles Cheatham was rising out of an expanse of choppy water. Rather than the usual trident, he bore a fishing-spear. His grandchildren were nothing less than plagued, as all mothers had universally decreed "no touching" its large, serrated bone teeth.

"It's not as if I have else to do," he pointed out. "Walk the dog, perhaps?"

The dog in question understood basic English. Her large head lifted up, but a moment later it lowered in patient disgust for having been fooled. Clea chuckled under her breath. "I suppose I'm worried about Geoffrey," she admitted. "The work he's on right now . . . Well, I don't think I've seen him this troubled in . . . *years*." That said, she began to feel a bit better. Outside the window, she could see her boys with Elizabeth's *childer* out in the back garden, romping with some sort of game that they no doubt made up as they went along. Clea devoutly hoped Elizabeth's herb-beds survived the attention.

"Troubled in what way, Clea?" Elizabeth wondered in her usual gentle voice. Just having her in the room was like having balm on the skin.

"He's talking nonsense." Clea shocked herself, and was glad the children were nowhere near. "He's talking of *retiring*, if you can believe it! What's he going to *do* when he leaves? He'd go mad within the week!"

Elizabeth's charcoal stick had stopped scratching over the paper. Even her Father looked impressed. *Small wonder*. Clea and Geoffrey never fought – not since their marriage, at any rate. Her brother Andrew was still surprised it had happened at all.

"The first point aside, dear," Elizabeth began, "have the two of you ever discussed his retirement?"

"Yes." Clea sighed. "And I'm being rash with my words . . . We *have* plans made for when he leaves . . . We've even made some allowances for if he's disabled, God forbid. It's just . . . ." She shook her head, frustrated. "He won't retire," Clea repeated. "He's not ready for it." Now that she was talking it was too late to put the cork back between her teeth – Clea rose and tried to find a place to pace without stepping on paper. "It's the business he's in, whatever it is. He hasn't looked this worried in a very long time."

"I hope he's coming to the Viewing tonight," Elizabeth fretted. "It will be mostly friends and family who show up anyway . . . ."

"Don't worry, I'm sure he'll be there." Clea chuckled. "He isn't about to get into a fratchin'[1] with his wife! I even gave him spare cards so he can toll a few of his friends along with him." She laughed at the thought. "But he *will* be at your showing, Elizabeth. He promised."

"Free food ought to draw a number of people," Elizabeth said practically. She sighed and stood. "Mr. Cheatham, I should permit you a rest before we take you out and parade you before the public, and then of course, there's my young ones that require severe herding techniques if they're to bathe and dress properly." She frowned at the tiny gold watch hanging off her lapel. "My apologies for keeping you."

"You're just like Robert." Charles Cheatham answered. "You have to have something to do with your hands when you're nervous."

Elizabeth stopped, awash with nerves again. "Oh, I *hope* everything goes well," she stammered. "Robert's bringing in his new line of paper for the Exhibit . . . ." She nervously ran her fingers through her long hair. "And they'll all be staring at me." The normally unflappable woman stated. "What will I do if they all stare at me at once?"

Charles Cheatham stood, unbuttoning the sea-cloth. From the waist down he was still respectably dressed. "Just do what I do in such a situation, Elizabeth," he said calmly. Clea moved to hand him the remainder of his clothing. "Don't look at them."

"That was well done," Clea chuckled once they were alone. "It's hard for Elizabeth to feel nervous when you say something so *outrageous*."

"All in a good cause, dear." Charles rolled his shoulders slowly, snapping loose the stiff spots. The bronze torc and wristlets clattered into what had once served as a wooden fruit-bowl on the table. "Now that we're alone . . . can you talk about what's troubling you?"

Clea handed him his shirt. He shrugged himself into it, staring into the void before his space. "He's speaking of retirement because I think he's afraid . . . that if he doesn't retire soon, they'll force it on him."

Charles Cheatham paused. "Can they do that? I understood that the Yard is a meritocracy of sorts . . . ."

"There's nothing wrong with his performance, Father. That I'd pick up from the gossips soon enough! No, he solves as many cases as ever, which is largely how their status is decided at the Yard. And there've been no complaints about his work, which is another. The fact is . . . he's at the same level of activity as he was twenty years ago, and he won't be able to keep that up for much longer. There's no hope for advancement. He won't get promoted without the approval of the Home Office . . . and his superiors seem to feel he's more useful where he is." Clea found his high collar and necktie and held them up. She waited while he deftly tied everything about his large neck.

"I thought he was getting less work when he started taking on those extra cases outside of the Yard." Charles Cheatham admitted.

"No, he's working as much as ever . . . I'm afraid there are too many detectives in the same boat, Da. As long as they take care of their own expenses, the Yard doesn't mind . . . Here's your cuffs . . . ." Clea sighed. "That money gets put aside for the future. It's not a bad savings, but if he's retired early from an injury . . . Well, it's up to the discretion of the Yard if there will be a disability pension to follow it."

"And you aren't confident of that form of support, seeing as how it's their same discretion that keeps him from a promotion." Charles Cheatham guessed.

"I shouldn't let that bother me so much." Charles heard his daughter make a clicking noise as his waist-coat buttons scraped against the surface of the desk. "He keeps himself busy. Perhaps he doesn't have time to think of it . . . but it's so frustrating, Da. He has a drawer full of letters of recommendations from the best people, and it isn't enough."

"You shouldn't let that pull you into a black mood, dear-heart." Charles found the buttons of his waistcoat without trouble, and shrugged on his coat.

"I'm trying not to, but to see him killing himself . . . it isn't easy." Clea rubbed at her eyes for a moment.

Charles let his coat hang open and put his large arm around his child-sized daughter. "We're alone," he pointed out as she leaned against him. "Whatever you say will go no further than this room."

Clea was silent for a moment, that particular quality she learned as a child, trying to see if she could analyze an algorithm in her mind first before trying to break it down on paper. "Da, he's . . . been having nightmares."

"Nightmares," he repeated.

"He would have them on occasion, and as long as we've been married, [2] but . . . ." She shook her head, her sleek black hair whispering against his chest. "*Feyther*, he's having them at least three times a week now."

"That's . . . unusual," Charles said carefully. "How long has this been going on?"

"Since April."

"*That* long?" Charles Cheatham was alarmed at the implications. "It's a wonder he isn't ill."

"He's *beginning* to get ill." Clea confessed. "He's hardly ever victim to the germs of London, but this summer he's been down twice with ordinary colds . . . He's spending money on those wretched Tinker remedies because they're cheaper than the regular doctors . . . ." She shook her head against her father's ribs. "He's wearing down, *Feyther*. The worst part of it is, he doesn't remember the nightmares when he wakes up. He just wakes up tired, like he's been running all night long."

"My girl, I'm no doctor, but I've never recalled anyone ever mentioning recurrent night traumas that cannot be remembered on the next day."

"I haven't either." Clea admitted. "But I know what it is." She took a deep breath, like she would very much like to find time in her day to go

127

off and have a short spell of tears. "It's *a* nightmare. Just one. Over and over again."

"Go on, dear girl." Charles patted her on the back, feeling awkward and out of his depth and not liking it one bit. "It could be important."

"He acts just like he did when he was in the hospital back in '83." Clea whispered. Her face was moist. "He doesn't remember those nights either."

"Clea . . . *those* weren't nightmares. That was a delirium from poisoned morphine, exacerbated from the trauma of nearly drowning in the Thames and then being drowned for real by that monstrous Mr. Quimper. The doctors explained that to all of us."

"I know. I *know* it was an hallucination, but somehow, it's stopped being a drug-induced delusion and it's now . . . a steady source of nightmares." Clea was at a loss to explain it. "And he's never been able to take the opiates since '83, so that isn't the reason for it." She took a deep breath. "He doesn't really remember them. He just . . . works himself to pieces until he falls asleep too deeply for dreaming. But that doesn't happen nearly enough and . . . well . . . he's wearing thin."

"I can imagine." Charles Cheatham used his free hand to stroke his jaw. "And it's one nightmare, the same one?"

"The same one." Clea's voice muffled against his waistcoat. "Drowning in the Thames while the warehouse burns above his head. It never changes." She reached up to embrace him, short though her arms were for the task. "I certainly don't know what to do. There's only so much chamomile and skullcap tea one can give a man!"

"Let me think on it, my girl." Charles Cheatham said slowly. For her sake, he lowered his head so she could see his soft smile. His white orbs meant nothing to her, after all, other than "Father".

"Are you sure, *Feyther*?" She asked softly.

"It's been a while since I had a problem to wrestle," Charles Cheatham smiled.

*Greensward Gallery, Pall Mall Street:*

"*There* you are! We were looking for you!"

In the confused semi-semblance of order in the gallery, Clea's practiced eye picked out her husband with ease. His very energy set him apart in a crowd as broadly as if he were seven feet tall. Geoffrey smiled, bare-headed from his visit with the hat-check man, and threaded around a knot of champagne-armed patrons, nipping through their course on the marble floor as quickly as an urchin navigating a snicket. The men never even noticed his presence. One last step and he was clear, holding out his gloved hand to his wife as well-dressed children swarmed around him. He ignored them with easy tolerance. (Gruff with adults, patient with children, he was the reverse of the Victorian male ideal.)

"Hazel re-sends her regrets," he explained. "And she's been back at the shells, so she brought a new collection for yourself and Elizabeth. I left the box with Robert in the back."

"I'll be sure to thank her." Clea smiled into his eyes. "You need more rest," she said *sotto voce*. "Are you going back to Paddington tonight?"

He hesitated. "I don't know yet," was the confession. "I'm waiting for a word."

"Very well, we shan't press it." Clea pulled him further into the crowd. "Shall we find something to eat? There're savouries more than sweets at this to-do."

"You always act as though I forget to even eat in your absence," Geoffrey complained. "I assure you, I do not."

"You might be eating, but are you eating *well*?" Clea charged. "Man does not live on kedgeree alone!" She found an empty spot and swept them both into it. A waiter primed to pay attention to all of Elizabeth's Court emerged from nowhere with a tray of flutes.

"I don't *always* eat kedgeree," her husband protested, but faintly. "But I wouldn't complain if I had to."

"I know you wouldn't." Clea poked him in the boutonniere with a lace-gloved forefinger. "I'm the one who took care of you during the influenza, remember? Oh, hello, Mrs. Watson." Clea grinned. "Do you remember the influenza last year?"

John Watson's wife was not yet to the point where her condition would sequester her from the outside world. Her healthy glow was quite evident as she smiled at the poor man pinned by the eyes of two women. "I remember it quite well," she said. "Four straight days, and John could do nothing but drink watered tea and scrambled eggs with hot-pepper sauce!"

"Well, Geoffrey didn't get it until late, and for *him* it was a solid week of ginger-water and smoked fish. He couldn't even be in the same room with anything else!" Clea grinned up at him fondly. "Where is your husband? Did he survive the first wave of newspaper writers?"

Mary sighed with the good-natured patience that was part of her very being. "I am pleased to say he is on good relationship with some of the men present." Her smile was never free, and yet, always warm. "I'm quite sure I saw the editor of *The Traveller* in the group."

"The one who published your husband's account of the river-ports along the Thames?" Clea wondered. "I quite liked it, but the illustrations were wanting."

"I felt so too, but it is a common problem . . . ."

Lestrade wondered if anyone in the crowd with John Watson would be pestering him to publish more of his adventures with Holmes. Watson was churning them out at an amazing rate as it was, but he was also writing interesting articles, medical monographs, and short fiction on a wide variety of subjects. As he'd once put it (while flinging a ferocious game of darts into an innocent dart-board at the Malmsy Keg):

> *"For the love of God, Inspector! As if I would publish any of the stories he didn't give me permission to use!'* (Thwunk! – *A dart plunged into the cork.) "Writing of nothing but* (Thwump!) *Holmes would not only be the route to* (Thwump!) *madness, it would be poor* (Thump-*thump!) penmanship.'* (Twunk!) *Have another Grozet –* (Thump!) *. . . Hmm . . . How* does *one score a dart that bulls-eyes on top of* another *dart on a bulls-eye?"*

"Do you think he needs to be extricated?" Lestrade offered sensibly.

Mary chuckled. "If we don't see him soon . . . the answer shall be a resounding *yes*."

"Have you been here before, Mrs. Watson?" Clea asked. "There's a beautiful exhibit up on Norwegian stitches."

"I'll take *that* as my cue," Geoffrey said hastily, "And I'll see to your husband, Mrs. Watson." Clutching his flute as tightly as any priest with a rosary, he waded through the crowd.

Even from the back, John Watson was easily found. He still contained the lean physical carriage of a man who prefers to live his life by experience rather than the armchair, and Lestrade mentally shook his head to see the contrast between the doctor and the majority he was with. *They swarm around him the way people swarmed around Sherlock Holmes. He compels them with his own nature.*

The small man wondered what the ratio of carrion-eaters was in this particular lot. Aged like a wheel of cheese, formals fashionably old-fashioned to show their bourgeois freedom with their waxed mustaches and oiled hair the most lavish extension of their vanities, and – *Good God! Tinted carnations!* – most of them made the detective think of someone's overstuffed horsehair furniture. He'd be surprised if the most action they'd ever seen was a game of squash. My God, Watson was approaching his fortieth year, and he looked more alive than that stick-thin, washed-out sod who was *obviously* fresh out of school. If he were a plant, his owner had kept him in a dark room for far too long.

"But you *must* agree as a writer that we *owe* it to our reading public to maintain the highest standards of language and grammar," the boy was saying. On second glance, Lestrade realized he was *much* older than he looked. But he was . . . well, *unused*. Someone who spent his life indoors and curled up with a nice, warm, friendly dictionary instead of an actual encounter. The detective revised his initial plant-kept-in-dark image to a man who spent his life in a sunless, cheerless room with the curtains drawn for "ambiance". *A few more years of that, and Elizabeth will have a perfect model of an Egyptian mummy . . . .*

"I agree that we are the keepers of the trust as far as language and grammar go," Watson was speaking in that calm, pleasant tone that Lestrade had heard him employ when dealing with potentially hazardous beings. "At the same time, we as writers must be accurate in our story-telling. You will agree that the two of us have very different methods and inflections. Were I to write of a say, a vendor born East of Aldgate as if they had spent their life in Kensington, I would hardly be doing the character or myself justice."

"But you use an example that is false!" the other man responded with such unholy eagerness that the others in the group flashed quick looks of glee over Watson's head. "The vendor's language isn't *real* English! It's an artificial construction, an illiterate aping of what the ear has heard without any training!"

*Oh, marvelous. Everyone draw lots to see who gets the gadfly, and so sorry, Watson.* Lestrade thought to himself that nothing ruined an evening of Fine Arts as thoroughly as the Fine Artists. *Hopefully, Watson won't leave too much of a mess on the floor . . . Oh, right. Mary's with him. Watson would behave, even if it killed him.*

*Just have to make certain that doesn't happen . . .* Lestrade sighed and signaled the nearest waiter and took another flute for the doctor, then quietly threaded himself straight into the little group.

"The English language is not Latin, Mr. Grover." Watson spoke firmly, still courteous, but he was too honest to hide the fact that his opponent had distressed him. "It is not dead. Therefore, it *must* grow, change, and adapt. Accents and dialects are merely a part of that growth." He blinked. "Ah, thank you, Lestrade. Mr. Lestrade, allow me to introduce you left-to-right, Messrs Harris, Grover, Throckmorton, Collins, Sevrin, and Todd. Gentlemen: Mr. Lestrade. We were just discussing the differences of the verbal portion of the English language."

"I'm afraid you've chosen a bottomless topic, Dr. Watson." Lestrade passed over the flute. "But don't stop on my account."

"But Mr. Lestrade is a perfect example of my earlier point," Mr. Grover – the wilting plant-man-leaped. "For example, he has a *French* name, yet he speaks a consistent form of English that is typical of the rising workers' class. He has been swallowed up, absorbed by the common masses of London, whereas in other circumstances he should be employing the rich Romantic language of his ancestors!"

*Have I just been insulted?* Lestrade decided just as quickly, *No.* The man was so *drunk* on the topic of English that nothing else existed. *And do I even* want *to get involved in this?*

"But the French do not all speak alike, Matty." The man Watson had pegged as Collins – a sere-looking man who looked like he really ought to be polishing a claymore while plotting the downfall of the House of Stuart – hefted up a water-tumbler to score his point. "There is Parisian, and Provencal – "

"Even the lowliest peasant in France wishes to speak perfect French!" Grover quickly shot back with an alarming rise of volume. Lestrade cringed to see more and more people were being drawn into their conversation. They were ceasing their own polite debates in favour of the free show that was erupting by the potted topiary. "That is the difference between the French and the English! The poorer classes of England do not wish to better themselves!"

"My good sir." Watson, yes, was beginning to show more than just annoyance. "May I respectfully remind you, the current French policy that 'encourages' everyone to speak the finest language is rooted from the bloody days of the Revolution, when the Rebellious elite decided that the Sun-King's tolerance of his country's many tongues was merely an insidious tool in order to keep them ignorant of each other and thus, easier to control." Watson's walking stick quivered, just a bit, under his large brown hands. "Once that was decided, millions of people woke up to find the languages, inflections, and tones – and yes, poetries, songs, and ballads – that were the pride of their forefathers were a *disgrace*, something to be ashamed of!"

"It is unfortunate that the people felt pride in an inaccurate and flexible method of communication." Grover lifted one hand, dismissing fifteen-hundred years of culture in one fell swoop. "But alas, as painful as such changes can be, it will only be more painful later. The longer the campaign for a Universal English is delayed, the worse off it will be for the Empire."

"You are taking the tactic of the Rebels who fostered the Revolution," Watson protested. "It is not applicable for England. We are the world's largest city, with a daily influx that reflects the entire world! A mobile and variable form of English is the only possible outcome!"

"I tell you, a Universal English is possible," Grover persisted. Those limpid eyes re-fastened on Lestrade just as he was taking a peaceful sip of his drink. "Public Education is the key. Again, I put it to you that if the *Lestrades* of this world speak the English of their upbringing, they will rise no higher in the world. It is a matter of political equality to unite England in language!"

"May I respectfully ask we not use me as an example?" Lestrade snapped, sharper than he'd meant to. "The French Government would be the first to tell you, I am not one of theirs. I am English, and my verbal skills are appropriate to my chosen profession – which, I may add, does not have to be exclusive to the English I speak in my own home." This was remarkably like chewing-out some upstart at the Yard. Lestrade was surprised at how good it felt. "Be assured I have no quarrel with the personal choice a man takes on how to communicate with his neighbors." He may as well finish getting into trouble. *I hope he's not here to write up about my in-laws . . . .*" Language is a useful tool, sir, no one would disagree with it. But the spoken language is only one portion of it." *Your body language is fairly interesting, from a policeman's point of view . . . .*

"Wait a moment!" Todd blurted. His voice was young and impressionable, a contrast to his rather dignified physical features. He blushed to be the man of attention. "Are you the *same* Lestrade Watson mentions in his . . . *writings*?" The man looked extremely doubtful. "Excuse me, it isn't a common name . . . ."

Lestrade pulled open the front of his formal evening jacket. The seven-pointed starburst-crowned badge gleamed on the other side – a rather skillful trick of the sewing on Clea's part once she realized her husband would never, *ever* be "off-duty".

That she positioned the chunk of metal directly over his heart was "merely a coincidence" in her own words.

"I didn't know the two of you were friendly." Grover had all but taken a backwards step. For some reason, he was acting like a man who realized he'd been duped. Lestrade had no idea why. "I was under the impression that the two of you disliked each other from reading about those cases."

*A-ha, so that's it.* Lestrade had caught on and he smiled politely. "We're friends off-duty," he explained. "Otherwise would damage the working relationship." He turned his full attention to Watson – who looked perilously close to getting thrown into a holding cell for the night. "And with that in mind, Dr. Watson, the Cheathams would require your presence up front."

"I believe I owe you a *long* favour for that," Watson said as they forged through the crowd. He was much calmer now that he was away from the human nest of – well, gadflies still seemed to fit. "One weekend in the company of George Bernard Shaw and it's like an irreparable tampering with the brain."

"No offense, Dr. Watson, but the gentry can keep to themselves. They live complicated lives, and mine is enough."

"Inspector . . . ." Watson stopped, forcing Lestrade to follow suit. Unlike Lestrade, Watson dealt with crowds by ignoring them. His size and presence made that quite possible, and the little detective was privately amused to see how the entire flow of traffic was forced to bend around him. "Thank you for that timely rescue. I was beginning to wonder if I would next write up an account of a drunk and disorderly charge from inside the nearest gaol."

"Your wife implied the possibility of entrapment." Lestrade grinned at him over the lip of his drink – Oh, all right, smirked. "But you don't think it was worth it to see the look on their faces?"

Watson tried hard not to look approving of mischief. "I don't know . . . I rather enjoyed Mr. Todd's confusion when he mistook you for the piano-tuner."

"Oh, that's an easy enough mistake to make." Lestrade said lightly.

"Thank you for the tickets." Watson paused to nod a greeting to a passing acquaintance in a florid cummerbund. "It was good to bring Mary out of the house. She always draws a bit melancholy when her roses begin to wither for the year."

"Understandable." Lestrade recognized a few faces in the crowd. "Elizabeth was honestly worried that no one would come . . . ."

Watson snorted his stance on that. "Mrs. Cheatham is not only the daughter-in-law of a celebrity, but she is well-connected. Her husband supplies most of the ink and pigments among the limners. I should *also* state for the record that her subject matter is the least inoffensive topic to air this year."

Lestrade lifted his hands, laughing softly. "I surrender, Dr. Watson. You win." At the other's rueful smile he lowered them. "And if we don't want to have both our wives to enact some creative form of retribution, Elizabeth's tour is about to start. Shall we?"

# NOTES

1. *Fratch*: Fight
2, Nightmares were mentioned very moderately in *Test of the Professionals* where Lestrade had one rotten night indeed, with falling through a burning warehouse into the winter Thames, surviving that to find himself a victim of gang execution by a psychotic madman who preferred to drown his victims in a frozen fish-pond, and then after everything was said and done, was laid up with bad morphine and several days of cruddy nightmares. He's blocked most of the events from his memory (stubborn people are good at that) but *Things Are. About. To. Come. Out.*

# Chapter XIX – The Hour is Coming

Dr. Watson hadn't the pleasure of meeting the tall, soft-spoken woman who thanked them all for coming, and to please make certain they do their part in enjoying the refreshments. Men chuckled with their glasses and women smiled in restrained amusement. Mary smiled as well. In the more permissive tone of the art world, she was able to stand quite close to her husband.

Charles Cheatham emerged with his trained dog to applause that was quiet and appreciative. The dog may have been the reason why no one was overly effusive. Watson was amused to see a few of the newspaper-illustrators busily at work. He did not envy them. Illustrating an event about an illustrator *had* to be a bit awkward.

"I wonder how much it eats?" Mary whispered to John's ear, still staring at the dog.

"Or *who*?" he whispered back. She squeezed his hand for being fresh.

Just as most men cannot remove their professions from their lives, even in the after-hours, Watson frequently found himself viewing the world from a triple perspective: That of a doctor, a soldier, and a writer.

Somewhere in the overlap existed Watson who was the man, the husband, and future father.

Conversation stilled as humans settled into the temporary auditorium comprised of many polished wooden chairs. The guest artist responsible for the show stood on an artificial stage done-up in *papier-mache* and crepe and plaster to give the impression of a segment of riverbank. Behind her loomed the slightly fearsome statue of the Main Piece, the oil painting that Elizabeth had spent almost a year on – more if one counted the sleepless nights, planning, timid beginnings, failures, reversals, and bouts of sobbing.

Old Father Thames lounged across the canvas in a pose that no one would possibly mistake for calm, or lazy-lordly. The river spirit brooded like the dark background of his watery realm, his contemplation as heavy as the bronze ornaments at his throat and wrists. Elizabeth had, in a last-moment fit of frightened compulsion, stitched delicate woad tattoos on his canvas skin: Hissing serpents coiled up his wrists and to his shoulders. Barnacles slowly grew up his massive legs, pale and delicate.

It was the Thames in the flush of the tide. Sea-creatures swirled about him, enjoying their brief moment of play. Large grey limestones made his equitable throne. But behind the painted giant was the unsettling skeleton of a wrecked ship, its oakwood black and worm-rotted. Watson found himself more than unsettled. The impassive countenance of the water-spirit implied nothing so much as a minor foot-note in the existence of His River. The trace of mortal human was nothing worth regarding. Indeed, the spirit had his back to it. Inconsequential business.

Watson couldn't help himself. He kept looking back to the original model for the piece, who was cleverly wearing a bronze torc about his throat instead of the usual formal tie. Utterly striking. And completely intimidating.

"John, *what* are you thinking?" Mary whispered in his ear.

"I'm thinking that Lestrade is a much braver man than I, if *that* is his father-in-law."

Mary shot him her "*Youareaterribletease*" look. "I think he looks quite charming," she informed him.

"Are you so certain?" Watson couldn't keep his astonishment out of his eyes.

"John, *really*. His bark is worse than his bite."

"Dearest, I believe his bark would be *plenty* enough . . . ."

"Your prospective sons-in-law will say *exactly* the same thing about you, my dear."

"Never," John protested. "I would be nothing less than fair-minded."

"*Shh!*" Mary politely pretended to believe him, and faced forward as Elizbeth Cheatham cleared her throat.

"England is an ancient land . . . ."

Elizabeth Cheatham began with her voice high and unsteady, her hands clasped before her with the perfect display of nerves typical to those who would rather demonstrate their art than explain it. Her husband Robert glanced up from their knot of children and smiled at her. Her shoulders lost some of their board-stiffness, and she continued.

"And no less ancient are its waterways. It has been said that for every river, stream, brook, and well there is a *genius loci*, a guardian spirit of the place. For millennia, the people of this island have drawn inspiration and creative processes from this concept. While I do not presume to join that considerable and large company . . . I took my inspiration from their inspiration, if you would. My wishing-wells, my cursing-wells, my sacred springs and freshets that you see here are all of a piece. An effort to display the emotions its human stewards have kept.

"My one exception to the rule is what you see here." Elizabeth stepped once to the side, to give her painted partner his due, "Old Father Thames." She cleared her throat again. "Or should I say, *Tems*, which the Romans turned to *Tamesis*. No one can say for certainty what its original meaning was, but the closest we can get, we believe, is '*dark*', and its waters truly are that . . . ."

For the remaining half-hour, Watson was agreeably spellbound as the woman wrapped the audience in a condensed version of what the waters had meant to early man, and why they were still capable of provoking symbols providing food for thought in today's modern and enlightened times. When it was over, he joined the rest in standing ovation. By then, Mrs. Cheatham looked quite ready to collapse into a chair and be waited on for the rest of her life, but she paused and opened the stage to the "considerable model" that was patient enough to work with her. Charles Cheatham took his cue, and the clapping turned masculine and approving.

*Then*, Mrs. Cheatham took to her chair and was promptly given a tumbler of iced water by her husband, who was all too happy to give a two-minute explanation on the special canvas that was used for this particular exhibit, and promptly ended all on a pleasant note by offering up another line of refreshments.

"Remarkable work," Watson opined, dazed with admiration – art could do that as long as it wasn't effete. "But yet again, remarkable subject matter."

"Yes," Lestrade echoed in a low voice. Watson glanced at him. The little man was taking *another* glass of wine. How many had he had? Watson naturally looked for the tell-tale flush of alcohol in the face, but if anything, Lestrade was looking *pale and withdrawn*. It was a reversal from his last talk, and Watson couldn't remember seeing any clues beforehand.

"Did you know your sister-in-law was capable of such evocation?" Watson aimed by guesswork, but it appeared that the exhibit had to have struck some sort of chord.

"View a work before the artist was ready?" Lestrade tried to make humor. "My life wouldn't be worth a tuppence violet."

"Did you wish to speak in private?" Watson spoke as quietly as was possible in the cheerful clatter of the reception. Most of the talking was going on above their heads. Mary had joined the women thronging around Elizabeth, collecting signatures on their playbills and then going to Charles Cheatham for his signature . . . and lastly, finishing up with their own signatory exhibit with a shameless plea for his son, Bartram Cheatham, the *current* reigning wrestling champion, to add his name to the paper.

It all looked as though it would take a long time.

Lestrade put his empty glass down and reached for water. Watson wasn't fooled. It was a common trick to dilute the alcohol's effects without putting a hold on the drinking.

"No," he said quietly. "I did want to talk with you, but now is hardly a convenient time for either of us." He hesitated, on the cusp of something, and Watson literally saw him think, *hang it*, and say it. "I don't need the excuse of business to find a reason to speak with you, you know."

Watson felt ashamed of himself. "I know," he said. "I do consider you a friend, even if it resembles the last thing in my writings."

Lestrade smiled for the first time in over an hour. It almost countered the uneasy, shaken guise he now wore. "As well as you should," he said. "It's *because* of those writings the Chief Inspector is so cheerful of late."

Watson sighed. "Lestrade, I feel that – "

Lestrade lifted an eyebrow. "Doctor," he said with a sort of dignity that was far too sober for the amount of wine he'd just consumed, "you write what you see. That's all you *should* do." His dark eyes pinned the bigger man like a butterfly against a cork, and Watson realized that these were waters he could not hope to ford.

"Thank you again for coming. It meant so much to Elizabeth." Clea Lestrade was so much smaller than Mary it was absurd to *not* draw a contrast. With her husband by her side, it was as if two separate races were standing and speaking: The Watsons from average to medium height in all warm tones of blonde and gold to John's cinnamon and oak colouring . . . and then to the Lestrades, small and dark-eyed, dark-haired, people of the dusk who burned with private animation, as if they contained the electrical force for much larger people.

*This was an exhibit about water spirits . . . but rock and fire would be the ones to suit these two,* Watson thought with utter certainty. "Now that we're all back in London, come and see us soon." Besides the natural courtesy, he was also thinking ahead to the inevitable boredom of Mary's incipient confinement. Watson honestly doubted there were enough embroidery in the world to contain her restlessness when she was truly under orders to stay put.

"We'll do that surely," Clea spoke for the Lestrades. In the relative privacy of the mad throng as everything wrapped up, her husband was content to stand and smile, close to her side as one of their sons decided to use his back like the Matterhorn. Watson was glad the fey mood had ceased to hold him, though there were still traces of its presence hanging like a dull cloud. With nary a blink, Lestrade settled the boy on his shoulders. Watson didn't envy him – Lestrade's son *clearly* took after the Cheatham's massive size of the family.

But large or small, Mary's eyes sparkled at the sight of the child, and John could well understand the reason why.

*Little Venice, Clea's old bedroom, now converted guest bedroom:*

"I'm glad you could come back with us. Will you be able to stay for the rest of your week-end?"

139

Clea was no longer used to her old bedroom, and was actually relieved that it had been redecorated to a cool, bland interior of blues and greens. The oak furniture was still the same. She sat before the vanity and pulled pin after pin out of her locks until a tiny pile of metal thorns collected atop the magnet like a small cactus. In the reflection Geoffrey stood behind, gently loosening her high collar and combing out each long black length as it was freed.

"I'm glad I could come," he smiled. "Hold still . . . ." He rarely initiated conversation while in the company of her family. But she intuitively understood a Very Bad Day when she saw it crash on him. Everyone else believed his persona of being very tired, but Clea knew better. He was as rattled as a child's toy, and that meant he wanted to be close to her and the childer (who were pretending to sleep in the Nursery with the other grandchildren. Lord knew when they *would* finally sleep.)

A thin stream of metal poured like a ribbon to the table. Geoffrey had finally puzzled out the catch to her necklace. "Be careful," she advised. "Elizabeth insisted I wear that."

"So she's in charge of your wardrobe now?" Geoffrey gave the chain a second look. It was bronze and finely worked, but Celtic in inspiration.

"I'm always amazed there's something I can wear," Clea scowled at a difficult pin. "My complexion is forever at war with my hair. You'd think I was Welsh."

"You're all snow and roses. It's not a bad thing." Geoffrey scolded amatively. [1]

Clea stood and stretched slowly. He set the comb aside and worked on the buttons. "Were you able to have your little talk with Dr. Watson?" She guessed. "That *was* who you were awaiting word from, is it not?"

He was far too used to her perceptibility to be astonished. But she could *surprise* him every day. "Partly," he admitted. "Times aren't ripe just yet." A flicker of whatever it was haunting him showed up again. She saw him blink it down and concentrate on her. Fingers grown deft with practice had the long line of buttons released. She sighed her way out of the constraints with a great deal of relief as the silk rippled to her feet. He leaned into her hair. In the mirror his eyes closed and he breathed in the scent of her lily-of-the-valley.

"Mmm, *Well* . . . ." Barefoot, Clea had to stretch if she wanted a kiss. She did. She wanted a *particular* sort of kiss. It didn't take him long to realize what kind . . . "I missed you," she whispered, perhaps unnecessarily. Most men never complained about having to help their wife achieve a state of undress at the end of the day. Hers was no exception. The kiss grew as deep as her propensity for mischief. She felt his smile against her lips as he caught on: She had a firm grip on his formal tie with one hand and wasn't about to let go of it. If he was going to step away, he would have to find a way to break the connection.

Clea, he had once said in equal-parts exasperation, fondness, and amazement (under similar circumstances as now,) had the loyalty of a Samothracian, the sly cleverness of a French simonist, and the nerve of a bank robber.

Clea had naturally thanked him for noticing, and continued with her single-minded seduction.

He managed to slip one hand between them without breaking the kiss, as that was now part of the rules for her game, and found the other end of the tie. He tugged once and the knot released. Just as quickly her *other* hand found his *collar* with an equally tight grip.

"Point to Cheatham," he gasped faintly, before their lips met again. Again he reached up and managed to tip the button holding his collar in place. This time her free hand switched to his cummerbund at the same time her lips found his neck. To break free from her grip there, he would have to peel out of his jacket first. "I mean . . . that's . . . three to *zero*, Clea . . . not . . . fair!"

"I learn from my mistakes," she murmured against his throat.

"What mistakes would *those* be?" he wanted to know.

"In that case, never mind." She ran a nail under his ear. He abruptly moved his hands to a dancing position, spinning her into a brief pirouette as if the rug was a dance floor. When he lowered her backwards, it was to the top of the bedcovers.

"You gave up rather easily," Clea teased. He remained sitting up on the edge while she stretched out her full length in her silk and crinoline. "So you don't feel like a battle of wits?" Their fingers entwined together like the leaf-design on their rings.

"With *you*? Give me credit for learning *something* since 1883!"

"Oh, very well . . . if you insist . . . ."

"Oh, *shush*." He kissed her into silence.

*Kensington Street:*

"My poor feet will never be the same." Mary regarded her footwear with a great deal of rueful sorrow as John (at last) was able to pull her toes free from the confining yet pretty shoes she had worn. He carefully lowered the offending footwear to the floor by the settee along with the button-hook. She sighed in bliss as his strong, careful fingers worked deeply into the sore spots. "That feels marvelous, John." Mary sank back, her hair loose against the stuffed cushion. "But I fear that I will be unable to wear those again until after Arthur comes!"

141

"You just intimated I would be a bear of a father protecting a daughter," John protested, but mildly behind a smile. "So, dearest, which shall it be? We know it isn't twins."

"Do we?" Mary chuckled.

"As a doctor, I – "

Mary had found the other cushion. She tossed it at his face.

"Would a cup of tea help you feel better?"

"Won't it make my ankles swell up even more?"

"Darling, that's to be expected. There's still some bilberry leaf we can throw in if you're truly worried about that."

"My only issue with bilberry is it doesn't taste *nearly* as good as it smells!" Mary protested. "Rather like . . . liver always tastes better than it smells."

"*I* think it tastes like a hayflower meadow." John protested. "A little sweetening and it should be fine."

"More of that terrible treacle you insist on?" Mary wasn't really being difficult. It was just amusing to watch him defend his position.

"Treacle is good for you in small amounts." He leaned over and kissed her forehead, still rubbing her sore feet. "You looked marvelous today. I'm glad you enjoyed yourself."

"Mrs. Forrester will be quite jealous." Mary paused for a tiny yawn. "And I always enjoy the company of Mrs. Lestrade. She's as far from *faineant* [2] as her husband, that is certain!" John chuckled at the aptness of the assessment. "I didn't truly get to know her until that awful chess tournament. Strange how adversity can bring out the best in some people."

John shuddered. "I shall never be able to look at a chess-set for the rest of my life without a contaminated thought," he declared. "Chess for charity . . . that is the last time we'll fall for *that* trap!"

Mary giggled. "You performed creditably. Mr. Holmes would have been proud."

John smiled, his gaze suddenly downward and he paid attention to a blister fermenting on her little toe. "Shall we set you arights for bed?" he asked. "Now that you've scorned my kind offer for tea . . . ."

"I need nothing but by own pillow," Mary yawned again. "Goodness. And since you'll be up tonight, you may compensate by setting some coals in the warming-pan."

"Am I that transparent, Mary?" John was honestly curious.

"I shan't call it transparent, John. You're restless. We may blame the phase of the moon if you like."

"What *is* the phase of the moon?"

"I haven't any idea, but we can still blame it."

John laughed. "Very well. I have some ideas that I would like to take down while the events are still fresh. But I will be in to join you when I'm finished."

"I hold you to no promises." Mary kissed him as she rose. "Your 'James' face is emerging. That means you're more likely to be up all night writing. Mind you make a little racket once in a while, so Ivy doesn't mistake you for a prowler again!"

John valiantly tried not to laugh at the memory of their poor maid's nerves, but it was easier to laugh than go through the usual self-examination of his painful nights of insomnia. "I do love you, Mary. There's no one else in the world like you."

"I would hope not." Mary dimpled as she held out her hand and he pulled her to her feet. "As my husband is a *rara avis* himself." [3]

"Birds of a feather," John quoted sweetly. "Now let's see to that warming-pan . . . ."

The clock ticked its way to the third hour of the morning. Charles Cheatham was wide awake. The fire crackled, barely alive but producing that bone-deep heat of hot coals. He remembered the colours of the coals. Some of it he could still discern when the room was very dark and the fire the only illumination.

Aida's ears were sharper than his, but not by so much. She lifted her head, listening. He rested his large hand on her back and waited. She could tell someone was descending the stairs. Her tail moved, very faintly and he knew who it was.

Perhaps he could fulfill his promise to Clea sooner than planned.

Charles had spent little time in his life contemplating who his son-in-law would ever be. And he certainly *wouldn't* have guessed his daughter would have a match in a policeman. After a life of struggling hard to rise above the Middle Class, the old wrestler had been startled to turn around and discover his only daughter was taking a single step backwards into the status they had just left.

Still, honesty was better than the lubricious corruption of her other suitor, a man who appeared in all ways to be Lestrade's better when he wasn't anything near his quality of character.

Light footsteps. The door pressed open and the footsteps stopped.

"Mr. Cheatham." Lestrade's voice sounded rougher than it should. A tired voice. Another nightmare. Charles had suspected something in the wind that evening when faced with his uncharacteristic silence. Attuned to sound to make up for his eyes, Charles had perceived Lestrade as a total *lacuna* in the hours between the exhibit and bed-time.

"Myron left the latest sample of cigars by the fireplace," Charles Cheatham said calmly. "I should like one myself. And there's plenty of brandy and ice left by the table . . . the maid forgot to clean it up, but I suppose that means she won't be coming to work in the morning with a hang-over."

Pause. The old wrestler listened to the younger man's steps on the floor. His stride was just barely uneven. A moment – liquid pouring, a dash of ice. The light scratch of a match against a thumb-nail, and Lestrade was handing it over, already lit. His fingertips tapped the paper band around the cigar, letting Charles know where it rested in space so he could reach for it himself. Charles often wondered who had taught him that particular trick of "sounding" for the blind.

"This is not an easy night for sleep." Charles puffed slowly. "Bartram left nearly an hour ago to his practice room. I daresay he'll have the wool punched out of his punching-bag by the morning."

"It's almost like a disease, isn't it?" Lestrade said quietly. "I didn't want to pull Clea into it. She can tell when I'm not sleeping."

"In my case, I am old and prone to little rest. Bartram is quickly following my example. There are some nights when doubts and memories emerge with the fog and corrupt our right to rest." Charles exhaled smoke to the fireplace. "The same fog is about you. I would venture it has to do with your work."

"Yes . . . ." Lestrade settled on the opposite couch from Charles. The leather whispered softly as he leaned back, and Charles could imagine him closing his eyes, resting them from the weary dry burn.

"There are times when a case is plain and simple," Lestrade said at last. "What you see is what you get. I know that the popular conceit is against that, but honestly . . . many of the matters we deal with *are* taken care of by their own circumstances." Charles could "hear" contemplation in the tenor voice. "Almost a biblical justice at times. For every item that we lose, it seems like another one is discovered."

"But this is not that sort of matter," Charles guessed.

"Mr. Cheatham," the voice was calm and matter-of-fact and grim, "I'm wrapped in a case right now that *will* be dangerous. Add to the problem . . . For the first time in my life, I'm not well-focused on it . . . I *can't* seem to focus on it." Charles heard him inhale the smoke. "And that I've been called to support *another* case that's unrelated, this may be the last 'vacation' from work I'll be taking in a good long time."

"I seem to recall your vacations involve hospitals." Charles commented. "Not that I'm criticizing your work ethic. But it does look like it takes a force of nature to make you stop for a moment." He chuckled behind his smoke. "Clea mentioned your sleep was no longer your own."

"That," Lestrade said carefully, "is a glorious way to put it. My sleep is no longer my own."

"Can you talk about it?" Charles stroked Aida's large head absently. "We needn't worry Clea. She said that you seem to retain the trauma of being poisoned by Quimper's people."

"I still don't remember much about it . . . ." Charles Cheatham heard a thick swallow. "There are only bits and pieces of it, fragments I can't trust . . . Some of it, I can make sense out of it. When I thought I was burning up in the warehouse, well, that had to have been inspired by the mustard-plasters they had on me to prevent pneumonia. Clea says she came to visit me while I was raving out of my head, and to this day I'm not certain if I remember her or if it's a memory I wanted to have . . . ."

Lestrade stopped talking for nearly a full minute. Charles Cheatham waited patiently.

"Where do nightmares factor in imagination?" Lestrade asked suddenly. "If you have nightmares, does it mean you're imaginative?"

"An interesting question," Charles Cheatham answered slowly. "It's common knowledge that too much imagination can lead to nightmares, but does one need imagination to have a nightmare? I don't know. Forced to respond on short notice, I don't believe so. It think more than one thing can inspire an unsettling dream."

"I always thought I didn't have an imagination. I'm still not sure I even know what the bloody word means."

It was serious business, but Charles had to keep from smiling. For Lestrade to be able to swear in his presence was quite a breakthrough. "In my day, the word implied a plot," he confessed. "Nowadays, it seems to mean a mental image."

"Imagination is not a quality that is trusted in a policeman." Lestrade's voice had changed. He was no longer facing Charles. His words were being directed in another part of the room. The wrestler guessed it was probably the floor. "I was glad not to have it. Some men can solve cases completely in their heads. I never could. I had to see what was in front of me. I didn't trust anything but what I could collect and catalogue."

Another period of silence. Charles said nothing, waiting with his cigar.

"For years, I couldn't remember much about what happened in the hospital." Lestrade admitted. "It was easy enough to say the fever had burned the memory out. It's certainly happened enough in common life. I decided that was the truth and that was the story I told."

"But you believe something else now?" Charles *knew* he did, but he asked as a way of prompting support.

Lestrade's voice dropped. "For God's sake, I don't want Clea to know this. She worries too much as it is."

Charles didn't think *anything* would stop his daughter from worrying, but understood. "Absolutely."

A deep breath, and the sound of the fire crackling the stained pine-cones. "I don't like going to the canals. It isn't so bad in the summer, even when it reeks of garbage. It's when we have a cold winter, and the ice crawls like a mat over the top of it all, making it look like a smooth, neat road – that's when I get edgy about being near it. I suppose it's because it looks like a road. People can walk on it, but it isn't safe for long. The ice melts, or it grows weak, and there's a dark, cold death waiting underneath.

"When we pulled out that little lead-thief Quimper killed, it was a bad moment for me. I couldn't say why, except there was something pitiful about him, Mr. Cheatham. Utterly . . . solitary and . . . abandoned. Murder victims are *never* a good thing, Mr. Cheatham. Even when there's a dead man that you know well and truly deserved it a hundred times over, there's the sad consequence of the person who finally did what the law couldn't do. Someone was forced to take justice into their own hands, and the Yard must shoulder the blame for that, and the anguish the killer must feel.

"Every time we look at a murder victim, the most prevailing thought is, 'They're dead because they were *alone*.' There was no one with them to save them from that end. On some level, it's the most total abandonment. There's something unspeakably lonely about it, and that lead-thief was one of the worst. Throughout the case, I'd catch myself beginning to go back to that memory, and I'd quickly move on to other, more important subjects. Yet it must have stuck tight in some deep place where I couldn't see it well enough to root it out.

"When Quimper was drowning me in the fish-pond, that lead-thief's face kept coming back in front of me. I realized I was going through everything he had. He was so full of lead he wasn't sane at all when he died, and perhaps his irrational words and actions from the lead is what led to his execution. But I didn't have anything like that to go on. It doesn't seem like it was possible, but I started . . . blacking out. I wouldn't have lasted for much longer if Clea hadn't distracted him." Swallow.

Long silence. A leathery movement. Lestrade was standing by the fire. His body blocking some of the heat on Charles' skin.

"What I remember from the hospital . . . is the drowning. Over and over again. I'd be back under that clear ice in the pond, watching his stick hold me down only a few inches from the air. And I'd re-live going under the Thames while the flames of the warehouse burned the sky above me. It happened over and over, and they say it was *only three days*. To me it was a lifetime . . . but that wasn't the worst part of it. It was the part I'd . .

. stopped thinking about because I just couldn't." Lestrade stood and finally reached for the offered tumbler. Charles heard the ice glitter inside. A long swallow and a deep breath.

"It must have been from the cold, and the shock, the blood-loss, or the loss of oxygen. *Either one* of those would have been enough to cause an hallucination. I investigated that to ease my mind. And since that's so, there's the chance that *all four* of those factors could have banded-up to make one particularly powerful delusion, because to this day I can't think of it without shaking like a leaf." The settee creaked faintly as Lestrade returned to it. The dog rustled softly at his return.

"There was a moment . . . as I was blacking out in the Thames. It was just a moment, Mr. Cheatham. But it was the last moment I had before I found myself washed up on the Limehouse spit like so much driftwood . . . .

"*The Thames spoke to me.*" Lestrade said faintly. "It was a *voice*, like a human voice, but that was because it wasn't real . . . It only existed inside my head. I could tell that much . . . but it was a voice that was . . . *large* . . . larger than anything. In that single moment of delusion, I felt as though the River had a . . . *consciousness*."

*Skritch.* A match was struck. Lestrade had noticed his cigar had gone out and was re-lighting it. Charles could tell his hands were unsteady as they worked.

The old wrestler was a moment collecting his voice. "If the river spoke to you, what did it say?"

Lestrade chuffed like a condemned man trying to find a joke. "This is where you're supposed to agree with my insanity."

"You won't get *that* from a Lancashire man," Charles Cheatham pointed out, sober as a Mandarin. "My generation *still* kills an animal by the Ribble to keep Peg O'Nell from taking a human life. Every seven years she takes her toll. Next year will be the seventh year." For the first and last time in his life, Charles *heard* a man shiver. "You've told this much of the story, man. You may as well finish. What did the Thames say to you in your delusion?"

"Something that didn't even make sense," Lestrade confessed in a dry, harsh whisper. "I have to appreciate the irony – ! When your own hallucinations can't make some sort of sense . . . ." He tried to laugh, but judging from the sound of his voice, he wasn't even succeeding with a smile. "It spoke just once, and thank God. But *when* it spoke . . . .

"When it spoke, *nothing else in the Universe existed*."

Charles heard the tap of the cigar as ash fell softly into the tray. Lestrade was so close he could smell the drink in his hand, feel sweat of horror coming off him in a wave against his own skin, hear his heart pounding like a fist-sized drum.

"It said," Lestrade whispered, "'*The hour is come, but not the man.*'"

Charles Cheatham felt as though someone had doused his warm fireplace with ice.

He understood then, with a sick sense of terror, what haunted his son-in-law. *He* understood. *Lestrade* did not, although he had a comprehension that death had weighed him in the balance and cast him aside for its own reasons. Geoffrey Lestrade was not *English* enough to understand. That terrible phrase was heard, time and time again throughout Charles' life throughout Great Britain, hearing the tales of history, legend . . . and hungry water spirits. It meant something quite specific. It meant that the River Thames was ready to take its sacrifice . . . but the life to be taken had not arrived.

And if the sacrifice was not met . . . the last person spoken to might do.

## NOTES

1.  Amatively: Pertaining to love
2.  Faineant: Idle, lazy, doless
3.  *Rara avis*: Latin for "rare bird"

# Chapter XX – Deadtheft

"As requested, Inspector."

Lestrade looked hardly rested for his two days off. He took a space at the end of the makeshift conference table and lined up his own notebook and pencil as Hopkins opened the folder up to several pages of neatly copied entries. Gregson entered a moment after.

"It says here that the conflict involving the Tinkers was . . . due to a lack of understanding on their death customs?"

Lestrade nodded, his arms across his chest. "The customs vary from family to family."

Hopkins cleared his throat and steadied himself. "Gregson, Lestrade recorded there was a battle over misappropriated belongings of a dead man, a veteran of the Second Afghan War."

"Sounds interesting." Gregson frowned. He poised his own pencil over his leather notebook and began writing the day's date. "Lestrade, now that your memory's refreshed, what do you recall?"

Lestrade grimaced. "It was awful." He warned them. "First of all, the Dooleys keep to the strictest form of death-customs. Padriac's Tribe actually has some marriage within the other sort of Gipsy . . . you know, the *drom*-folk. It's made some of their superstitions . . . well . . . boiled them down, as it were. They're very particular on what to do in case of funerals, and the most important thing they do is burn the dead man's possessions until it's all a pile of ash. The things that one can't burn, such as dishes . . . a cooking-pot, perhaps a little sculpture . . . that sort of thing is destroyed or flawed in a way that it can't be used anymore."

Hopkins' eyes were bright with interest. "But as poor as they are, wouldn't it make sense to pass on what they have? Heirlooms?"

Lestrade shook his head. "Heirlooms are *memories*. They'll give you two answers to that question, depending on who it is and how they feel at that moment. The most common one is they must break the deceased's things or the spirit will be unable to rest. The objects are ties . . . doors between this life and the afterlife, and to break these things is to make sure the dead can continue to where they're supposed to go without distraction." Lestrade had found the water jug. He poured a small amount into a cup and sipped reflectively. Someone had thin-sliced a lime into the cold water and he appreciated the flavour.

"If that's the usual explanation, I'm afraid to ask for the other one." Gregson had lifted an eyebrow.

"The second answer may be closer to the real truth." Lestrade smiled slightly. "They hold that if the possessions are destroyed, there's no reason to be greedy over them." His smile grew at Hopkins' expression. "Ask a Gipsy the same question twenty times . . . you'll probably get twenty different answers."

"Interesting." Hopkins made frantic notes with his right hand. "Are you saying they're not as superstitious as they'd have you think?"

"They're about the least fanciful people you'll ever meet." Lestrade warned. "Superstition is a disguise that protects them. Pretend along with them whenever you can." He set his cup down. "As I recall this case, the possessions of a dead man were given to the tribe in an act of charity. The tribe didn't know they were from a dead man, and when they did, you'd best believe they were upset . . . Hopkins, I'm serious. They even toss their funeral togs to the rag-and-bone man when they're done with the ceremony!"

"It's not that London's the largest city," Gregson clarified. "It's the largest *port* city. There's probably more different varieties of people on these streets than say, the City of Cadiz. Lestrade specializes in CID work that lets him mingle among certain types. Tinkers and Gipsies trust him like they don't most of us. I specialize in organized crime, but to be frank, I prefer to stick to either the home-grown English variety or the Italian – Corsicans frighten me out of what little growth I've got left.

"In a few years, you'll be finding yourself consulted in fields you didn't know existed yesterday."

Hopkins looked dubious indeed, but continued to skim through the information. "So what did they do when they realized they were given a dead man's possessions?"

"They were shocked and horrified and fair to ill. The first thing they did was hie out of city limits and set the caravan that held the goods on fire. Burned everything to the bare rock. They asked me to go to town and buy them cloth to replace what had been made unclean. That meant *new* clothing, right off the bolt. For several days there was a veritable frenzy of stitch-work. They lived off hedgehogs and the occasional badger until they had their working wardrobe replaced. If all that wasn't bad enough, the dead man had been a friend of theirs . . . someone they didn't know completely well, but they'd been friendly with each other." Lestrade lit a thin cigar and puffed briefly. "*This* is where it turns into a sticky wicket."

"Good God." Gregson passed his hand over his brow. "*I can't wait.*"

Lestrade ignored him. It had taken decades of practice, but he had finally achieved this personal goal.

"The dead man, Matthew Rooskstool IV, had been a student of language. Lived off Godolphin Street, the stone's throw from the important Whitehall offices. Translators ran in the family. Rookstook III specialized in the Latin-based languages, so he was called on whenever clear language was needed for the Foreign Office matters. Rookstool II, who was still alive at the time of this tragedy, preferred the Eastern-European and Central-European tongues, and 'our' Rookstool, the fourth and the last, was somewhat inspired by his grandfather's example because he began with Magyar, Hungarian, a little Finno-Ugric, and moved from Romanian to Romani – the latter being one of the names the Gipsies call themselves. From there he started acquiring an interest in the Irish tinkers."

"That . . . ." Hopkins cleared his throat. "That sounds like a remarkable family."

"One would think so, wouldn't one?" Lestrade said wryly. "Oh, there's no inherent cruelty to them, but they were to a man . . . rather alien to the rest of us. At any rate, Matthew IV was the last of a good line, but funds were poor, so he took the Queen's Shilling with the intention of coming back and joining the family business of translating. Unfortunately, he was killed in one of the opening skirmishes of the war in Afghanistan, and the family had to rely on a sympathetic charity – St. Michael's Veterans Rest – to have his body sent home in a condition they found acceptable."

"God." Gregson said in disgust.

"The Veterans Rest ran through a string of funeral homes that agreed to operate on a slightly lower pay. There were conditions attached to their work. They had to be brought to London, and the deceased's non-essential possessions were turned over to the charity . . . but the Killing Fog had hit." Lestrade shuddered slightly at the memory. "*All* these morgues were swamped with the dead. Making matters worse, Rookstool the III unexpectedly died of a heart attack the same night his son was shipped to London. He'd been feeling ill but was keeping his upper lip stiff . . . and when a prowler thought to take advantage of the cover of the fog, he sent the beggar off with a flea in his ear and a blunderbuss of swan-shot in his backside! You might say, that was how I'd officially joined the case . . . Any suspicious death has to be investigated . . . It wasn't hard to investigate. The poor old man was lying half-off his own porch, the antique still in his hand, in a paroxysm of a chest pain."

"Was the prowler found?" Hopkins asked with little hope. Gregson, who certainly remembered the more sensationalist part of the case, was hiding a smirk behind his cheap fag.

"Oh . . . yes." Lestrade said evenly. "We picked him up at Saint Pancreas [1] after the doctor finished plucking the swan-shot out of that aforementioned backside." He pretended not to hear Gregson's choke of amusement. "The powder-charge was weak, thank goodness. Might have been two casualties that night . . . ."

"That really is an unusual case." Hopkins glanced at Gregson and came to some sort of private resolution. "Go on, I'm fascinated."

"Well. With the father unexpectedly dead, the body of the son went briefly unaccounted for. Everyone had thought his body had been taken to the pre-selected Veterans Rest-funded funeral home for the usual treatment [2] but they didn't have the time or mental clarity to think of the boy until they took the father to join his son in death . . . ."

"Hold on," Gregson was rising to his feet. "I think this requires a few diagrams . . . ." He pulled the chalk out of the tray and began quickly scrawling notes.

Lestrade sighed. "To make a most unpleasant story at least brief, the confusion was *finally* straightened out, but in the meantime, and unknown to everyone, the dead veteran had on his person his *own* desires written for his possessions. One of them was to have his things donated to the first charity case than went by."

"Was that . . . the Dooley's tribe?"

"Awful, isn't it?" Lestrade noted. "The Dooleys didn't know their friend was dead. They were minding their own business when a man on the street presses a soogin sack, into the nearest scissors-grinder's hands and says, 'Compliments of Matthew Rookstool the Fourth, gentlemen,' tips his hat, and goes."

"It almost beggars belief, but we've seen stranger than that." Gregson wrote as he spoke with the ineffable confidence of a man who fully intends on being surprised by others for the rest of his life. "Remember that silly blue rock Peterson found in that lost Christmas goose?" [3]

"And an even sillier robber." Lestrade had to snort at pleasant memories. "It was worth it to know Sherlock Holmes could make an emotional decision . . . Misplaced though it was." He grinned as Hopkins grimaced. "But to continue . . . I'm almost finished but it gets just a *small* bit stranger . . .

"I mentioned the Veterans Rest-sponsored funeral homes were supposed to turn over all the dead man's possessions to the St. Michael's Veterans Rest. This agreement was made and signed by the deceased's next of kin and responsible legal parties. It was how they recoup'd much of their financial costs in sending the soldiers back home. Objects of an obvious sentimental value were returned to the grieving kin of course, but non-essentials such as field kits, accessories, a few books, that sort of thing . . . Well, the charity wasn't very charitable to learn they were missing these things. The contract made the Rookstool family culpable for any errors, so, faced with a potential lawsuit and a scandal, the already-beggared Rookstools rather moved out of their authority and accused the Tinkers of stealing. The Tinkers thus learned the hard way what was happening, and they too, acted impulsively. They were burning their wagon when I got to the outskirts."

Hopkins had quite forgotten to write by this point – he didn't worry. He doubted he could forget one gram of this bizarre story. "Is *that* the end of it?"

Lestrade only shrugged. "Who's to say?"

"Aren't you a help?" Gregson leveled.

"Just being honest." Lestrade protested mildly. "But there was one last thing." He scowled even as he thought about it. "The Veterans Rest insisted there was some jewelry missing from the body. The problem was, they refused to be specific about it . . . just kept giving the same circling accusations about how they had been told to expect some jewelry! Well, other than the watch, which was recovered, and the poor boy's mourning ring [4] for his fiancée that preceded him in death while he was abroad, that was all we found."

"What about the other funeral home? The ones that took Rookstool and made such a botch of the business?"

"We thought of that. We couldn't get a search warrant for something that we wouldn't even recognize if we saw it!"

"Good grief!" Hopkins decided. "What was the name of this funeral home anyway?"

"The Dew of the Sea Funeral Home – allegedly so named because it's right at the waterfront and thus gets a healthy amount of business for the coffins delivered off the boats. But I asked them, and they were really named that really because it's the common euphemism for rosemary."

"Rosemary," Hopkins quoted softly. "That's for remembrance . . . ."

"Mmm-hmm." Lestrade nodded. "And to hinder your case even further, gentlemen, I'm afraid I checked into both funeral homes before coming here. Both of them are out of business." Gregson muttered something under his breath. Lestrade had heard the man often enough in their association that he didn't feel sorry to miss out on him just once. "Does this have any bearing on this case you mentioned, Hopkins?"

Hopkins looked weary. "Actually, yes."

Lestrade blinked. He honestly hadn't expected that.

"Elderly senior citizens are being rooked out of their savings – Oh, bother, I wasn't making a pun, I swear – and the sanctity of their dead by some unusually unscrupulous funeral directors." Gregson had turned sober. This wasn't something to chuckle at. "Usually they're widows, but I'm afraid there's a fair number of poor old spinsters who were put inside such sheltered conditions that they really don't know what to do with themselves once their male benefactor dies. Several of them have been directed to a few approved charity houses, but that's if we can find them in time. Otherwise, they're swallowed up by the grudging largess of distant relatives. We're talking about women who have no idea they have the right to their own property!"

"Good Lord." Lestrade was nauseated. "There's no end of scandals in that business, but still."

"There you are. You can see a few parallels for yourself." Gregson was satisfied at Lestrade's nod of agreement. "I'm afraid this is going to turn into one of those old-fashioned sweeps where we're all to be running around on foot and getting our information the tried-and-true way."

"Wasn't aware there was any other way." Lestrade smirked slightly.

Gregson smirked back. "Then I needn't tell you what has to be done." He put the chalk down and dusted his hands. "And, it bothers me to say this, but we're going to be in need of a little outside help. That was made rather clear to me this morning."

Lestrade had an uneasy feeling. "How so?"

"Doctor Roanoke's taken a brief convalescence to settle some family affairs." Gregson held up his hand quickly at Lestrade's wince. "I know, he's the best . . . but he told me who he recommended for taking his place in the meantime. In his book, Watson's the best hand there is."

"We don't know how busy Watson is," Lestrade protested. "And . . . well, there's also the fact that it sounds like we'll be searching old boneyards! Do you think the man will want to expose his wife to that sort of secondary risk? He's about to become a father, and his wife isn't the most robust woman . . . not with London air as grey as it is."

"I know, but I'll settle for the other two men on Roanoke's list if I have to." Gregson sighed. "They're good, but they dislike the work immensely . . . With Watson, all you have to do is tell him you need help and he's right there."

"That doesn't mean we should take advantage of him . . ." Lestrade muttered, but he was thinking. A sigh escaped his finest intentions. "Do you want me to speak with him?"

"You're closer to him than we are." Gregson said the obvious with a callous lack of tact. "The Colonel's targeted both of you. It might be a good idea for the two of you to start working together. It wouldn't hurt to get to know each other a bit better." He sniffed, everything neatly arranged. "Since I'm making it clear I'm requesting the two of you together, no one can really say there's favoritism going on."

Lestrade realized his mouth had dried up. Gregson's gall had that effect on him. The worst part about it was he'd already been leaning tentatively in that very direction.

*"No, I did want to talk with you, but now is hardly a convenient time for either of us."*

*"I don't need the excuse of business to find a reason to speak with you, you know."*

*"I know. I do consider you a friend . . . ."*

Lestrade bowed his head in agreement, but he felt a thin uneasiness descend on his shoulders, like the shadow of the cedar tree that had silently, finally, grown tall enough to cast its shadow over his grave.

# NOTES

1. St. Pancras Hospital.
2. Funeral directors prepared the body for *home viewing* – cleaning, shaving, washing, basic cosmetics, and then dressing it in appropriate clothing. The body was sent to the home of the bereaved, and the director also draped the house in black as a courtesy to the family.
3. "The Adventure of the Blue Carbuncle" – late 1880s by all reckoning . . . .
4. Rings inscribed with the date of death of a loved one, and usually an inscription like "*Weep not*".

# Chapter XI – Disquiet Before the Storm

Scotland Yard could be a miserable place to work at times.

Three hours of staring at two fat folders of too much useless information.

*Three . . . hours.*

A needle in a haystack? A needle would be *simple – Get a ruddy magnet!*

This was worse . . . so, so *much* more aggravating. Hopkins' skull ached despite the fact he was situated in a relatively cool, sun-sheltered office. (It was awful in the wintertime, but at least he could breathe in the worst of the summer and autumn weather.)

And now . . . Even *breathing* was growing difficult as the pressure moved against London. Hopkins had been watching the coloured water in the thunder-glass drop lower and lower. When it finally hit the tiny line etched below the centre, he was certain a ferocious storm would be the result. Up and down the cool blue water had moved . . . up . . . down. And each time it went down . . . it went down a little lower. Atmospheric forces were not at work today – they were at war.

Unfortunately, London before a storm was often non-productive, aggravating, stressful, and prone to a high amount of human error. Violent crimes went up. So did public disturbances. Hopkins was no different from his cohorts in that he felt as edgy as a cat collecting static. Even the papers stuck to his fingers, and he found himself re-stacking them with crisp whacks to jolt out the atmospheric charges.

The young man hissed through his teeth softly. *So many people dead.* So many common names. He had given up making lists over an hour ago, and his final defeat was marked by an aimless paging and reading through report after report. Adding to the paper-trail, many complaining bereaved had included copies of every transaction they'd ever had with the business in question. Thoroughness was admired, but still . . . .

*"There has got to be some sort of tie in all of this!"*

Hopkins was ready to scream from his frustration. His knuckles went white about the offending scraps of paper and, impulsively, he flung the whole mess into the air. Foolscap rained down like the malediction from an angry, bureaucratic deity. The young man watched it all re-settle to his desk, the floor, and the top of the coat-rack with a furious scowl.

*Wait . . . ?*

His fingers slid over a paper that had fallen loose from its complaint-form. It was from the defunct Dew of the Sea funeral home.

*Stationery. St. Michael's Veterans Rest* was stamped firmly across the invoice, sealing a transaction between the funeral home and the long-defunct charity.

*Brown . . . Corporal Silas Brown, Died of fever the day after embarkment . . . .*

Hopkins felt a scowl shrink his face as he read through the paper (and its horrific hand-writing) with new eyes. The boy – young and not immune to disease – had been a posthumous applicant for the burial-charity on behalf of his mother, the nearest and only kin.

*Brown . . . .*

Brown was a common surname, even for the English. There were also *dozens* of variations . . . spellings that revealed their source of origin. Plain, ordinary old "Brown" was the most common of the common . . .

Gregson was opening the door to find Hopkins' office papered like a London snow – just a cleaner shade of white – while the thin young man was on his hands and knees, scurrying across the floor like a bloodhound or terrier. For one appalled moment, the imaginative Gregson wondered if Sherlock Holmes had returned to The Living long enough to possess his comrade.

"Sta – "

"*Don't touch anything!*" Hopkins all but screamed.

Gregson jumped backwards out of the doorway so fast he collided into Morton, [1] just coming in with a box of new photographs of criminals for the archives. The man grunted, less annoyed than he was shocked to see Gregson move like that.

" – Sorry," Gregson apologized to either Morton or Hopkins, no one was certain which. He gingerly shut Hopkins' door, leaving a crack to peer through. Morton peered too.

"What in the world is *wrong* with the boy?" Morton whispered. "Looks like poor Mr. Holmes when he's on the floor like that."

"That was my thought too," Gregson whispered back. "He ought to rest easy . . . His legacy's in good hands, eh?"

They watched in silence, neither man moving for another minute. Several constables passed by, giving them curious looks.

"*I found it!*"

Hopkins was clutching a piece of paper in each hand – *clutching* being the only word for it. High spots of colour danced in his cheeks as he rose up, still managing not to step on any paper on the floor. "Gregson! I think I found it!"

"What is it, Hopkins?" Gregson felt a smile coming on.

"Mrs. Holywell, one of our deceased victims, used to be *Mrs. Brown*, mother of a soldier who died in Afghanistan!" Hopkins waved the pages in the air like little flags. "It can't be a coincidence! Corporal Todd Brown was processed through the *SMVR*! The Funeral Home that the Veterans Rest went through was the *Dew of the Sea*! The Dew of the Sea is out of business just like Lestrade said, but – " He dropped his papers and scrabbled briefly, found what he was looking for, yanking it aloft. "But if you look at the names on the stationery from the *Dew of the Sea*, there's a few parallel names on it to the funeral home that processed Mrs. Holywell – Misters *Robinson* and *Peake!*" He scurried again, and somehow found what he was looking for. "There's also a Mr. *Bayard* listed on this stationery – the secretary himself for the business. Well, his name is also in the name of another funeral organization, the *St. Rupert Memorial Service* – also a partner of the SMVR!"

"In other words, *the same men* are processing the dead relatives of soldiers they did up for the SMVR, only under different organizations . . . If it's a coincidence, it's a bloody long one." Gregson grinned like a shark and slapped his palm on the jamb. "If you're right, Hopkins, then all we have to do is keep looking – Where there's one case there has to be another!"

"Alphabetize . . . need to alphabetize . . . ." Hopkins dropped to the floor again. "Gregson – don't step there!"

"I'll . . . Ah . . . I'll let you go, Hopkins . . . ." Gregson considerately retreated.

"Good evening, Inspector." Mrs. Watson stood at the door, her luminous eyes reflecting in the evening's gaslight. "I'm pleased to see you at our doorstep. It's been too long."

Soaked to the bone by the appallingly warm rain that had struck London with all the force of a tropical storm, Lestrade had heard many people say such words in his life. They didn't always mean it. After his promotion it had grown *worse*, as people were obligated to prove their breeding by being gracious about speaking to an undesirable such as a Scotland Yard detective. But with the Watsons, he knew firmly the sentiment was honest.

"Such a particular expression on your face, Inspector." Mrs. Watson moved to take his wet coat without the least hesitation. "Whatever could have caused it?"

"I was thinking of the nature of honor, Mrs. Watson." Lestrade smiled as he held his damp hat in his hands. Bowlers *shed* water – another thing to love about the things. "That to some, their honor demands they be gracious to someone even when that person is not befitting to their station or their life. On the other hand, there is another form of honor where a person is gracious by nature. What would you say?"

"I would say that the former is far too common, although it does help get things done," Mrs. Watson's mouth quirked in a quiet smile, "but the latter, rare though it is, makes the most difference in the world. But why do you ask?"

Lestrade hid his smile in the un-fastening of his gloves. "A man of the law can come to some peculiar thoughts when it's himself and his musings on the street, Mrs. Watson."

"John says much the same thing." Mary looked at him as though she understood. "Now, please, I would be remiss with the womenfolk of your family if I did not have you sit by the fire with a cup of tea in your hands. And while I am a doctor's wife and not a doctor, my experience bids me prescribe Darjeeling in this weather." Her smile increased as the maid came, belatedly. "Ivy, please set the tea – in the green tin, this time. Mr. Lestrade awaits the return of the doctor."

Lestrade felt his heart sink. "I do beg your pardon, Mrs. Watson. Had I known . . . ."

"Tush." It was the harshest criticism he had ever received from her. "John is engaged, and he will return as soon as he is able. It is a necessary duty, but not one he particularly enjoys." She favored him with her eyes again. "But I am certain he will enjoy the surprise of your visit to us."

Ivy's faults were no doubt legion, but Lestrade had to admit that boiling water was not one of them. After a few moments of relaxing the best chair in the house, with a steaming cup in his hands, he had to confess to his hostess that he felt nearly invulnerable to come what may.

Mrs. Watson laughed over her sewing. Unlike some women, she could speak, pay attention to the world around her, and stitch at the same time. "I'm sure John would agree. He tells me of his adventures while stationed in India, when the first flush of the leaf came in." With another chuckle, she made another stitch. "The commanding officers had a terrible rivalry going on with who would get the first crop of tea in . . . and each small region had its own distinct taste. A Colonel or General would be known for the kind of tea he was serving, and it would be expected of him to supply his guests when they came to visit."

Lestrade felt himself grinning at the image she painted. "It sounds perfectly stimulating, and a situation ripe for some less than sterling behavior," he offered.

Mrs. Watson looked up at that point, and *smirked right back*. "'The finest stories never see print,'" she quoted. "Someday, you should ask John the story about the tiger-hunting tea smugglers of the 84th. I guarantee you'll believe that a higher motivation is also a motivation for many a crime."

Lestrade smothered a laugh. "Mrs. Watson, I confess I've long expected such."

Again, a peaceful, contented smile of amusement as she pulled another stitch through the cloth. "It is difficult enough for him to disguise the truth for the protection of those involved. But there are some escapades in which no one could disguise the identities."

The room descended into a comforting silence. Lestrade noted without envy that the doctor was doing fairly well for himself. The furnishings were sparse but of design more than lack of funds. It spoke of the swift efficiency of a male-oriented business, but Mary's softer touches in lace and flowers were ostensively placed for the reassurance of the female clients. Lestrade tried, for the sake of argument, to imagine the Watsons as frivolous, squandering individuals and naturally gave up. Watson had struck him as a man without complicated tastes when he first met him. There was simply *something* about that erect posture that not only had no patience for frills, but a distinct lack of understanding.

"Mary, you really must stop your sewing once in a while," Watson's voice chided faintly in the hallway, rousing Lestrade out of a light doze.

"John, you know how I am when I've got new thread." A pause, and Lestrade could imagine the kiss exchanged. "And I was hardly bored. Your friend from Scotland Yard is here on a visit."

"Inspector Lestrade?"

Not Gregson, but Lestrade. As flattered as the small man was, he wondered again at Gregson's role in this case. Was he avoiding Watson?

"The very same. And I'll bring you a cup of something hot to drink."

"Something low in theine. A large leaf, dear."

"And a short brew. I still have some twig tea set aside for you."

A moment, and the Watson's entered with enough time for Lestrade to finish waking up.

"Inspector, if you're here for business, I will bid you leave for the night if you promise to return on a purely social call later."

"Most gracious of you, Mrs. Watson, and I will surely do that."

"I bid you a pleasant night, then."

Lestrade waited until they were alone. "You're up a bit late, John."

Watson exhaled through his lips, his eyes clouding in sadness for a moment. He too was damp from the outdoors, but there was an unpleasant savour to his odor that spoke of the less soothing portions of London. "I was at the opium dens along the wharf tonight, rescuing a man from his own foolishness."

"You went alone *again*?" Lestrade truly struggled to keep the criticism out of his voice, but the concept of Watson leaving his wife to wait up for him was stunning.

Watson skewered the other man with a look that lasted less than one second. "I am never there in a capacity that could be seen as . . . ." He paused, searching for a word, which was something he hardly ever did. "Regulatory."

Lestrade chuckled without humor. "I must remember to use that word. One of the fallen, I take it. Was it the same gentleman I met at Bethnal Green?"

"It grieves me to say such." The brief pain only darkened in Watson's eyes. "He is a good soul, but a slave to the drug. And he investigated that drug only in the spirit of scientific inquiry."

Lestrade shook his head. "I am sorry to steal more sleep from you, then. You've had enough of a night without my intrusion."

Watson's eyes darkened for quite another reason. "My dear Inspector," he said sharply – it would have been pompous in another man. " A medical man is rarely intruded upon. What brings you to Kensington?"

"We're wondering if you could give us a hand at the Yard, Doctor." Lestrade smiled a little nervously. "I know you have your duties, but we're a little at odds at the station – "

"Heavens, Lestrade," Watson said patiently. He finished pouring off the brandy and pushed one forward. "Just settle down and take this. You're worn to the bone." He scowled as he took in the smaller man's being. "When are you going to stop spending the entirety of your days out in weather like this?"

Lestrade scowled at him. "What makes you think I was?"

Watson did not roll his eyes, but Lestrade got that *distinct* mental impression. "I am no brilliant deducer. However, one of the first things that impressed me about you was the fact that while Gregson pursued his leads in his mind, you were off on your own two feet, getting covered in clay and chasing down your own suspicions in the Jefferson Hope case." The dark brown eyes were soberly worried on him. "This time of year, you shouldn't push it. It's dangerous with all the miasmas floating around."

"Well, London seems to be prey to one miasma or another," Lestrade pointed out. Watson grimaced his submission to that sally.

"But you met me before Clea. I assure you, I'm not allowed to keep on my former carelessness." Lestrade sounded disgruntled, even to his own ears.

Watson threw back his head and laughed. "You shouldn't be surprised that your wife is as formidable as you are!"

161

"There are times when I think I've married a cross-cousin of Sherlock Holmes," Lestrade admitted with honest embarrassment. "

"Then I commend you. It takes a strong man to marry a strong woman." Watson's smile was genuine. "Your family is out of London, I take it?"

Lestrade sighed. "This time of year she spends nearly every weekend with her family. This time it's a return to the country on a sort of informal reunion."

"And line up all the grandchildren for comparison?" Watson guessed. "Even so."

Watson brushed his mustache – a mannerism Lestrade was positive he had never seen before. "Well, you are luckier than I am, to know your in-laws."

"They aren't the easiest people to get to know."

"I'm speaking from a medical viewpoint," Watson admitted. "I swear, half the solutions to a medical problem could be solved with a good knowledge of one's family legacy."

"That makes sense." Lestrade said, while at the same time he thought, *"And here Watson always painted Holmes as the paranoid."*

"Mary is returning to Kent in a few days." Watson said unexpectedly. "It is to our benefit that she sees to her health, and I'm pleased that her former employer thinks so highly of her. But when she leaves, I will be at your disposal."

"We look forward to you then." Lestrade stood to shake on it.

## NOTE

1.  From "The Adventure of the Dying Detective", wherein Watson refers to him like an old acquaintance, but this is the one and only time he's ever mentioned in The Canon.

# Chapter XXII – Hungry Ghosts

In these strange mountains, he breathed dry cold air and watched as tea came from China, pressed into dense black bricks and carried in packs. The people moistened fine barley flour with the tea, and a little sugar, butter, and curds for flavour. They ate the confection, *tsamba*, every day. Bread did not bake in these higher elevations, where water boiled at an amazing ninety-degrees Celsius. Cooking with water was impossible in the higher lands, where he frequently discovered his nose bled and his head throbbed at night until his bones finally settled inside his skull.

Here they made or did without. They grew their lamp-oil in the form of butter. Beef and mutton were almost *all* one ate at the highest part of the world. Vegetables only existed in the lowlands of the mountains. He grew accustomed to ginger in the potato soup, and leaves of spinach when it grew. The meat air-dried, safe for consumption (they assured him).

In his first month, he was the guest and grew reluctantly resigned to being served the breast and ribs at meals – largess had never sat well with him, but a guest could not deny his position of honour. Their main utensils were personal knives, used to cut the food away. But just like it was back home, they made four kinds of sausage: Blood, meat, flour, and liver. He drank fresh milk or yogurt, and gradually grew accustomed to the reddish white tea thickened with more of the same thick butter.

News collected in a strange way to this highest point. When the winds blew against the tents at night, and the meat rested in cool caves, they spoke of the things that interested them, or recited family histories before the tiniest of fires – so small it appeared to be made of smoke.

He often wished for Watson's presence. Watson would have listened to the old men explain their medical procedures. They could not cut into the body, but they knew what was inside it. Roots treated bones. Bark treated muscles. Branches treated the nerves – themselves branchlike in shape and function. At times he wondered how far back was he viewing these concepts. But there was no particular sense of time that paralleled his own.

They understood disease, but his usual guide held that unclean spirits used disease as a doorway to enter the body. Overall they spoke of the three mind poisons – Desire, hatred, and delusion – that led to illness.

Here there was no crime as he or Watson, or even Lestrade, could have seen it. Witchcraft was the primary force of imbalance, for manipulation of outside forces had selfish motivations.

Here Time itself did not stop. It merely became internal. The dead were buried in the air, if they were ever found. Caravans vanished off the face of the earth. Slides buried as much as it revealed. In a way, it reminded him of his flight in the Alps. But while the small chalets and hamlets kept church records of avalanche victims of centuries past, these people merely spoke of mountain-rumbles that swallowed this person or that person, in their grandfather's grandfather's grandfather's time. Often he came across the dead, lying serenely in death as they dissolved into the dry soils and dryer winds . . . *Wind*, their word for *breath*, their word for the life force itself. What was their true concept of the afterlife, if it was not watching their loved ones return to the original forces that shaped the world? He did not know. Here the carrion-eaters had a purpose.

Here they painted their prayers on cloth flags. He stepped across a small place, a mound of rock and earth in the middle of nowhere, and was startled at the sight of the cluster of brightly-painted flags with words and Buddhist advice. The older flags were melting into the wind that never stilled. *Air burial*, he thought then. The prayers were buried in the air like the dead themselves. Here ghosts walked among the living, as vital to the world as the corporeal were.

The man who called himself Sigerson now, knew his own mind and body was out of balance. That one particular ghost pursued him. The dry mountain air was far from the Pleistocene chill of the Swiss Falls . . . but Moriarty's scream still echoed across the planet and hovered just out of his hearing.

*You cannot give a ghost your life force*, his guide said. Sigerson did not know how his problem was so transparent, perhaps it was because his gaze tended to linger a little longer in the dark corner of the tent where the wind whistled. Or how he watched, reluctantly mesmerized, as a pale scrap of cloth broke free and danced off a cliff, its fibres the same tint of dead flesh.

*The Hungry Ghosts await.*

He had thought it superstition, like the zealots of various fates he had encountered in the past. Little had he known, the harsh severity of this land had driven out such abilities in the humans who lived here.

But it was *not* superstition. It was permitting power to exist within your enemy, and little matter if that enemy was dead. If you allowed him to follow you in your mind, then it truly was the third Imbalance: *Delusion*.

*A hungry ghost is the voice of undoing.*

He knew that . . . now. Knew he was out of his depth at the top of the world. Knew he could not mend this rift inside his soul alone. With all of that torn soul he ached to speak to Watson. To a lesser extent, he wished his brother were able to listen, but he knew full well what his brother was, and to distract the Queen's Government itself during such a troubled time was selfish beyond his sense of duty.

But Moriarty's voice was undoing him, thread by thread.

He had never killed anyone before. He had never imagined he *would*. At the edge of the Falls, he had not expected to survive – How could he? At the Edge of the World, he had trouble remembering anything outside the scraped-raw details.

*A hungry ghost has a belly as large as a mountain, but a mouth as small as the eye of a needle. A hungry ghost, then, is a metaphor for those who try in vain to satisfy their physical desires. There are many ghosts in the world, many* pretas.

With Moriarty, the physical desire had been *power*.

*The* pretas *will frighten you, or haunt you, frighten you and disturb you. It will feed on the energy your fear produces.*

With himself . . . his hunger had been *knowledge*, the key to understanding the human race. That hunger still rested within himself, but in a world without clocks, it was muted somehow. For how long? As long as he stayed here.

Wouldn't the people who knew him find it ironic that he, the brilliant Great Detective, craved to understand the human equation? Yet he did. They said he was inhuman because he placed the mind before the body, but they were as opaque to his understanding as he was to them.

He settled himself against an anonymous stone the colour and tint of the mountain range itself. To the south was Bengal, and the Bay of Bangladesh. The eastern border of India. Watson had been there once. In a way, the land was a piece of Watson, for it had shaped the young soldier into the hardened and resolute lines he wore now.

This would be a good place to melt away . . . to dissolve. Here the hunters would never follow him. Moran would *never* come this far. John Clay's royal ties could never carry him even as far as . . .

Or did he even know? Had John Clay outgrown his ambitions by now? His nature was not well suited to control large amounts of people, but his arrogance demanded it. Such a conflict was venomous. He was a clever but weak point in the dead Moriarty's gang.

He sat there, by the cairn of stones, as small mammals scurried for cover. Eventually they bored with his presence and continued with collecting seeds. He did not know what these tiny things were, but here capture and dissection was revealed for the abomination it was. Something that was alive should be allowed to live.

*Om mani padme hum.*

The mantra of compassion in the Universe. *"Praise to the jewel in the lotus."*

The world was, to his delight, far stranger, and richer, and more complex than his greatest hopes and fears. He recognized his own hunger. That of his fellow man, his brother, his closest friend, the city that had stood stead for an entire world. He missed them the way he missed his Stradivarius, the way his tobacco curled in his hand when he packed his pipe, and he knew it was not a hunger to be dispelled and exorcised by a ceremonial meal. It would cure him no more than it would have cured Moriarty. By the reckoning of this ancient people, he and the Professor were both mentally ill, and incurable until they accepted their delusions as delusions.

But this land, kind though it was, would not hold him forever. He had no choice but to eventually return to the world he came from. A Tibetan would say that healing took priority. He could not say that. As soon as it was safe to return home, he would.

His fingers ached for the sight of a newspaper in a language he could fathom at a glance. English, French, Italian . . . .

He found himself waiting for the caravans, looking for the papers they used to pack their wares.

Once in a load of pottery he found a single folded paper in Gallo French. In a load of smoked tea there was half a torn page in Russian. He understood a few of the words, enough to whet his need for more.

How did the Irish newsletter get packed inside a box of silk? The rounded letters stunned him like a blow between the eyes. Likewise, the Arabic papers in their delicate left-to-right script. He found Chinese, Mandarin, Nippon, Dutch trading words in the crumpled forests. After the Chinese languages, he saw the Arabic and Russian the most. For some reason, the Arabic drew him like the others did not. Perhaps it was the sheer beauty of the script. Or its reverse writing-direction? He did not know. It was the easiest language to be tutored in. His guides all knew some of the tongue, and were willing enough to teach him. A most hasty young man, they thought of him. Hasty if his family sent him money every six months! Very quick-moving and thinking. Did they ever stop to pause, and ponder the Universe around them?

The answer was yes. They did stop and ponder. Quickly as they moved, they thought faster. But the world itself was moving at a frightening pace. And there was no choice but to keep moving . . . .

The story continues in:
*The Narrow Path*

## MX Publishing

**MX Publishing** is the world's largest specialist Sherlock Holmes publisher, with over six-hundred titles and over two-hundred authors creating the latest in Sherlock Holmes fiction and non-fiction

The catalogue includes several award winning books, and over four-hundred-and-fifty have been converted into audio.

MX Publishing also has one of the largest communities of Holmes fans on Facebook, with regular contributions from dozens of authors.

www.mxpublishing.com

@mxpublishing on Facebook, Twitter, and Instagram